Break in the Storm

Sherryl D. Hancock

Copyright © Sherryl D. Hancock 2016

All rights reserved. No part of this publication may be reproduced, stored in or introduced into a retrieval system or transmitted in any form or by any means, electronic, mechanical, photocopying, recording or otherwise without prior written permission from the publisher.

This is a work of fiction. Names, characters, places and incidents are either the product of the author's imagination or are used fictitiously, and any resemblance to any person or persons, living or dead, events or locales is entirely coincidental.

Originally self-published by Sherryl D. Hancock in 2016

Published by Vulpine Press in the United Kingdom in 2017

ISBN 978-1-910780-36-7

Cover by Armend Meha

Cover photo credit: Tirzah D. Hancock

www.vulpine-press.com

Acknowledgements

Once again, thank you Google for all your wonderful options and abilities. Google Earth is a life saver! Also to my wonderful wife without whom all of these stories would just be computer files that no one would ever read! I love you!!!

For my mom who has been my biggest fan since I started writing books. She's the person who taught me to love storms, even sitting outside in our backyard in San Diego when it would rain just so we could feel it. Thank you Mom for all the love and support you've shown me all through the years, I don't think I'd still be writing if you hadn't supported me by reading every single page I wrote and 'loved' it every time.

Chapter 1

Quinn Kavanaugh sat outside the bar on the patio smoking a cigarette, waiting for the man that would be considered her boss. In truth, Quinn didn't consider anyone her boss, and if anyone attempted to force the issue, they were usually sorry they did. She wasn't what most people would expect from a girl from Belfast. She was by no means a 'wilting flower.' In fact her Irish blood was likely the cause of her short, fiery-red hair, with a style that lent itself to the likes of the actress Ruby Rose. The many tattoos that appeared on her forearms, biceps and even one on her neck also gave Quinn a rough, 'not to be messed with' appearance. She wore jeans and biker boots, as well as a black denim sleeveless vest with the Harley Davidson logo on the front pocket and dark sunglasses. Her motorcycle helmet was on the table next to her. Adding to the tough appearance was the black thick banded watch with studs, and plethora of silver rings.

To lesbians, Quinn was considered butch. To most other people, she was considered off-putting and a bit dangerous; which was what she wanted. She was, in fact, dangerous. She was lethal if she needed to be, but she tended to save her deadly skills for the job, not for every day. Even so, it amused her endlessly that the waitress seemed both afraid of her and attracted to her at the same time. It happened a great deal, even with straight women. It was the draw of the 'bad boy' persona, regardless of her sex.

"Out here hunting for cancer I see," came a voice from behind her, which had her grinning immediately.

Glancing up, one emerald-green eye framed by a dark red brow narrowed. "Don't give me that American shit," she growled, her accent clear as a bell.

Mackie laughed, moving to sit down across from her, pulling out his own cigarette.

"Thought you quit?"

"I have," Mackie said, rolling his dark eyes, "hundreds of times, you try being married to Cassie Roads."

Quinn threw her head back laughing. "Gladly, mate!"

John Machiavelli, also known as Mackie, was married to the tiny little powerhouse of a singer that was Cassie Roads. He'd met her while acting as her body guard and had fallen for the tiny fireball. The woman was forever driving him insane with her antics. It was a source of amusement for those that knew the couple. Quinn had commented on more than one occasion that she'd happily attempt to tame the girl if he couldn't handle her. Cassie had threatened to take Quinn up on her offer a few times, when Mackie wouldn't give in to her on something.

"Yeah, yeah," Mackie said as he lit his cigarette.

When he didn't say anything else, Quinn narrowed her green eyes behind her sunglasses. "I'm really not gonna like what ya got for me this time, am I?"

Mackie chuckled, shaking his head. "Probably not."

"So yer gonna make it up to me, ain't ya?"

"You'll get to name your price."

That statement had Quinn's mouth dropping open, then she began to grin. "Holy shite, man, am I gonna be guardin' the queen?"

Mackie laughed outright at that, then shook his head. "No, but you're not gonna like it, all the same."

"Tell me," Quinn said, taking a long drag off her cigarette.

"She's a singer."

"Jesus…" Quinn breathed, shaking her head, "you know I hate fuckin' industry people."

"I won't tell your girlfriend that."

Quinn was dating a well-known movie star, Valerie Henning. She shrugged it off. "She knows."

Mackie rubbed his chin, not sure how that worked, but unwilling to ask. He needed Quinn for this job, so he needed her thinking good, positive thoughts.

"Look, you'll meet with BJ Sparks, he can explain everything."

"BJ Sparks?"

Of course she'd heard of the man, he was a legend in the music industry. BJ Sparks was an all-around master of music. He ran Badlands Records, and he was also the lead singer of his legendary band, Sparks. He was responsible for many highly successful bands and solo artists. BJ Sparks was not someone you turned down a meeting with, he was a legend.

"He's the one requesting you," Mackie said.

"Why?"

"Because he needs a woman, and he needs one that can kick ass if the need arises."

"Holy Hell," Quinn said, "what did this singer do, piss off the Taliban or what?"

"No," Mackie said, his face a mask of contempt, "but her previous body guard was a Navy Seal."

"What happened to him?" she asked, though unsure if she wanted to know the answer.

"He's been removed."

"Voluntarily?"

"Nope."

Quinn nodded, this was not a simple protection job, and she could feel that there was more than what Mackie was saying. A Navy Seal was well-trained and usually pretty lethal. If he was no longer this singer's body guard, there was a reason, and part of her didn't really know if she wanted to know the story. A sense of dread crawled up her spine, and she found herself nodding her head.

"When?" Quinn asked.

"Tonight, eight o'clock at his house," Mackie replied, relieved that Quinn wasn't asking too many questions, and that she appeared to be willing to listen. "I'll text you the address."

"Who's the client?"

"Xandy Blue," Mackie replied.

"Never heard of her."

"You will," Mackie said. "BJ just took over her contract."

Quinn looked back at Mackie, impressed.

Later that night Quinn arrived at the home of BJ Sparks and his wife, Allexxiss. As Quinn was led to BJ's study, she looked around amazed. The house was an incredible combination of warm wood paneling and opulent antique pieces. The walls were hung with various paintings, many of which were made up of wild kaleidoscopes of colors. Quinn noticed in the study that there were various framed artworks for album covers, along with the platinum records and signatures of all the artists. It was an impressive sight, as was BJ Sparks himself.

BJ strode into his study, wearing black leather pants, boots and a half open black and green patterned shirt. His hair, a dark auburn was slightly shaggy, and his light blue-green eyes trained on Quinn Kavanaugh immediately. She was from his homeland of Northern Ireland and he recognized it in her immediately.

He walked directly to her, extending his hand out. "I'm BJ."

"Quinn," she replied, nodding and masking her awe sufficiently.

"Let's sit." BJ gestured to the comfortable chairs near a large fireplace.

BJ noted that Quinn did not sit back and relax; she seemed to be on alert, and he wondered if that was a constant state for her. He'd read the file Mackie had provided. She'd been Irish military, part of their Army Ranger Wing and had worked with US Special Forces. She was heavily trained in hand to hand combat, sharp shooting and use of weapons such as knives. Looking at her, BJ determined he'd be afraid of her if she was his enemy.

Quinn waited, realizing that BJ was sizing her up. She was used to that, people rarely knew what to make of her, she liked that.

BJ knew that Quinn was waiting him out and it impressed him. Most people were either nervous in his presence or so awestruck they didn't think to be strategic.

"So Mackie says that you're good at your job," BJ said, leaning back comfortably in his chair.

"Haven't lost anyone yet," Quinn replied confidently.

"Good to hear. Mackie says he's worked with you before."

"I just don't usually do this end of it."

"This end?" BJ asked.

"Industry people."

"Like me?"

Quinn hesitated for a moment, then sardonically said, "Your type of industry, yeah."

"You think we're all a pain in the ass?"

Quinn's look didn't waver. "I think industry people are higher maintenance than regular people."

"Our lives are different than regular people."

"Granted," Quinn said equably. "But it tends to make protecting them harder."

"I'll give you that one," BJ agreed. "But I can tell you Xandy isn't like that."

Quinn nodded, not looking convinced.

"She's scared."

That pulled Quinn up short. She hadn't expected to hear that and a grimace crossed her features as she nodded.

"The bodyguard?" she asked.

BJ nodded, not looking happy.

"Mackie says he was a Seal?"

"Yeah," BJ said, disgusted. "He was."

"Can you tell me what happened?"

BJ looked indecisive for a moment, but then nodded. "I'm gonna leave the details up to Xandy, if she wants to tell them, but suffice it to say that he attacked her."

"Sexually?" Quinn asked, narrowing her eyes.

BJ looked back at her, his eyes answering for him.

"Son of a…" Quinn muttered, in disgust. "That's not the experience I have of Navy Seals."

"Nor I."

Navy Seals were usually very disciplined, with a great strength of character. It disheartened her to hear that one had been so far off the mark. With Special Forces, it was a source of pride that they were always on the right side of things, be it the law, the country or in any situation with the opposite sex. It rubbed her the wrong way that his man not only had gone against that conditioning, but that he'd taken advantage of his position as a bodyguard..

"So, you'll take the job?" BJ asked.

"I will."

"Name your price."

Quinn grinned. "Well, there's this sixty-nine Charger I've had my eye on…"

"Oh," BJ said, smiling broadly, he was a car man himself, much to his wife's chagrin. "Into American heavy metal are you?"

"Among other things."

"Well, then," BJ said, standing. "You should have a look at my garage."

"Lead on," she said, her eyes bright with excitement.

Cars were one of her major vices, motorcycles being the other. Having the opportunity to see a collection that was as renowned as his was an unexpected pleasure.

Walking into the well-lit garage, Quinn was sure she'd died and gone to Heaven. Spread out before her was the most incredible set of vehicles she'd ever seen.

There was a rich bright red 2011 Aston Martin V12 Zagato, its sleek lines just screamed power. Quinn walked over to the car, her eyes taking in every inch.

"Zero to a hundred in four point two seconds," BJ confirmed.

"Bloody hell…"

"She'll do three hundred five," BJ added.

"So hot…" Quinn whispered.

She turned then to the next car, a Porsche 918 Spyder in racing yellow.

"Is this a Spyder?"

"Yup… my latest acquisition."

"That put a dent in yer wallet I'll bet," Quinn said, her eyes never leaving the sleek low-slung vehicle.

"Just over a mill."

Quinn whistled appreciatively. "She fast?"

"Not as fast as the Aston," BJ replied, enjoying the young woman's reactions to his cars.

"But fast."

"Yeah, six hundred and eight horses are usually pretty fast."

Quinn nodded. She moved on to the other cars, encountering BJ's 'American heavy metal.' BJ also owned a black 1969 Mustang Boss 429, a red 1970 Plymouth Hemi Barracuda, and a 1968 Corvette Stingray in British Racing Green. It was an astounding collection of cars. On top of that he owned some motorcycles.

"Is that an Indian Head?" Quinn asked, pointing to the red and tan Harley Davidson.

"Yep, nineteen forty-one," BJ replied proudly.

"Nice…"

He also had a Ducati 1199 Panigale R; one of the fastest production bikes on the market.

"The wife gives me a lot of grief over that one."

"I imagine."

The last of the bikes was a custom chopper; a cruiser style bike in shades of blue and green with flames licking out from the edges and "Sparks" written in script on the tank. It was an awesome sight to behold.

"The guys over at Orange County Custom did that one for me," he said, watching Quinn admire the bike.

"It's awesome!"

BJ nodded, quite happy that she was able to appreciate his collection. "So what are you driving?"

"Right now," she said, rubbing her eyebrow, "a sixty-nine Mach one."

"What engine?" BJ asked, immediately interested.

"Three-ninety CI, big block."

"Nice, so you drive American muscle too."

"Well, that and a Harley."

"Which Harley?"

"A sportster, Iron eight eighty-three," Quin said, grinning as BJ looked surprised. "Not exactly a girly bike."

"Nope, nothin' wrong with that," BJ said. Then he pinned her with a look. "What's that Charger running at that you've got your eye on?"

"Bout fifty k."

"Sold."

Quinn narrowed her eyes at him. "Why do I think I just lost a deal here?"

BJ didn't respond, his eyes sparkling as he smiled.

That night, back at Valerie's place, Quinn had to explain it to her.

"You made a deal based on you wanting to buy a car?" Valerie asked, shocked. "Seriously?"

Quinn grinned, knowing that Valerie would never understand.

"Are you crazy?" Valerie shouted.

Quinn laughed. "Sometimes."

"BJ Sparks could afford a lot more than fifty thousand, Quinn."

"I know," Quinn said, getting annoyed that Valerie was now talking to her like she was an idiot.

It was a bad habit of Valerie's and it got on Quinn's nerves no end. Quinn had met the up-and-coming movie star at a party; they'd gotten along and had ended up back at Quinn's place in bed that same night. They'd now been together for a few months. Valerie was a control freak and wanted Quinn to move into her mansion in the Palisades, but Quinn refused. It was a constant argument with them.

Valerie was a classical dark-haired beauty with an edge to her. It landed her roles in movies such as the 'dark seductress' or the 'hard core bad ass.' With long flowing black hair, dark eyes, and a lithe body, she was a lesbian's dream physically, but a nightmare when it came to her angry fits and dramatic tendencies. Valerie and some of her friends were the main reason that Quinn didn't like working for industry people. They thought the world revolved around them and it got really old really fast.

"Don't give me that look," Valerie snapped, knowing Quinn was getting angry, and wanting to stave off the fight likely to ensue.

Not that she minded fighting with Quinn; the makeup sex alone was worth the fight, but it had been a long day and she just wanted to relax. Reaching for a glass, she poured herself a drink, offering Quinn one as well. Quinn shook her head.

"So who are you guarding?" Valerie asked when she'd settled on the couch with her drink.

"Some singer named Xandy Blue," Quinn said, moving to sit on the couch a couple feet away from Valerie.

Valerie noted the distance, which meant that Quinn was still pissed at her.

"What's she like?"

"Got me," Quinn shrugged. "I've never heard of her."

Valerie sighed, shaking her head as she pulled her phone out to Google Xandy Blue. "You've never heard of anyone in music that doesn't play rock."

"And?" Quinn queried with a raised eyebrow.

Valerie just shook her head again, scooting over on the couch and handing Quinn her phone.

Quinn looked at the picture Valerie had pulled up. She had to admit the girl was definitely beautiful in a wholesome, bubble gum kind of way. Xandy Blue had a perfect heart shaped face, peaches and cream skin, honey blond hair, and big cornflower-blue eyes.

"Guess we know where the 'Blue' part came from, huh?"

"Ya think?" Valerie said, snidely. "Could she be more of a pop princess if she tried?"

Quinn didn't respond, knowing that Valerie disdained anyone that wasn't new and edgy. She also dismissed them as having no real talent and just trading on their looks. Though, Quinn was fairly sure that if Xandy Blue was talentless, BJ Sparks wouldn't be interested in signing her. So there had to be more to the girl than just looks.

Quinn pulled up the bio portion of the page. Xandy Blue was from the Midwest and had been found on a talent search in a shopping mall. At the age of fourteen she'd come to Los Angeles to work on some of the Disney network shows, but not in any starring roles. At nineteen Xandy married Tommy Shay. They'd been married for two years before divorcing. Xandy Blue was twenty-two years old. That was all the bio said. It was fairly lackluster, but Quinn knew that her official bio would be a lot less interesting than the real thing. She guessed she was about to find out.

Their first meeting was at Badlands Studios where Xandy was putting the finishing touches on her first album with BJ's label. Quinn arrived at the studios early. She signed in with security, who checked the list to see that she was on it.

"Go on back," the security officer said. "She's in studio three."

Quinn nodded. "Thanks."

Walking away she didn't see the security officer watching her go. *Wouldn't want to mess with that one,* the man was thinking.

Quinn was dressed in all black, including black Harley Davidson boots. She wore a collared shirt, a black and orange Harley Davidson leather jacket and black jeans. Around her neck was a thick silver chain from which a silver and black Celtic cross hung. Her silver rings were in place as well. The sleeves of the jacket were pushed up to expose a large gun metal black watch. She looked imposing.

Imposing was the first thing Xandy thought when she saw the woman that had to be Quinn Kavanaugh standing on the other side of the sound booth. Quinn's hands were in her jacket pockets and she leaned indolently against the wall, her face a mask of calm as her green eyes took in everything around her.

Quinn did her best to stay out of the way in the small sound booth. As she stood by, she listened to the playback that was being run. She was surprised to hear the quality of Xandy's voice. The girl had some serious pipes on her, that much was evident. Quinn imagined this was what BJ had seen in her.

After twenty minutes, Xandy finally told the guy in the sound booth, "I gotta go."

"But we need to finish this track," the guy shot back.

Xandy looked indecisive, and Quinn waited to see if she was going to pull a star trip on the guy. Surprisingly she didn't.

"Can we pick it up after lunch?" she asked, hopeful.

The guy looked at his watch irritably. "I have other stuff to do."

"She is the talent," Quinn found herself saying in a low tone, without even looking at the guy.

He glanced back to where she was stood, ready to snap at her too, then he saw her and his eyes widened as she pushed off the wall, giving him a direct challenging stare.

He swallowed convulsively, and then nodded. "Yeah, yeah, I can do that."

"Great!" Xandy said smiling brilliantly as she set her headphones on the music stand in front of her.

Walking out of the sound booth, she looked directly at Quinn. "You must be Quinn," she said with a shy smile.

She was several inches shorter and very petite compared to Quinn who stood at five foot eight. Quinn suddenly felt like a giant.

"I am," Quinn replied, her accent clear.

Xandy nodded. She was hesitant and clearly a bit intimidated. Quinn noticed that she was clasping her hands together nervously as well.

"Let's step out of here," Quinn said, gesturing for Xandy to precede her.

Xandy nodded and walked out of the studio, with Quinn following her into the hallway. She could sense quickly that Xandy was unsure of herself.

"Why don't we go have some lunch?" Quinn asked, trying to reassure Xandy a little. She had no need to be nervous around her.

"Okay," Xandy replied, all big blue eyes and unease.

Once again Quinn gestured for Xandy to precede her. They got out to the parking lot and Quinn led the way to her car.

"Wow!" Xandy said, sounding very young as she stood stock still and stared at the black and sapphire-blue Mach 1 Mustang.

Quinn couldn't help but to grin proudly. She loved her car and had done a lot of work on it herself to get it in the pristine condition that it was in now.

"It's a Mustang. My uncle had one, but it wasn't nearly this nice," Xandy said, in awe of the car.

"Thank you."

"What year is it?" Xandy asked, as Quinn unlocked and opened the passenger door for her.

"It's a sixty-nine," Quinn replied, closing the door after Xandy had climbed inside.

She walked around the driver's side, and even as she got in she could see Xandy looking around the interior wide-eyed. It was impossible to describe the joy Quinn felt that someone appreciated her car. Valerie didn't like the classics; she preferred fancy cars like

Mercedes and Bentleys. Quinn pulled herself up short, why was she comparing them?

"This is so nice…" Xandy said, her Midwest accent coming out, as she said "nice."

"Did you restore her yourself?" she asked.

"I did," Quinn said, noting that Xandy used the word "her" to describe the car. Maybe this wasn't going to be so bad after all.

When Quinn started the car up, it let out a deep rumble from the engine, and she saw Xandy smile.

"I love that sound… that rumble."

Loud rock music blared from the speakers. Quinn immediately reached over to turn the music down. "Sorry."

Xandy smiled. "I like my music loud too."

Quinn nodded, accepting that excuse. Putting the car in gear, she backed out of the space and headed for a local restaurant that she knew wouldn't be too populated.

Xandy looked down at Quinn's hand resting on the stick shift as she drove. She noticed the rings that Quinn wore. They were gorgeous. The ones on her right hand were a band style, and it was obvious they were all from the same designer as they had a similar style. The bands were silver, with beautiful colors in channels within the band.

"How beautiful." Xandy reached her hand out to touch one of the rings with her finger lightly.

Quinn lifted her hand off the stick shift glancing at them with a grin. "Thank you, I'm rather fond of them."

"Who's the designer?"

"Her name's Sheila Fleet," Quinn answered.

"Her work is amazing," Xandy said, touching the rings again.

There were four in all. One band had rainbow colors running through it which Xandy could easily determine represented the symbol of the gay lifestyle. The next ring was two shades of blue with what looked like silver hash marks across it, but they were uneven.

"What does this mean?" she asked, indicating to the blue ring.

Quinn canted her head, thinking it was interesting that the girl picked up on the subtle difference in the ring's markings. Most people just wrote it off as a design.

"It's called ogham. It's an old alphabet, the word essentially means 'a blessing on the soul.' "

"Wow… that's pretty cool."

Quinn smiled broadly, inordinately pleased by this girl's fascination with seemingly everything.

"And what about this one?" Xandy asked, touching the next right which held red, orange and gold colors in its channel, the silver around the color was textured silver.

"It represents lava. I just liked it."

"And this last one?" The ring was another that had the blue hues, but there were very definite raised letters in silver within the blue band.

"They're Viking runes. It says 'dreams of everlasting love.' " Quinn added, her look circumspect.

Xandy looked over at Quinn, her look inscrutable, but she nodded.

"Well they're very cool. I'll have to check out the other hand later."

Xandy felt like she was being far too nosey about her new bodyguard. She was always fascinated with new people and new experiences. Sadly some people simply didn't hold her attention very long. Living in Los Angeles, Xandy had quickly found out that many people, especially in the music industry, were very superficial or very self-centered. That type of personality tended to put Xandy off and lost her interest quickly.

Quinn was definitely fascinating. Xandy easily detected that she was a lesbian; it didn't bother her in the slightest. In fact, she was curious about it. She'd never really gotten to know anyone that was gay, so she thought this might be a new learning experience for her. At this moment, though, she was curious about Quinn's accent.

"Is your accent Irish?" Xandy asked almost timidly, afraid she was wrong, as she'd had bad experiences with misinterpreting accents.

Once she'd thought a man from England was Scottish and had said so, he'd been quite irritated by the comparison. He'd responded, "I ain't no dirty Scot!" From that time forward she'd tried to be more careful.

Quinn noted the hesitancy. "Yes," she replied, softening her voice a bit.

"What part of Ireland are you from?"

"I'm actually from Northern Ireland, Belfast," Quinn answered as she pulled into the parking lot for the restaurant.

"I've heard it's beautiful."

"It is."

"Do you get homesick?" Xandy asked, sensing Quinn's affection for her homeland.

"Oh yeah," Quinn said, as she turned off the car. "But when it gets bad here, I just go home for a bit."

Xandy smiled sadly and nodded. Quinn detected the sadness and wondered at it, as she got out of the car and walked around to open the passenger door. Xandy was surprised by the very gallant gesture, but liked it all the same.

"Thank you."

Quinn inclined her head and gestured for Xandy to precede her into the restaurant, scanning the area around them as she did.

Already on duty, Xandy thought to herself, comforted by that fact.

Inside the restaurant, Quinn turned to Xandy. "Do you mind if we sit outside? I need a fix," she said, holding up her lighter.

"No problem."

They got seated at a corner table. Quinn made sure that Xandy was seated in the corner so no one could get close to her without going through Quinn. Quinn pulled a cigarette and lighter out of her jacket pocket, put the cigarette in her mouth and lit the tip. The lighter was a Zippo so it made that famous clicking sound.

Before Quinn could pocket the lighter, Xandy asked, "Can I see that?"

Quinn gave her a quizzical look for a moment, but handed over the lighter all the same.

Xandy took the lighter looking at it in fascination, touching the raised Celtic cross on its face. The cross was enamel and painted in shades of green.

"This is beautiful. I seem to be saying that a lot today," she said self-consciously.

Quinn grinned as Xandy handed the lighter back to her. "It's good that you still think things are beautiful. Most people who've lived in LA for more than a year tend to become immune to beauty."

Xandy canted her head, giving Quinn an amused look. "You know, I've never thought of it that way. Most of the time I just walk around feeling like a dork."

Quinn leaned back in her chair, taking a long drag of her cigarette, assessing Xandy. This girl was indeed very damaged, even if she looked like she did her best to put on a brave face.

After the waitress took their order, Quinn snubbed out her cigarette and leaned forward, her forearms on the table as she looked at Xandy seriously.

"Okay, so let's get down to business," she said.

Xandy nodded, suddenly somber.

"BJ wants you to have twenty-four seven protection. He feels that with the unhindered access your previous b…" Quinn's voice trailed off before she said the word 'bodyguard' because she saw the stricken look on Xandy's face.

Reaching her hand out, Quinn covered Xandy's hand that rested on her lap. Xandy looked down at Quinn's hand, desperate to focus on something other than the conversation. She nodded to show Quinn that she was still listening.

"I'm sorry," Quinn said, her tone softer. "But if I'm going to protect you, I need to take everything into account."

Quinn paused, lowering her head to try to get Xandy to look at her again, which after a long pause Xandy did. Quinn could see the glazing of tears in those big blue eyes and she winced at the sight.

"You don't have to tell me anything right now," Quinn said, her tone soft, eyes on Xandy's. "But it's something we're going to need to talk about at some point, okay?"

Xandy nodded, blinking as a tear escaped and slid down her cheek. Quinn reached up brushing the tear away gently. Xandy looked back at her, it was obvious her mind was trying to grasp Quinn's overtly chivalrous gesture. It made Quinn realize that she was already being to drawn in by the young ingénue.

After a long few moments, Quinn moved to sit back, pulling out another cigarette and lighting it.

"Thank you," Xandy said quietly after a long pause.

Quinn didn't answer, but her expression said that she understood Xandy's gratitude and accepted it. Their lunch arrived not too long after that, Quinn noted that Xandy ate delicately. She sensed that she was going to have to handle this girl with kid gloves. It was going to be a shift in the way she did things, but Quinn also knew that this childlike woman was traumatized by her experiences and the last thing she wanted to do was scare her more.

When they finished lunch, Xandy looked over at Quinn. "So would you need to stay with me, or do I need to come to you?"

"If it's alright," Quinn said, rubbing her eyebrow with her thumbnail, "I'd rather stay at your place. It's easier, and I'm sure you have better security than I do."

"I do have a security system."

"Good," Quinn said, thinking she needed to make sure the codes had been changed since the last bodyguard was in place. "All I'll need is a room, preferably close to yours so I can keep an eye on things."

"Can you move in today?" Her eyes sparkled expectantly as she asked.

"I'm yours as of this morning, so I definitely can," Quinn said, giving the girl a wink.

Xandy smiled at the jaunty wink. "Great! I just have to finish up at the studio…"

"I'll go grab some stuff while you do that, then swing back by to pick you up."

"What about my car?"

"I'll get someone to bring it back to your place," Quinn said, always thinking three steps ahead.

Xandy nodded again, feeling relieved. She really didn't want to spend another night alone in her house.

Chapter 2

Quinn was pleasantly surprised by Xandy's house; it was not at all what she'd expected. Far from ostentatious, like Valerie's Palisades home, Xandy's house was a modest traditional style house, certainly not a mansion by any means. It was located in the affluent Brentwood area, but it wasn't a "star" type of home. It was a single story set back from the street, painted a cream color with seafoam-green trim and front door. The front yard was beautifully landscaped and it reminded Quinn of an old English garden with purple and white wisteria trees, a white painted park bench and a white picket fence surrounding the yard. It really seemed to fit the image Quinn already had of the young singer.

Inside, the house was also beautiful with hardwood floors, elegant arched doorways, crown molding throughout, as well as a chair rail set midway down the wall. The bones of the house were incredible, but Quinn noted that there were few personal touches. The walls were beige and there were no paintings or decorations on the walls or on the furniture in the living room. It was as if Xandy was living in the house, but not really moving into the house.

"Did you just move in?" Quinn asked.

"About six months ago, you know, after…" Her voice trailed off as she looked away.

"Oh." Quinn nodded. She was surprised that BJ hadn't told her that Xandy hadn't had a bodyguard in over six months and that she'd moved in that time as well.

Xandy could see what Quinn was thinking. "BJ made sure I had a security system installed. It was fine, until… well, lately."

"What's happened lately?" Quinn asked, realizing that maybe there was a lot more to this story than she'd been told.

"Well," Xandy said, moving to the kitchen and busying herself with putting dishes away as she talked. "I've been getting calls. You know, obscene ones…" Quinn nodded, waiting for Xandy to go on. "And then there's been someone kind of lurking around…"

Quinn's senses perked up at that. "Have you seen who it is?"

Xandy shook her head, and Quinn noticed that her hands were now shaking. Walking over to the girl, Quinn carefully took the plate Xandy was holding and set it aside, afraid she was going to drop it.

"Do you think it's him?" Quinn asked.

Xandy shrugged, her eyes lowered. "It's always dark."

Quinn nodded, drawing in a deep breath and blowing out audibly.

"Okay… why don't you show me where you want me to stay."

Xandy nodded, and led Quinn down the hall of the house. Stopping, she pointed to the master bedroom. "That's my room," she said, then pointed to the room right next to it. "You can stay in there."

"Good," Quinn said, and she took her bag into the room.

An hour later, Quinn had not only unpacked her few belongings, but had prowled around the house checking security cameras and familiarizing herself with the house and the surrounding grounds.

There was a nicely secluded courtyard at the back, surrounded by tall walls. She noted that there was some greenery that needed to be cut back, and she wanted to add a couple of cameras to eliminate blind spots in the security system, but for the most part she was satisfied with the system that had been installed.

Walking back inside the house, Quinn went to locate Xandy, it was now getting dark outside. She found Xandy sitting in her bedroom on a chair in the sitting area of the room, lost in thought. Quinn took in the lack of decoration in this room as well. There was a nondescript bed with a simple beige bedspread and a dresser with a mirror. There were also boxes shoved to the side of the room and a few items such as shoes or clothes scattered around. The only other furniture in the large master was the beige and gold patterned arm chair Xandy sat in and the matching ottoman.

Quinn walked into the room, and stood by the ottoman. Xandy snapped out of whatever thoughts she was lost in and looked up at Quinn. The look of utter devastation in the girl's eyes had Quinn moving to sit on the ottoman, her look searching. Xandy's lower lip started to quiver.

Without stopping to think, Quinn reached out touching Xandy's knee, her look beseeching.

"Talk to me," she said simply.

Xandy seemed to pull back into herself; physically she pulled her knees up to her chest defensively wrapping her arms around them, shaking her head. She averted her eyes.

Quinn sat back, sighing. Her need to fix things was causing her to want to push harder than she knew she should.

"Okay…" Quinn said, nodding as if Xandy had actually spoken. "I'm getting hungry, do you want dinner?" she asked as casually as she could.

Xandy looked back at Quinn, her look both cautious and apologetic as the same time. Finally, she nodded.

"I'm gonna order in," Quinn said, pulling out her phone. "Anything good around here?"

"There's…" Xandy began, but her voice came out as a low gravelly whisper. Clearing her throat she started again. "There's a good Chinese place nearby that delivers."

"That works, what'll you have?"

"Kung pao chicken."

Quinn nodded, scrolling through options on her phone. "Got it."

Xandy watched Quinn walk out, her look contemplative. She knew that Quinn wanted to help her, and part of her wanted to let her. Unfortunately, the side of her that wanted to hide away from everything was stronger, and in her mind talking about things would only make things worse. It occurred to her belatedly that Quinn may have thought that she'd shrunk from her touch because Quinn was a lesbian and she wasn't. That was a new source of worry that had her distracted until she went to bed.

Quinn was just dozing off when she heard a muffled cry from Xandy's room. She was out of bed and in Xandy's room a second later.

"What's wrong?" Quinn asked from the doorway, her senses on high alert.

Xandy sucked in her breath in surprise, embarrassed suddenly. "Nothing."

Quinn walked over to the bed where Xandy lay, her eyes scanning the room and Xandy herself. It was evident the girl had been asleep.

"Nightmare?" she asked.

Xandy looked back at her for a long moment, then she nodded slowly.

"Wanna talk about it?"

Xandy shook her head immediately.

"Wanna talk about the weather till you fall asleep again?"

Xandy laughed softly, even as she moved over in the bed to give Quinn room to sit down.

Quinn sat on the bed, her back against the headboard. She was wearing black sweat pants and a black tank top with the word "Hooligan" across the chest.

"Nice shirt. Is that you? The hooligan?" Xandy asked.

"Back in the day."

"Were you a troublemaker?" Xandy asked, moving to sit up.

Xandy was dressed simply in baby blue lounging pants and a white tank top.

"Uh…" Quinn hesitated, her thumbnail rubbing at her eyebrow. "Somewhat."

"Which translates to a lot?"

"Too right. I was forever getting into trouble, climbing ruins and faffin' about."

Xandy smiled, then her eyes fell on the tattoos on Quinn's arms. Reaching out she touched the one on Quinn's right bicep.

"What does this represent?"

The tattoo was a black shield shape with a gold colored anchor in the upper left hand corner and a more central red saber with a symbol underneath that Xandy vaguely recognized as being Celtic. The saber was bracketed by gold garland.

Quinn looked down at her arm. "The Irish Army Ranger Wing."

"You were in the Irish army?"

"Yes."

"And this?" Xandy asked, touching the black curved band above the shield with the word "Fianóglach" in gold.

"It basically means Ranger," Quinn said. She could see that Xandy was waiting for more of an explanation. "It's Gaelic, it comes from Irish mythology, there was a band of ancient warriors and they were called the Na Fianna, so 'fian' translates to warrior and 'oglach' translates to young volunteers."

"So how do you say it?"

"Fianóglach," Quinn said giving in to her full accent so Xandy could hear it properly.

"That's so melodic."

"Gaelic is a beautiful language."

"Do you speak it?"

"Oh yeah, me ma wouldna allowed any diff'nt," she said, her accent thick in an impression of her normal speech.

"Wow!" Xandy said, surprised by the switch in the thickness of Quinn's accent. "That's really neat."

Quinn smiled, looking somewhat embarrassed. "It's how I'd talk if I was home."

"So you Americanize it for us?"

"If I wanna be understood, yeah, I kinda have to."

"Can you say something to me in Gaelic?"

"Dè tha thu ag iarraidh dhomh a ràdh?"

Xandy stared back at her dumbfounded. "What does that mean?"

"It means, 'what do you want me to say?' "

"Oh. How about, 'why did I get stuck with this girl?' "

"Carson a faigh mi steigte le nighean seo?" Quinn said, pausing, then continued with, "Oir bha i feum dhomh."

"What was that last bit?" Xandy asked, having noticed the pause.

"I said 'because she needs me,' " Quinn said, seriously.

"I do need you, you're right."

Putting her hand out, she touched the shield on Quinn's arm. "I'm sorry about earlier," she said, her tone soft, her eyes on the tattoo. "There's just things I can't talk about yet." She lifted her eyes to Quinn's. "It's not you, though," she said, her tone stronger, then she looked hesitant, her eyes dropping again. "I mean, it's not because…"

Quinn watched her as she talked, her small smile circumspect. "Because I'm gay?"

Xandy's head snapped up at that, her blue eyes wide. "Right," she said, looking apologetic again. "I'm sorry, it's not that you're gay."

Quinn gave the girl a stern look. "For one thing. You need to stop apologizing for one, having issues and two, for not wanting to talk about them." She reached out a hand and took Xandy's hand and looked directly into her eyes. "You have the right to your own thoughts, your own counsel, and your own feelings on things, okay?"

Xandy looked back at her, the look on her face telling Quinn that no one had ever told her this before. Quinn breathed out a sigh, shaking her head.

"I'm in the habit of trying to fix things and people," Quinn told her, her tone a bit self-effacing. "And that's sometimes a problem, because not everyone wants to be fixed, or wants me to fix them. You have the right to say 'no,' you can just tell me to back off and I will, okay?"

Xandy blinked a couple of times, like what Quinn was saying was physically touching her. She swallowed a couple of times as well, which told Quinn that she was unsure of things.

Quinn blew her breath out and dropped her head shaking it back and forth. "And we're back to intense conversation and not the weather a'tall," she said, her tone so self-castigating that Xandy couldn't help but laugh.

"It's okay," Xandy said, finding Quinn's mannerisms so endearing. "I think I was just as guilty in that as you were."

Quinn leaned her head back on the headboard, stretching her legs out in front of her, crossing them at the ankles. "So, what do you think the weather will do this week?"

Xandy laughed, leaning over to put her head against Quinn's shoulder companionably. "I think it will rain and rain and rain." Xandy sighed deeply.

Quinn put her arm around the smaller girl. "You'll be okay."

Xandy leaned against Quinn, turning her head to look up at the other woman. "Are you sure?"

"Dìreach," Quinn said in Gaelic. "Absolutely."

Xandy settled more comfortably against her bodyguard. They talked for a while about inconsequential things and before long, Quinn realized that Xandy had fallen asleep again. Xandy's lips twitching with anxiety, Quinn leaned back with her head against the headboard, and feeling Xandy shift to relax against her again. They slept that way that first night.

Quinn woke the next morning to the feeling of someone touching her neck. Glancing down she saw that Xandy was still lying against her, and her finger was touching the tattoo on her neck.

She grinned, anticipating the question. "Family crest."

"Knew I was going to ask, huh?"

Quinn nodded, moving her head around to stretch her neck muscles a bit. Then she glanced down to see the bluest, almost lavender. eyes watching her.

"Wot?" Quinn asked, her accent clear.

Xandy smiled at that. "You know I need to know what the stuff on the family crest means."

Quinn made a noise in the back of her throat to indicate impatience even as she grinned. Reaching up she touched the tattoo. It was a white shield shape with a red lion and two red crescent-shaped moons below.

"White indicates peace and serenity, red is a martyr's color, it symbolizes military might and generosity. The lion is a symbol of courage, and the crescent is a subject who has been enlightened by his king."

"Wow."

"Yeah, yeah…" Quinn said, as she moved to stand.

"It's cool that you're that connected to your family and country," Xandy said, sitting up to stretch.

"Aren't you?" Quinn asked glibly and immediately regretted it when she saw Xandy blanch. Stepping back toward the bed, she gave Xandy an alarmed look. "Are you okay?"

Xandy nodded too quickly, and moved to get out of bed and headed for the bathroom. Quinn watched her go and wondered what was wrong. She was still wondering when Xandy appeared out in the courtyard twenty minutes later.

Quinn was sitting at the table in the courtyard, drinking the coffee she'd made and smoking. Xandy walked over, carrying her coffee and sat down at the table. To her credit, she didn't apologize, having taken in what Quinn had said about her not having to apologize all the time. They both sat silently for a couple of minutes. Quinn noticed that Xandy fingered her cup fretfully, when she looked over at the girl, she seemed deeply focused on her coffee. So Quinn waited.

After what seemed like hours, Xandy began to talk, her voice hesitant.

"My family is dead," she said, barely above a whisper.

Quinn sat up at hearing that, her look intent, but she didn't say anything, imagining that this was hard enough for Xandy to talk about.

"They were killed by a tornado," Xandy continued, her eyes focused on her cup. "It was an F4, it came up so fast that they didn't have time to get to shelter. At least that's what the police said."

"Jesus…" Quinn breathed, unable to fathom losing an entire family; she knew she'd die if she lost her family like that.

Xandy pressed her lips together, not wanting to cry, but not sure she could control it.

"It was three years ago. I begged them…" she said, her voice breaking. "I begged them to move here, I told my dad I could buy them a farm out in the country…" Her voice trailed off as she shook her head, then she gave a short mirthless laugh. "My dad couldn't cotton to these Californians; they were all crazy as far as he was concerned. What the hell did they know about growin' stuff?" She shook her head. "I told him that California has a huge amount of agricultural exports, but he wouldn't listen. He liked his farm, he liked his house, his land…"

Quinn had no idea what to say, the magnitude of what she was hearing was on a scale she didn't feel equipped to handle. Then Xandy lifted her head, tears filled her eyes. "My three baby brothers and two sisters died that day, along with my mom and dad…" The tears overflowed. "How do you get over that?"

"You don't, at least not for a long time."

Xandy shook her head, letting her tears flow. Quinn couldn't stand it, and moved to hug her. Xandy leaned into Quinn and sobbed.

When it came to women crying, Quinn Kavanaugh could not handle it; to her it was completely wrong for a woman to cry with anything but joy. She knew she got that from her mother who was forever telling her that women were the "good lord's gift to the world" and that she'd better treat them right.

When Xandy had finally calmed, Quinn moved back to her chair, immediately lighting another cigarette while Xandy composed herself.

"So. What's on the agenda for today?" Quinn asked solicitously.

"Not much," Xandy said, appreciating the change in topic. "Just the gym."

"Sounds good."

Quinn took Xandy to the gym she usually worked out in, and Xandy found a class to take while Quinn went and worked out with her regular trainer. Since Quinn knew the owner of the gym fairly well, she was comfortable with Xandy being able to move about the gym safely. The owner, Rob Wolfe, was an ex-Army Ranger so when Quinn told him that she was protecting Xandy, Rob understood and kept an eye on her.

An hour later, Xandy walked into the room where Quinn was training with Todd. They were in the boxing ring, and Quinn and Todd were battling it out. Quinn was wearing the customary sports bra and black gym shorts; she was barefoot with black fingerless gloves on. Xandy was astounded at how much lean muscle Quinn had, she found herself envious that there didn't appear to be an ounce of fat on the woman.

Lean muscles flexed and relaxed as she bounced and moved during the sparring match. At one point she moved in looping her leg around Todd's left leg and taking him down to the mat. She spun and moved so quickly that Xandy could barely track her movements. This woman was definitely a fighter and she held nothing back in her training. Neither did Todd, they were both bruised and red from where they'd made contact with the other during the match.

When Quinn walked over to Xandy her skin was sheened with sweat even as she toweled off.

"Hey," Quinn said, smiling. "How was your class?"

"Not nearly as intense as that," Xandy said, in admiration.

Quinn grinned as she reached for her shirt and put it on. "You ready to go?"

"Sure."

A few minutes later in the car, Xandy looked over at Quinn. "You take your workouts pretty seriously."

"I have to."

"What do you mean?"

"Well, when all else fails, this is my only weapon," she said, indicating her body.

Xandy grimaced at that thought.

"Wot?" Quinn asked.

"I can't imagine doing what you do."

"That's the job… deciding who you'd be willing to die for."

"Die for?" Xandy repeated, shocked.

"That's the idea of a bodyguard."

"But…"

"But what?"

"What if the person you're guarding isn't worth dying for?" Xandy asked.

Quinn looked over at her, narrowing her eyes slightly. "You mean what if you're not worth dying for?"

"Okay, yes."

Quinn looked back at the road, then canted her head giving Xandy a sideways glance. "You are."

"I don't think so."

"Fortunately you don't get the say in that."

"I could fire you."

Quinn snorted. "No you can't."

"I could get BJ to fire you," Xandy shot back.

"Good luck with that."

Xandy gave a deep sigh. "I don't want anyone to die for me."

"Happens all the time. You just don't see it."

"What do you mean?"

"Your armed services, your fire fighters, your cops."

Xandy nodded. "That's true, but why?"

"Because it is the job of those that can protect people, to protect the people they can."

Xandy stared back at her, unable to fathom such unshakable courage. "Boy they really got the courage part right on your coat of arms."

Quinn simply chuckled and drove them back to the house.

Later that night, Quinn was checking the house before going to bed and when she looked in on Xandy and saw that she was tossing and turning. Stepping into the room and over to the bed, Quinn said Xandy's name and startled her awake.

"It's just me," Quinn said, holding up her hands.

Xandy closed her eyes, nodding her head.

"'Nother one, huh?" Quinn asked.

"Yeah."

"Move over," Quinn said, moving to sit on the bed with her.

Xandy chuckled, even as she moved. Within a minute, Xandy was settled against Quinn's shoulder.

"This is becoming a habit," she said.

"Indeed," Quinn said, grinning all the same.

After a few minutes Xandy glanced up at Quinn. "What's Northern Ireland like?"

"It's incredible," Quinn said, wistful.

"Tell me."

"Well," Quinn said, settling more comfortably against the headboard, "It's always green, just like they say, but it's rich in people. The people are full of life, and they love to sit and talk for hours and hours. There's no hurry there, people take their time."

"Big difference from LA."

"Got that right."

"What about castles?" Xandy asked, her expression childlike.

Quinn grinned. "Oh yeah, we got those too. Hell, I grew up a stone's throw from Carrickfergus near Belfast."

"Really?" Xandy asked, unable to fathom that. "How old is that castle?"

"It was built in eleven seventy-seven, so pretty old. My brothers and me used to go and play, acting like the castle was bein' attacked. We'd work the canons and yell orders at each other, it was pretty grand."

"How many siblings do you have?"

"Oh, quite a few," Quinn said, rubbing her eyebrow with her thumbnail. "I have five brothers and three sisters."

"Nine kids?" Xandy asked, astounded. "I thought my parents were bad with six of us."

"Well. In Northern Ireland there isn't a lot to do, but drink and make babbys."

"Babbys? Oh, babies," she said, getting the slang.

"Very good."

"So, what are the houses like there?"

"Well, I can tell you that some of these movies were pure bollocks when they portray the Irish as poor potato farmers in nothin' short of mud huts. My da did pretty well for himself, we lived in a very nice manor in Belfast."

"Your da?" Xandy repeated. "That's your dad, right?"

"Right."

"So it was a big house?"

"It was… is, they still live there. All the same it was only five bedrooms so we had to double up a bit."

"Are you the oldest?" Xandy asked, fascinated by Quinn's background.

"No, I'm round about the middle, three of my brothers and one of my sisters is older. The rest are younger than me."

"Wow," Xandy said. "Your parents had their hands full."

"Nah, the older kids usually kept the younger kids in line. Usually."

"You were trouble, weren't you?"

Quinn laughed. "I had a tendency to forget that I was supposed to be home, I was forever out after dark, playing and adventuring."

"Is that why you joined the army?"

Quinn considered the question for a minute. "Yeah, I guess that's probably why," she said, as if she'd never really considered that before. "I always wanted to go on adventures, different lands, different experiences, I was insatiable."

"Never thought you'd end up stuck with someone like me, did you?"

"You're not so bad," Quinn said equably. "Now some of your fellow industry folk..." she said, as she rolled her eyes.

"You really don't like people in the business, do you?" Xandy asked. she'd picked it up from a few of Quinn's comments.

"No."

"But didn't I hear you're dating a movie star?"

"Heard that, did you?" Quinn said, narrowing her eyes at the younger girl.

"It's the business. Even I'm not immune to gossip," Xandy replied.

"Ah-ha… Well, yeah, I am currently dating a movie star."

"But you don't like movie stars?"

"I don't even like her sometimes," Quinn answered honestly.

"Oh, that's not good," Xandy said, grimacing.

"That's why I have my own place."

"Much to her annoyance?"

"Oh yeah. If she could, she'd have me stuffed and installed in her home permanently."

"Stuffed?" Xandy queried horrified.

"Shellacked, mounted, framed, hung…" Quinn listed, teasing.

"Oh my…" Xandy said, widening her eyes. "She's that much in love with you?"

"I wouldn't call it love."

"What would you call it?"

"Obsessed, possessive, gotta have what no one else has…" Quinn said, not sounding too impressed.

"But you don't think she loves you?" Xandy asked, unable to understand the logic.

"I'm not sure she even knows what love is. She's about acquiring things. I'm just one of the things she's acquired."

"That's terrible, people aren't possessions," she said with such vehemence Quinn caught the implication.

"Is that what happened to you?" Quinn asked gently.

Xandy paused, surprised by the question. She looked like she was thinking about it, but then she nodded her head. "In a way. Tommy thought I was going to be his ticket."

"To everything?"

"Pretty much, but I didn't make enough money for him to get everything he wanted."

Once again, Quinn detected an undertone to what Xandy was saying. "So…"

Xandy pressed her lips together in a frown. "He decided a sex tape would be just the ticket."

"Are you fecking kiddin' me?" Quinn exclaimed, shocked.

"I wish I was," Xandy said sourly.

"Manky blackguard," Quinn muttered.

"A what?" Xandy asked, unable to keep from smiling at the utter contempt written all over Quinn's face.

"Suffice it to say I think he's a dirty son of a bitch."

"Well, that's true."

"Is that why you divorced him?"

"That was definitely the final straw, yeah," Xandy said, nodding.

Quinn nodded too.

"Fecking?" Xandy asked.

Quinn curled her lips in a grin. "What we say to keep from getting a beatin' from ma."

"Awww."

A short while later Xandy was once again asleep, and Quinn found that it was rather endearing that the girl seemed so comfortable in the arms of a butch lesbian. Quinn imagined that Xandy hadn't had a lot of exposure to gays, at least not of the female side. Gay men were all over the industry, always accepted for their flair and style. Lesbians tended to be in the background, except in cases like Ellen DeGeneres or Ellen Page or most recently Holland Taylor, which Quinn put firmly as a win in the lesbian column. Someone like Xandy, however, would rarely be around someone like her and Quinn found it a testament to the girl's character that she adjusted to Quinn as quickly as she had.

Quinn had no way of knowing that Xandy hadn't made many friends in Hollywood. Her Midwest values and general naiveté, and her refusal to let those go, made her the odd woman out in most circles. Sadly, the people she'd trusted had betrayed her at every turn. While Quinn was indeed an unknown quantity to Xandy, she was also someone Xandy felt she could safely admire for her accomplishments and willingness to be who she was. In two short days, Quinn had shown her more thoughtful and gallant graces than most people had shown her in years. It was something, and Xandy appreciated the rarity of it.

The night passed into morning and Quinn woke to the feeling of a hand on her arm. She chuckled even as she opened her eyes to look down at Xandy.

"Always got yer hands all over me," Quinn said, a smile telling Xandy that she was kidding.

Xandy grinned, biting her lip in guilt. "I admit it. I was covetous of your arms."

"Oh-ho…" Quinn said, widening her eyes dramatically. "You diabolical git."

"I'm a what?"

"A diabolical git."

"An evil… thing?" Xandy guessed.

"A very terrible horrible person," Quinn translated.

"All that?" Xandy replied, mocking horror.

"Indeed." Quinn grinned.

"Okay. Really though, I was looking at these," she said, touching all the tattoos on Quinn's left arm, ending up on the ones on her forearm.

Quinn touched her forearm, running over the tattooed words as she pronounced them. "This is 'An làmb a bheir, 's i a gheibh.' It means the hand that gives is the hand that gets."

"Gaelic."

"Right."

"And this?" Xandy asked, touching the tattoo on the lower part of Quinn's upper arm.

Quinn couldn't help but grin, the girl's curiosity was boundless. "It's the symbol for the Northern Ireland National football team."

"Soccer."

"Football," Quinn said, narrowing her eyes.

"Okay…" Xandy said, grinning and then looking more closely at the symbol.

"And this," Xandy said, tapping the tattoo on the upper part of Quinn's upper arm. "I've seen this one a million times, but I don't really know what it means."

"It's called the Triquetra. Most people think that it came from that show Charmed where the symbol appeared on their 'book of shadows' but it has truly nothing to do with witchcraft. It's also known as the Trinity Knot."

"And what does it mean?" Xandy asked, sensing that Quinn didn't like that it had become such a common symbol, watering down her culture.

"The Celts believed that everything in life came in threes; past, present and future; three stages of life; and the three domains, earth, sea, and sky. The Triquetra represents the three in an endless line, no beginning, no end."

"I like that."

Quinn smiled at her in response, she liked that the girl seemed to take everything in and appreciate it for what it was.

"It's really rare for someone as young as you to be so open to things," Quinn said, thinking back to her thoughts the night before.

Xandy looked surprised by the comment, then shrugged. "I guess I just like to learn."

Quinn narrowed her eyes, sensing that Xandy was sidestepping the compliment, but not wanting to call her on it. Quinn's phone rang at that point, reaching over to the nightstand she picked up her phone, looking at it.

"'Lo," she answered, then smiled. "Ray Ray, yeah, what's up?"

Xandy watched as Quinn talked on the phone, moving to sit up and stretching as she did. Quinn found herself distracted by the movement, and then realized she was watching her charge in fascination. The girl was very definitely beautiful, and she certainly had a body on her.

Knock it off, her mind warned her.

Quinn immediately averted her eyes, moving to sit up to continue her conversation with her friend.

"Yeah, I should be up for that," Quinn said as she got off the bed. "Gotta fine tune her though, she was running rough last week."

She listened for another minute, glancing over at Xandy who was still sitting on the bed, watching her talk on the phone. The girl did that kind of thing a lot. Quinn wondered if Xandy just couldn't adjust to the way she looked or what. That thought had her looking in the mirror and running her hand through her red hair smoothing it.

"Got it, I'll call you later to confirm," Quinn said. She hung up the phone and turned to Xandy. "Got a favor to ask."

"Sure, what is it?"

"I need a ride over to my place, I need to pick up my bike."

"Bike?" Xandy repeated, thinking a bicycle didn't match Quinn at all.

"Harley," Quinn clarified, seeing the confusion clearly on Xandy's face.

"Oh. That makes way more sense. Of course."

An hour later they were at Quinn's apartment in Santa Monica; Xandy was surprised that it was on the beach. The apartment itself was small, but certainly a good enough size for one person. It was very upscale, and Xandy could only imagine how much it cost to live right on the beach. The apartment itself was nicely apportioned and seemed very much to be the Quinn she'd been getting to know. The furniture in the living room was black leather and the walls were a sea blue color. There were a few framed photographs on the walls, one of which caught Xandy's eye. Walking over to the photograph she looked more closely at it. It was a picture of a ruined castle, up on a cliff with the ocean below and the sky going to shade of blue and purple with the sunset.

"That's Dunluce castle," Quinn said from behind her.

"It's amazing," Xandy said, her voice nearly breathless.

Quinn smiled, then pointed another photograph. "That's Carrickfergus castle."

"The one you played at?" Xandy asked as she moved to the other photograph.

The castle seemed to rise out of the calm bay that it guarded, and it was reflected in the water of the picture. The sky was so blue it as almost unreal.

"That's so cool…" Xandy said, shaking her head, then she turned looking at Quinn, and gestured around her. "This place, it's very you."

"Yeah, I like it, when I'm here…"

"When you're not guarding some pop princess?"

"Or at Val's," Quinn said, her tone indicating how she felt about that.

"Does she come here?"

"To Santa Monica?" Quinn asked in mock horror.

Xandy grimaced "I guess not."

"No."

Xandy shook her head. She liked the Santa Monica area. Who wouldn't like an area with a Ferris wheel?

Quinn fished around in a blue and green glass bowl, on her kitchen counter, and plucked out a set of keys.

"Got 'em," she said, gesturing toward the door. "Let's go."

Xandy nodded, taking another quick look around. They walked out of the lobby of the apartments and back to the garage area of the complex.

"Two car garage?" Xandy asked, surprised. They were fairly hard to come by.

"Oh trust me, I pay extra for this," Quinn assured her, as she unlocked the pad lock and lifted the garage door.

The garage was another surprise to Xandy. To say that it was organized was an understatement. The floor was covered in textured tiles in greys and blacks. The back wall of the garage was lined with black and silver cabinets including a rolling tool container. There was a lift in one corner, and a couple of rolling cabinets tucked into another corner.

Parked on one side of the garage was a beautifully sleek Dodge Charger. It was painted a dark blue with the letters RT on the side in red. The chrome wheels sparkled; all the chrome on the vehicle sparkled. It was obvious that Quinn took very good care of her car.

Stepping into the garage Xandy could smell the mixture of gasoline and exhaust, and found that she really liked it. It had a kind of old school muscle feel to it that she found very striking, in a pleasant way.

"So you have two muscle cars?" Xandy asked, running her hand reverently over the fender of the Charger.

"This one's new. In fact this is my fee for your protection detail."

"Your fee is a car?"

"Well, the amount I paid for it was the fee, but this was what I told BJ I wanted the fee for."

"Sounds about right," Xandy said, winking at her.

Quinn grinned, then moved toward the motorcycle parked at the other side of the garage. Xandy followed her. The tank and frame of the bike was matte army green. It certainly wasn't a fussy bike, it seemed like it was all business. Xandy thought that it was just like Quinn, no-nonsense.

Quinn walked over to the cabinets, pulled out a backpack and started putting tools in it. Before long she returned to where Xandy stood and glanced over at her as she reached for her helmet. Looping it on the handlebars, she leveled the bike, pushed the kickstand back and nodded toward the outside. They walked out of the garage with Quinn pushing the bike. Once outside, Quinn put the kickstand down and walked over to close the garage door and secure the lock.

Walking back over to the bike, Quinn climbed onto it, starting it with the legendary Harley rumble. Xandy felt herself shiver. There was something about that sound and the very sight of this woman sitting on it that sent a visceral reaction through her.

"So you gonna follow me back," Quinn told her as she reached for her helmet, taking the leather riding gloves out of it and pulling the helmet on. Her helmet was the same matte army green as the bike.

"Yeah," Xandy replied.

"You want a ride to your car?" Quinn asked, grinning as she pulled on her leather riding gloves.

"Sure," Xandy said, her blue eyes sparkling with enthusiasm.

Quinn held her hand out to Xandy, Xandy took it, climbing carefully onto the back of the bike. Behind Quinn, she moved her hands to Quinn's shoulders to steady herself. Quinn reached around her, pointing to the spare helmet on the back of the bike.

"Put that on."

Xandy pulled the helmet on, securing it easily.

It was a simple half helmet, not like the full face one Quinn wore, but it would work for the short trip.

"Now, hold on," Quinn said, revving the powerful engine.

The ride was a short one, but Xandy loved it. She had her arms wrapped around Quinn's waist, hands grasping the leather of Quinn's jacket. She pressed her face to Quinn's back, and inhaled the smell of leather; it was a wonderful, if short, experience.

Climbing off the bike at her car, Xandy smiled brightly. "That was so cool! Thank you," she said, putting her hand on Quinn's gloved hand.

Quinn nodded, smiling.

"I'll see you back at your place, stay close," Quinn told her, then she reached up and put down the helmet's face shield.

The drive back to Brentwood didn't take long. Driving behind Quinn in her little blue Lexus SUV, Xandy did find her eyes constantly drawn to the figure of Quinn on her motorcycle. She knew she was far too fascinated with her bodyguard, but there was something drawing her to this woman. She wasn't sure if it was Quinn's overt gentility when it came to her, or if she just had no real experience with a woman of Quinn's 'type' before. As they drove down a two lane stretch of road, Xandy noticed another motorcycle coming down the other side of the road toward them. As the other motorcycle came close, Xandy saw Quinn drop a gloved hand and held it out slightly in kind of a 'low five' position. The motorcyclist on the other bike did the same.

Xandy waited for Quinn to walk the still-running bike backwards to get it parked where she wanted it in Xandy's garage. When Quinn cut the engine and took her helmet off, she could see that the girl had another question. She grinned in amusement.

"Wot?" Quinn queried, stripping off her gloves and taking her jacket off.

"What was that thing you did when that other motorcycle passed you back there?" Xandy asked.

Quinn looked back at her for a moment, at first trying to figure out what she was talking about, and then realized what she meant.

"Oh... just kind of a salute to a fellow rider," she said, shrugging.

"And he knew to do it back?" Xandy queried.

"It's pretty common among riders."

"Very cool," Xandy said, grinning.

Quinn just chuckled, the girl found the most inane things, fascinating. Setting down the backpack she'd brought with her, she began rummaging for the tools she wanted. Kneeling down she began working on removing the air box cover for the carburetor.

"So what are you doing to it?" Xandy asked, watching as Quinn worked.

Quinn glanced up at her, her expression indicating surprise as to Xandy's continued curiosity.

"The bike's been running a bit rough, so I'm gonna clean out the carburetor to see if that helps."

"You do your own work?"

"If I can," Quinn said as she laid aside the air box cover.

Xandy nodded continuing to watch Quinn work.

"Would you take me on a ride sometime?" Xandy asked, hoping she wasn't being too big of a pain.

Quinn glanced up at her again, looking amused.

"Sure," she said, as she picked the hex keys to remove the next set of bolts. "In fact I'm doing this to go on a run tomorrow, if you want to come?"

"That would be great," Xandy said, but then looked crest fallen. "But that's your day off. I shouldn't bug you on your day off."

"It's okay. I'll warn you though it's with a lesbian group called Dykes on Bikes."

"So?" Xandy replied, mystified.

Quinn laughed outright at the look on the girl's face. "Alright then," she said. "Let me get this taken care of, so we won't get stranded tomorrow."

Quinn spent the better half of the day cleaning the carburetor and cleaning the bike to get it ready to ride.

Later that night, Xandy wandered into Quinn's room after she had just settled down. Quinn was not at all surprised. With a knowing grin, Quinn moved to sit up and put her arm out to Xandy. Xandy looked a bit abashed, but climbed into the bed all the same, moving to lean against Quinn.

"Bad dream?"

Xandy shook her head. "No, just got lonely."

Quinn smiled mildly, the girl was definitely endearing. Quinn had music playing; it wasn't the harder rock that she usually played in the car. Xandy listened to the song playing.

"Who is this?"

"Chris Daughtry."

The song that was playing was called "Crashed" and it talked about how the singer was not sure what he was looking for, but then he crashed into this other person. It wasn't your usual love song, but it really did relate to people who maybe normally didn't fit together.

"I like it," Xandy said, closing her eyes and listening.

Quinn merely nodded. They both sat listening to the music, and the songs that came after that one. Without realizing it, Quinn stroked Xandy's arm with her thumb, lost in her own thoughts. Xandy felt the movement and found that she very much liked the feeling it gave her. It was amazing to be so relaxed in someone's presence, especially when she barely knew Quinn, but that's what she was, completely relaxed.

When she'd been in her own room, Xandy had felt a sense of loss. She missed the closeness that she'd become quickly used to with Quinn. Part of her knew she needed to look at those feelings more closely, but the other part of her that wanted to stop thinking so much about everything shoved that thought aside. In Quinn's presence she found peace and a feeling of safety she'd desperately needed for months now. It had been that need that had gotten her out of her bed and wandering into Quinn's room.

"I really liked your apartment," Xandy said, glancing up at Quinn.

"Thanks."

Xandy sighed, looking around her at the bedroom. "I guess I've been pretty bad about doing anything here."

"What's up with that anyway?" Quinn asked, having wondered that since she'd first walked into the house.

Xandy shrugged, moving to sit up and looking down at Quinn. "My other place was decorated. I loved that place."

"You don't love this one?" Quinn asked, pushing herself up to lean against the headboard.

"I do," Xandy said, glancing around the room, "it's just…"

"Just what?" Quinn asked gently.

Quinn was learning quickly that there were a lot of hidden landmines when it came to Xandy's past, and she was doing her best to navigate them as carefully as possible.

"I just don't feel like I've settled in," Xandy said, looking sad. "BJ had seen this place, and thought that I might like it, which I did. It was after… Jason."

"The bodyguard."

Xandy nodded, swallowing convulsively and breathing out slowly as if to calm herself.

"I bought it, but," she said, shrugging again. "I just never really had the heart to do anything with it after that."

Quinn nodded, understanding that problem.

Xandy looked hopefully at Quinn. "Would you help me do something with it?"

"Sure. What are you thinking of?"

"Just like paint and stuff, maybe some tile work in the bathrooms."

"I could probably help with some of that."

Xandy bit her lip, smiling, then nodding almost to herself.

"It's about time I do something here," Xandy said, her gesture indicating the house.

Quinn nodded, agreeing with that sentiment whole heartedly.

"What time do we leave tomorrow?" Xandy asked yawning.

"Six o'clock."

Xandy nodded, settling more comfortably against the other woman, putting her arm cross Quinn's stomach. Xandy felt the muscles under her arm twitch a little bit, but didn't think anything of it.

Quinn barely kept herself from outright jumping when Xandy's hand had slid across her stomach. The action and the corresponding feeling had been very unexpected. The sensations that radiated from Xandy's arm resting there had Quinn wondering if she was in some serious trouble. She fell into a fitful sleep with self-castigating thoughts of what she perceived as her complete lack of self-control. Little did Quinn know that Xandy being blissfully unaware of any of Quinn's turbulent thoughts was actually a testament to Quinn's self-control.

Chapter 3

The ride the next day was both fun and also a bit of a source of trouble for Quinn. While all the girls from the group knew that Quinn was dating Valerie Henning, a shining beacon of lesbian stardom, Valerie never went riding with her. When Quinn showed up to the run with Xandy, she was hailed with a series of catcalls and, "Whata, whata, whata?" from the head of the group, Sandy.

She'd explained that Xandy was a friend, and that she was not gay. "So don't try it, Pam," Quinn had said, winking at the dark-haired woman across from her. Once they'd cleared that up, they had gotten ready to begin their run. Quinn wore faded jeans with black leather chaps over them, her black leather Harley Davidson boots and a black leather vest under which she wore simply a black sports bra. Over it she wore an all-black classic biker style jacket.

Xandy had surprised her by wearing what Quinn would consider appropriate clothes for the run. She wore jeans with flat black boots and a long sleeved thermal shirt in light blue, as well as a pullover hoodie jacket that was also light blue. She looked very wholesome, but also looked like she'd be warm.

Unfortunately, they hadn't counted on the cooler weather in the mountains that they'd rode to and Xandy was shivering by the time they got to their destination. As they got off the bike, Quinn unzipped her jacket, took it off and put it around Xandy's shoulders, then she turned to rummage in her saddle bag and pulled out a black thermal shirt with the letters "HD" for Harley Davidson in orange on the chest. Taking the vest off and setting it aside, Quinn pulled on the thermal shirt and put the vest on over it.

"Quinn, you're going to be cold," Xandy said, trying to hand Quinn her jacket back.

Quinn gave her a pointed look, telling her without words that she wasn't going to argue with her about the jacket. Xandy sighed mightily, but gratefully put her arms in the arms of the jacket. It was big on her, but it still held Quinn's warmth, so it felt wonderful.

The group had lunch at a local restaurant and Xandy was entertained by the conversations going on. She noticed a few long looks in her direction, one was even intercepted by Quinn, who narrowed her eyes at the woman and shook her head slowly, even as she grinned. Xandy took the opportunity to talk to these women and found that many of them were really nice and very definitely from all walks of life. There were cops, nurses, a doctor, a lawyer, an architect, a few fire fighters, and even one judge.

She felt a wonderful sense of togetherness from the group, and they happily included her even though it had been made clear that she wasn't a lesbian. Xandy also noticed that not one of these women held a lot of interest for her, not like Quinn did, and that pricked at her sub-conscious.

Quinn noticed that Xandy became quiet at one point during lunch, she kept an eye on her without being too obtrusive, but when the girl wandered out of the restaurant. Quinn knew she had to follow her. It was unlikely that Xandy would be in any danger in this remote location, but Quinn wasn't taking any chances.

She found Xandy standing near the bike which was parked near a stand of trees.

"Everything okay?" Quinn asked from behind Xandy.

Xandy turned around, looking up at Quinn, her face shadowed before she smiled.

"Yes," she said, doing her best to shake off the thoughts that had been intruding on her.

Quinn narrowed her eyes slightly, not believing the girl, but not wanting to push too hard. "The girls can get to be a bit much."

"Oh, no," Xandy said, shaking her head. "They're great, really."

Quinn nodded, her green eyes on the girl.

"We'll probably be heading out here in a few minutes, so you might want to hit the ladies room."

Xandy nodded, starting to walk back toward the restaurant. Quinn watched her go and followed a few paces behind. She wasn't sure what was going on with Xandy, but she was going to make sure she was around if she wanted to talk.

That night Xandy was unusually quiet, but Quinn didn't push, wanting to give her space. They ate dinner quietly, and headed to bed early, the fresh air had made them both tired. Regardless of her quiet mood, Xandy found her way into Quinn's room all the same. For once they simply fell asleep; Xandy on her side next to Quinn, her head in the hollow of Quinn's shoulder, her hand next to her face on Quinn's shoulder, with Quinn's right arm around her.

The next morning Xandy got up before Quinn and went to shower and then make breakfast. Quinn wandered into the kitchen an hour later, having showered and dressed. Xandy was going through emails on her laptop computer when she gasped out loud. Quinn turned from getting her coffee and saw all of the color drain from Xandy's face. Walking over to her, Quinn could see an email open on the computer. She read it over Xandy's shoulder.

You dirty whore, I'm gonna fuck you up in ways you can't even begin to imagine...

It was all Quinn needed to read before reaching over to snap the laptop shut. By that time, Xandy was shaking. Quinn moved to kneel in front of the girl, taking her hands in hers; Xandy's hands were ice cold. Looking up into Xandy's eyes, Quinn gave her hands a gentle squeeze.

"No one is going to get to you," Quinn told her. "No one, do you hear me?"

Xandy looked back at Quinn, her lavender-blue eyes wide with terror. Quinn pulled the girl toward her, holding Xandy's tiny frame to her. As she moved to stand, she scooped Xandy up in her arms. Quinn carried her to the master bedroom, and sat down on the bed. She leaned against the headboard, and cradled Xandy against her. The girl was shaking like a leaf. Quinn held her, reaching up to stroke hair in an effort to calm her.

"It's going to be okay," Quinn told her, her mind racing as she did. "We're gonna take care of this."

"There has been others," Xandy whispered.

"There have?" Quinn asked, her tone almost angry that she didn't know that.

Xandy nodded, her face pressed against Quinn's shirt.

"Does BJ know?" Quinn asked, because she hadn't been told anything about this if he did.

Xandy shook her head.

"Xan…" Quinn breathed. "Why? Why didn't you tell him?"

Xandy scrubbed her face with her hand, shaking her head. "I've already been a royal pain in the ass to him."

"Fecking hell, Xandy," Quinn said, exasperated. "You are not a pain in the ass. You're probably the easiest client I've ever had, and I'm sure BJ feels the same."

Xandy didn't say anything.

"Do you still have the other emails?" Quinn asked gently.

Xandy shook her head. "I deleted them."

"Fuck…" Quinn muttered, cussing for the first time in front of Xandy.

It was enough to shock the girl out of her stupor.

"You're ma would smack ya for that," Xandy said, in a fairly good imitation of Quinn's accent, grinning.

Quinn glanced down at her, shocked then she chuckled.

"Got me there. Okay, let me go and make some calls," she said, moving to stand.

Xandy made a petulant sound in the back of her throat and tightened her hold on the part of Quinn's shirt that she had her hand wrapped around.

"Okay…" Quinn said, grinning, as she reached into her pocket for her phone. "I'll make the calls right here."

The first call she made was to Mackie, who told her to call BJ directly, giving her BJ's private cell phone that he "always answers, come hell or high water."

Mackie was not wrong, BJ answered on the second ring.

"Yeah?" BJ answered.

"BJ, it's Quinn."

"What's goin' on?" BJ asked, alert.

"Need your help," Quinn said, glancing down at Xandy.

"Name it!"

"Xandy's been getting threatening emails."

"She's *been* getting emails?" BJ cut in. "Since when?"

Quinn grimaced, knowing BJ was not going to be pleased with the answer. "Apparently for a while now."

"Bloody fucking hell!" BJ shouted. "Why am I just hearing this now?"

Quinn widened her eyes slightly, seeing Xandy wince. It was impossible for her not to have heard BJ's exclamation.

"Because I just heard about it myself," Quinn said mildly.

"Put her on the damned phone," BJ raged.

"Yeah, I don't think so," Quinn said, not willing to let BJ scream at the girl. She was already terrified.

"Excuse me?" BJ said, his voice having dropped to a dangerous octave.

Quinn was not intimidated; her emerald-green eyes narrowed slightly, a sign to anyone that knew her that meant she was digging her heels in.

"No," she said simply.

"Be wide Kavanaugh…" BJ said, telling her to be careful in Irish slang.

There was a long minute of silence on the other end of the line. Quinn waited, refusing to back down.

She heard BJ mutter something that sounded suspiciously like, "cheeky Irish…"

Finally, she heard a mighty sigh.

"Fine!" BJ said. "I'll make some calls and get back to you soon."

"Thanks," Quinn said, upbeat.

"Bean deacair," BJ fired back, making Quinn laugh. He'd called her a difficult woman in Gaelic.

"You bet," Quinn replied, which elicited a laugh from the record mogul and they hung up.

Within two hours, a cell phone was ringing across town in Malibu. Devin James answered her cell phone, not recognizing the number, but it was on her business line so she still picked up.

"Hello?"

"Is this Devin James?" BJ queried.

"It is," Devin answered, surprised by the accent she was hearing.

"Ms. James, my name is BJ Sparks, and I got your name from Attorney General Chevalier. She said you've worked with her agency with great success. I'd like to hire you."

Devin's eyes widened slightly at the mention of his name, and widened further when he mentioned who he'd gotten her name from.

She'd worked with the Attorney General's office a couple of years before, helping them to solve a major cyber case. She had no idea that Midnight Chevalier herself remembered her.

"Okay," Devin said, not sure what to say to someone that was a major player in the music world. "What exactly do you need help with, Mr. Sparks?"

"Call me BJ," he said, his tone warm. "I'd like to meet with you if I can, I'd rather not discuss this kind of thing on the phone."

"Alright, when?"

"This afternoon?" BJ offered. "My house? Can you make it for lunch? Say one o'clock?"

Devin was taken back, she didn't imagine people like BJ Sparks had that kind of time on his hands, but she had to find out.

Devin stammered. "I... sure, yes."

"Perfect. I'll text you the address."

"Mr. Sparks," Devin said, quickly before he could hang up.

"BJ," he reminded her, humor in his voice.

"BJ... can I bring my fiancée?"

"Of course."

Devin hung up the phone with a sense of unreality. Standing, she walked to the back sliding door of her house, opened it and walked outside.

Skyler Boché, Devin's fiancée and the love of her life, sat smoking, legs stretched out in front of her and her feet on the chair across from her. Skyler glanced over her shoulder, as her hand rubbed the head of the Husky that sat next to her. Benny turned his head, giving Devin a quick "aroo" as a greeting. Devin walked over, moving to sit in the chair Skyler had her feet in. Skyler shifted her feet to allow Devin to sit, a routine they repeated often. The backyard was Skyler's haven, where she escaped to stare out at the ocean. Benny was her constant companion. He had been named after a member of Skyler's helicopter squad that had been killed in Iraq. Benny was trained as a PTSD therapy dog. He could sense when Skyler was having a rough day, and would alert Devin when that was happening. He was a calming influence for Skyler, when she needed it. She had been through some horrific things in Iraq, and was also in therapy to deal with what had happened.

Skyler looked at her fiancée and grinned, Devin had been the best thing that had ever happened to her. Devin, with her black hair with the purple streak running through it, and multiple ear piercings, was her 'wild child.' Skyler had never had someone who loved her completely and unconditionally. If it hadn't been for Devin, Skyler was sure that she'd never have begun the process to heal some of the trauma in her past. It was still an adjustment not to run away, but Devin's love kept her grounded and she was forever grateful to her for that.

"So you're never going to guess who I just talked to," Devin said, reaching out to pet Benny as he shoved his muzzle under hand.

"Who?" Skyler asked, her light blue-green eyes narrowing in the smoke she blew out.

"BJ Sparks," Devin said, so evenly that it took Skyler a second to catch up.

"Wait, what? You talked to BJ Sparks? *The* BJ Sparks?"

"Yup."

"Holy Hell," Skyler said, smiling broadly. "What did he want?"

"He wants to meet with me."

"For what?" Skyler asked, stunned.

"To hire me, he said."

"Whoa."

Devin James was known in the computer world as "the Glimmer" because she was able to hack into the most secure systems without leaving even the slightest trace she'd been there. She was also well-known for cracking the most complicated of computer fraud cases. When the FBI needed help, they called her, when any law enforcement needed help... they saved up a lot of money and called her! Now BJ Sparks had called her.

"And," Devin said, excited, "I get to bring you."

Skyler was perplexed. "Me? Why?"

"The meeting is at his house."

Skyler gave her a sidelong glance. "And he's okay with you bringing me?"

"Yep."

Skyler contemplated the idea for a moment, then gave Devin a sly glance. "Think he'll let me see his car collection?"

Devin rolled her eyes. "Oh lord!"

Skyler laughed.

Quinn pulled up in front of BJ's house that afternoon. Xandy was sitting in the passenger seat of the Mustang. It had taken a little bit of convincing to get her to come, as Xandy was sure that BJ was going to yell at her like he'd wanted to on the phone earlier.

"I'm not gonna to let that happen," Quinn had told her, with a shake of her head.

"What if he fires you?" Xandy asked, her eyes wide.

"He won't."

Finally, Xandy had agreed to come.

As Skyler and Devin rounded the drive in Skyler's car, a Nissan 370Z sports car, she caught sight of the classic Mustang already parked there and saw the woman getting out of the car. She whistled appreciatively at the car, even as she put her car in park. Devin grinned, knowing Skyler had a thing for cars.

Skyler got out, walking around to open the passenger door for Devin, her eyes on the Mustang the entire time. She put her hand out to help Devin out of the low-slung vehicle.

"Go on," Devin said, chuckling at Skyler as she nearly trotted over to the car.

"This is hot," Skyler said to Quinn as she walked up.

Quinn inclined her head. "Thanks."

"What are you running?" Skyler asked.

"Three ninety CI, big block," Quinn replied, loving that she'd found another car nut like herself.

"Skyler Boché," Skyler said, extending her hand to Quinn.

"Quinn Kavanaugh," Quinn responding, grasping Skyler's hand and shaking it firmly. "This is Xandy," Quinn said, gesturing to the petite blond.

Skyler nodded to Xandy, smiling, as Devin joined them.

"I can always find her near the cool cars," Devin said, grinning and extending her hand to Quinn. "Devin James," she said introducing herself.

"Pleasure," Quinn said.

Devin walked over to Xandy as Skyler and Quinn went back to discussing the Mustang.

"I'm Devin," she said to the other girl, seeing that she was quite timid.

"I'm Xandy," Xandy replied, smiling at Devin.

"Well, you girls can drool over the cars later," Devin said, glancing over her shoulder at Skyler and Quinn. "We should get inside before we're late."

With that Devin turned, putting her arm through Xandy's to lead her toward the door.

"You gotta get BJ to show you the garage," Quinn was saying to Skyler as they walked toward the door.

"Holy shit, you've seen it?" Skyler replied in awe.

Devin rolled her eyes, looking over at Xandy. "It's gonna be a long afternoon." To Skyler she said, "Business first, babe."

"Yeah, yeah," Skyler said, grinning as she winked at Devin.

"Such a brat sometimes…" Devin said, shaking her head, her tone teasing.

Once inside the house, BJ came to greet the group. Introductions were made, and BJ gestured for them to follow him.

"We're out here."

Devin fell into step next to the mogul. "So, how do you know Attorney General Chevalier?" she asked, her curiosity getting the better of her.

BJ opened and held the French doors that lead out to the large pool and patio area of his estate.

"Midnight and I go way back, she loves me," BJ said, his grin suggestive as he winked at Devin.

"Don't let Rick hear you say that!" said a blond haired woman walking toward them.

BJ chuckled unrepentantly. "And this is my lovely wife, Allexxiss."

Allexxiss was a world famous actress known as Ramsey. There was no missing the beautiful woman that stood before them. Blond haired and blue eyed, Ramsey was considered one of the country's most beautiful women. She smiled graciously at them and motioned to the table that had been set for lunch.

"We're over here," Allexxiss said, nodding to all of them.

Once they were all seated and more introductions had been made, BJ looked over at Quinn.

"Is that the Mach?" he asked, referring to the Mustang Quinn drove.

"It is," Quinn grinned proudly.

"I'll need to check that out after our meeting," BJ said. Then his light blue-green eyes went to Skyler. "Is that a three-seventy?"

"Nismo, yes," Skyler said, pleased that he obviously knew his cars.

"Yeah, I want to add a Nissan to my collection," BJ said. "Been looking at that new GT-R model."

Skyler nodded. "Got a chance to drive that in Vegas, it's one hot car."

"And if you'd let me buy you one, you'd have one," Devin put in smoothly, grinning at Skyler.

"Uh, no," Skyler said, shaking her head at her fiancée.

Devin just shook her head, rolling her eyes.

It was evident to everyone that this was a regular discussion between the couple.

"I have been known to pay in vehicles," BJ said, grinning at Devin.

Devin looked like she was considering the idea.

"Yeah, I don't think so," Skyler said, reaching over to take Devin's hand, squeezing it gently. "No offense Mr. Sparks."

"None taken," BJ said, grinning even as his eyes sparkled mischievously, "and it's BJ."

"Well, BJ," Devin said, shooting her fiancée a *so there* look, "we'll talk."

Skyler made a growling noise in the back of her throat and rolled her eyes, sighing.

Everyone chuckled at the exchange.

"Skyler Boché," BJ said, narrowing his eyes for a moment, "are you the one that works for LAFD?"

"Yeah…" Skyler said her tone cautious, wondering to how BJ knew that.

BJ nodded. "I read about you in the paper a few months back, your team saved a group of hikers in the back country."

Skyler dropped her head, but nodded, never one to accept adulations.

Quinn looked over at Skyler. "Fire fighter?"

"Chopper pilot," Skyler said.

"Aw, Sláinte," she said, holding up the wine class that had just been filled.

Skyler looked back at the other woman blankly.

"Sorry," Quinn said , "it means, well, it's like cheers."

"How do you say it?" Devin asked.

"Sláinte," Quinn repeated slower, it sounds like slant-cha.

"It's Gaelic," BJ said, grinning.

Skyler nodded. "Cool."

The group was silent for a bit, then Devin looked over at BJ.

"I gotta say," she began, "I'm really surprised that someone like Midnight Chevalier remembers me. I think I met her maybe twice while I was working at the DOJ."

"Well, Midnight has a damned good memory," BJ said, "and when she's impressed by someone, she never forgets. And she was definitely impressed with you, young lady. She said you helped them close a case that had been giving her heartburn for a year."

"It was actually kind of fun," Devin said with a nonchalant shrug.

BJ shook his head. "I can't even begin to wrap my head around what you do," he told Devin honestly, "but if you can help us out here, I will be eternally grateful."

Devin nodded. "I'll do my best."

"What's Midnight doing these days?" Allexxiss asked, having previously met the tiny powerhouse that was the California Attorney General.

"Oh you know, same old thing, upsetting the bad guys" BJ said.

"She's got to be the best AG this state's ever seen," Devin said.

"She certainly kicks ass and takes names," Skyler agreed.

"She helped out the LGBT community more than once," Quinn added.

"One of her best friends is gay," BJ said, "she'd do anything for Kana, and anyone like her. That's just how she is. I'd like to see her do more…" he said, his voice trailing off.

"Is she gonna run?" Allexxiss asked, her blue eyes widened.

"Everyone she knows is pushing her to," BJ confirmed.

"Run?" Devin asked, a note of hope in her voice.

"For Governor," BJ said.

"Holy shit! That would be awesome," Devin said.

"You have no idea," BJ said smiling.

There was a lull in conversation again as everyone digested the information they'd just heard, which was fairly juicy gossip.

BJ looked over at Xandy then, he'd noted that the girl had literally not spoken the entire time.

"You're awfully quiet," BJ said, looking directly at the girl.

Devin noticed that Quinn's chin came up, and glanced at Skyler to see if she'd noticed. Skyler glanced back at Devin and shrugged slightly.

"I'm just listening," Xandy said, very softly.

"Interesting..." BJ said. His tone had an edge to it.

"Leave off..." Quinn warned quietly.

BJ narrowed his eyes at Quinn. "Oh, we're gonna talk," he said, his tone threatening.

Quinn just looked back at BJ, her look anything but compliant. Then she inclined her head. "Yes, the *three* of us will talk," Quinn said, emphasizing the word "three."

"I don't think you need to be involved," BJ countered, his tone dismissive.

"Then it's not gonna happen," Quinn replied, a rebellious smirk on her lips.

Quinn could sense Xandy tensing behind her. Without looking away from BJ's glaring eyes, she reached behind her, extending a hand to Xandy, who gladly took it. Xandy's hands were shaking hard and she was glad of Quinn's comforting touch.

BJ narrowed his eyes dangerously again.

Devin and Skyler had no idea what was going on, but it was obvious they were witnessing a battle of wills.

"Bren..." Allexxiss put in, her tone cautionary.

"I think you're forgetting who you work for," BJ said sternly

"I think I don't fecking care," Quinn replied, her emerald eyes blazing, but her voice completely controlled. "I'm not gonna let you have a go at her without me there to protect her. That is what you hired me to do."

BJ started to reply. "You'll fucking do—"

"Brenden James!" Allexxiss cut him off, her voice exactly like a scolding mother.

Whatever BJ was about to say died as he winced at his given name being practically screeched at him by his wife.

Quinn did her best to hide her grin, but failed. "Holy show…"

Everyone tensed at the perceived barb, everyone except BJ Sparks, who stared open mouthed at Quinn, but then began to laugh, shaking his head. The entire group relaxed then.

Devin watched as Quinn tilted her head down and toward Xandy, giving the girl a wink and a grin. Xandy shook her head, looking extremely relieved. Devin also noticed that she had Quinn's hand in both of hers and she didn't seem like she wanted to let go. Devin glanced over at Skyler and saw that Skyler was also watching the two. Devin grinned at her partner gleefully. Skyler merely shook her head, an amused grin on her lips.

The rest of lunch was less eventful, and afterwards Devin, Xandy and Quinn went to BJ's study. Allexxiss told Devin that she'd entertain Skyler. Devin noted that Skyler didn't seem to have the least bit of a problem with that proposition.

"I want her back when I get back out here," Devin told Allexxiss in mock jealousy.

"We'll see," Allexxiss said, winking at Devin.

Inside BJ's study, Devin couldn't help herself; she had to ask Quinn what she'd said to BJ out by the pool. She had heard what had been said, but she hadn't understood it. She pulled Quinn aside while BJ gathered up information from his files. Xandy had moved to sit on the couch in the sitting area, awaiting the rest of the group.

"It's just slang for a rather embarrassing situation," Quinn told her.

"Aw,' Devin said, nodding her head. "Did the trick."

"That was the plan."

"And if it hadn't worked?" Devin asked.

Quinn looked back at the other woman, her look assessing. Finally she shrugged, shaking her head. "Dunno."

"Would you have backed down?" Devin asked, pretty sure she already knew the answer.

Quinn tilted her head at the other woman. "Nope."

Devin grinned, nodding her head.

Devin and Quinn walked over to where BJ now sat across from Xandy. Quinn sat, once again, so she was between BJ and Xandy. BJ and Devin sat in the other vacant chairs.

BJ started the conversation. "Xandy has been getting threatening emails, apparently," he said, shooting Xandy a narrowed look. Quinn immediately tensed, her eyes widening slightly as if to say *really?* "She's been receiving these types of emails for a while now."

Devin nodded, looking over at Xandy.

"Do you still have all of the emails?" Devin asked, inadvertently stepping right into the source of BJ's irritation.

"No," BJ snapped, his eyes flashing, "she didn't even see fit—"

"Okay, okay," Devin said, holding her hand up to stave off the tirade she could sense brewing in BJ. He bemusedly stared at her hand, was there no end to the scoldings he was going to take from the women in his house today? He also caught Quinn's quick grin, and rolled his eyes at the woman.

"Xandy," Devin said gently, turning to look at the girl, "did you see the emails on a computer? Or was it on your phone?"

"On my laptop," Xandy said.

"Okay," Devin said, glancing at BJ, "it's not a problem. I can probably recover all of them."

"Can you find the person that's doing this?" Quinn asked.

Devin nodded. "I'm sure I can." She looked at Xandy. "I'm going to need your laptop though."

Xandy nodded. "Sure."

"How long do you think it will take to get some answers?" BJ asked.

"Hard to say," Devin said, shrugging. "I really need to get a chance to look at the information on the email footprint."

BJ nodded, "Okay. How soon can you get started?"

Devin looked pensive. "I'm finishing up some stuff for the DOD, and then I could start. I'd say maybe a week."

BJ nodded. "That would be great," he said, glancing at Xandy. "Xandy," he said, entreating, "I'm sorry, I'm just worried about you, okay?"

Xandy nodded.

"I should have been better about handling it," BJ said, looking a bit ashamed of himself.

"It's okay," Xandy said, shrugging nonchalantly, every bit the star. "I have a bodyguard who isn't afraid of you."

For the second time that day BJ was stunned into silence, his mouth agape. Then Xandy started to grin and the whole group laughed.

"She's getting that from you," BJ accused Quinn. "Bloody women!"

Quinn laughed, not looking the least bit offended.

They talked about details then, but the meeting was over in less than twenty minutes.

Skyler got her opportunity to tour BJ's car collection, and it took every persuasive power Devin had to get her fiancée out of the rock mogul's garage.

On the drive home, Devin looked over at Skyler. "So what did you think about Quinn and Xandy?"

"Quinn *and* Xandy?" Skyler repeated.

"Yeah," Devin said.

"Xandy's not gay, you know."

"None of them are gay, till they are."

Skyler chuckled shaking her head. "Not gonna be happy till the whole world is gay, are ya?"

"Nope… I need to get Xandy's laptop from her," she said, her eyes narrowing as she mentally planned. "I think I'll invite them to our place for dinner."

"As a couple," Skyler said, pointedly.

"Quinn is her bodyguard, Sky, I have to invite her," Devin said, winking at Skyler.

Skyler just shook her head, rolling her eyes.

"Oh, come on!" Devin said, reaching over and touching Skyler's hand on the stick shift. "You saw what I saw."

Skyler pursed her lips, but then nodded. "Yeah, they seem close, but if they're a couple, BJ doesn't know it, and you need to be careful."

"I'm not going to tell BJ Sparks a damned thing, that's not my job," she said, holding her hands up in a 'hands off' gesture.

"Good."

"So you're okay with me inviting them to dinner?" Devin asked hopefully.

"It's your house, babe."

"It's *our* house, Skyler," Devin said, narrowing her eyes at her fiancée.

Skyler made decent money as a rescue helicopter pilot for the Los Angeles Fire Department, but Devin made extremely good money as a consultant. She'd once told Skyler that she didn't even get out of bed for less than $100,000. Skyler didn't make that in a year, and Devin could quite literally make that in a week. The house in Malibu belonged to Devin. Skyler had moved in with her six months before, but she refused to consider it in any way shape or form hers. It was a constant joke between them.

"Blah, blah, blah…" Skyler said, reaching over to turn up the stereo, only to find that her usual music had been replaced with what she'd consider 'bubble gum' music. "What did you do to my iPod?"

Devin chuckled. "The stuff you listen to is too damned dark, you need something upbeat."

Skyler narrowed her eyes at Devin. "I like my music." Even so within moments, Devin noticed that Skyler was tapping her hand on the steering wheel in time with the song on the stereo.

Pitbull and Ricky Martin's "Mr. Put it Down" was playing. Skyler couldn't resist the beat.

"Careful, babe, you're almost dancing," Devin mocked.

"Don't make me pull this car over," Skyler said darkly, even as she grinned.

"Yeah, yeah," Devin said, waving her hand airily.

Chapter 4

The same night of the meeting, Xandy and Quinn had dinner together out in the courtyard as it was a nice evening. Summer was coming, and they both knew that the humidity of the LA summer would likely preclude such evenings in the future.

"I really liked Skyler and Devin," Xandy said at one point.

Quinn nodded. "Yeah, me too."

"They just seemed so comfortable together, you know?" Xandy said, her tone wistful.

"Yes they did."

Something in Quinn's look told Xandy that there was more to that statement. She cast a sideways glance at Quinn; she'd picked up the habit from the other woman.

"Is your relationship with Valerie like that?"

"Not even close."

"And that's okay with you?" Xandy asked, biting her lip in apprehension.

Quinn caught the gesture and wondered at it. Shrugging she shook her head. "Never really thought about it much."

Xandy's eyes fell pointedly on the ring containing the Viking runes, meaning 'dreams of everlasting love,' and then looked back up into Quinn's eyes.

Quinn curled her lips in a sardonic grin. "Yeah, I know," she said in answer to the unspoken question, "it's just not there with her. But I just don't have the energy at this point to do anything about it."

Xandy nodded, accepting the answer. "It would take a lot of energy?"

Quinn chuckled. "Yeah, breaking up in the lesbian world is something to avoid if you don't have large stores of energy."

Xandy widened her eyes at that statement. "It's that hard?"

"It can be."

Xandy frowned, but didn't pursue the subject.

"So…" Xandy said hesitantly.

"Wot?" Quinn asked, pushing back her plate and pulling out a cigarette and her lighter.

"How did you know you were gay?" Xandy asked.

Quinn gave a snort of laughter. "How'd you know you were straight?"

Xandy looked shocked by the question, and looked like she was trying to think of an answer.

"I'm sorry," Quinn said, putting her hand out apologetically, "that was a smart ass lesbian comeback." Sitting back in her chair she looked reflective. "I grew up with the same movies and shows that everyone did back then, that showed a boy and a girl getting together." Her green eyes had a faraway look. "I always played with the boys, doing all the same things they did… half the time I'd do better than them. But I guess at the same time the boys were starting to notice me, I was noticing Molly O'Shay down the street," she said, with a wistful smile.

"Oh my," Xandy said, smiling sympathetically, "did you ever do anything about that?"

"Oh hell no," Quinn said looking horrified by the thought, "I'd have been run out of town by a mob with pitchforks and torches."

Xandy grimaced. Quinn chuckled at the face the other girl was making.

"So, what did that feel like?" Xandy asked, her look curious. "When you *noticed* Molly?"

Quinn grinned, sighing. "Oh, God it was awful. I absolutely obsessed about the girl. I thought about her constantly; what was she doing? Had she even noticed me? What would I say to her if I could even be brave enough to talk to her? How would that conversation go?" she said, shaking her head at the endless questions she'd had swirling in her head. "I'd watch her in the play yard at break, watching her every move, just fascinated by everything she did, it was maddening. She was a blue-eyed girl, with red hair about two shades darker than mine, she had the cutest freckles..." Her voice trailed off as she shook her head, rolling her eyes. "To this day if I see that same shade of red hair on a girl, my heart skips a beat, thinking it might be her. It's crazy, because I knew almost nothing about her, she could have been the worst bitch on the planet for all I knew, but the sight of her would make me all nervous and my heart would flutter. It's stupid," she said looking embarrassed.

"No," Xandy said, shaking her head, "she was kind of your first love, right?"

"Even if it was from afar, *way* far, yeah," Quinn said..

Xandy nodded, like she was confirming something.

"Were you ever with a man?" Xandy asked, worried that she was getting too personal, but Quinn didn't seem to mind.

Again Quinn chuckled, looking abashed. "Well," she said wryly, "technically I made two attempts to be with a guy."

"Technically?"

Quinn sighed, taking a long drag off her cigarette and leaning back in her chair.

"I knew that I was supposed to like guys, so when I was about fifteen, I gave it a shot with a guy that had been flirting with me for months."

"How'd that go?"

"It was all arseways," Quinn said, shaking her head and laughing, in response to Xandy's blank look. She clarified, "It was a mess."

"What happened?"

Quinn paused, looking like she was thinking back on the time.

"It started out okay," she said, sounding circumspect, then she laughed softly, "but when he tried to touch me, you know, the diddies…" She indicated her breasts. "I lost it and punched him so he'd get away from me."

"Oh my God," Xandy said, laughing sympathetically.

Quinn blew her breath out, nodding her head. "Yeah, it wasn't good at all." She chewed on her lower lip, thinking of the awkward conversation with her brothers when they wanted to know why she'd punched one of their friends in the face.

"I tried again, a few years later, just before I turned eighteen in fact; this guy was kind of a friend, and a lot less aggressive sexually than the other guy. I thought that maybe I just hadn't liked being pushed, and I figured I'd matured a bit," she said, shrugging in her retrospection. "That got farther," she said her face and amused mask, "but as soon as he took off his pants, I was so completely done." The last was said with a laugh, as she put her hand to her forehead, shaking her head.

"Wow," Xandy said, grimacing again. "Yeah, it sounds like there was really no hope of heterosexuality for you."

"Amen!"

Xandy looked back at Quinn for a long few moments; it was obvious she was debating saying something. Quinn waited in silence, smoking her cigarette, her legs stretched out in front of her comfortably.

Xandy pressed her lips together in trepidation, she was indeed wrestling with the desire to say what she had on her mind, but at the same time afraid that Quinn would be angry. Looking at Quinn, she could see the other woman was waiting for the proverbial other shoe to drop. *Well, I've gone this far,* Xandy thought to herself.

"So I have a confession to make," Xandy said.

"Okay…"

Xandy twisted the cloth napkin that was in her lap nervously, looking like she'd rather be anywhere else at that moment. "I've kind of been obsessing about you," she said in a rush, then winced not sure what Quinn's reaction was going to be.

Quinn surprised her by chuckling, and inclining her head. "Okay," she said simply, as she waited for more information.

Xandy wasn't sure what to say next. "At first I really thought it was because you were so different from anyone I'd ever met. But it's not that, and now I'm wondering if it might mean that I'm gay."

"Other than your fascination with me, what makes you think you might be?"

Xandy was relieved that Quinn not only didn't seem to be angry or put off by her admission, but that she was actually willing to help her figure this whole matter out. Once again she was grateful to whatever unseen force had put Quinn Kavanaugh in her path.

"Well... what you were saying about Molly, about how you thought about her all the time and watched every move she made," she said shrugging self-consciously. "That's what I've been doing with you. I've been fascinated by the cars, by the music you listen to, the tattoos, the rings..." Xandy's voice trailed off, as she shook her head and looked away in embarrassment.

Quinn rested her elbow on the table next to her, her chin resting on her thumb, assessing as she watched Xandy talk. She smiled softly when Xandy talked about the tattoos and the rings. Quinn had been surprised by her level of interest in these things, but had dismissed it as simple curiosity of a young person who had never been exposed to such things before.

"I'm crazy, right?" Xandy asked when she'd gotten her embarrassment back under control.

Quinn shook her head, a kind smile on her face.

"No, you're not crazy. But tell me this..." Quinn said, moving to lean toward Xandy, putting her elbows on her knees. "What's been your experience with men?"

Xandy looked surprised by the question. "What do you mean?"

"I mean, how many men have you been with?" Quinn asked, gently, especially on the word "been."

Xandy pursed her lips. "Three."

"And how did that go?" she asked, repeating the question Xandy had asked her earlier.

Xandy looked pensive, then curled her lips up in disdain.

Finally, she shook her head. "It didn't go quite as badly as your experiences did, but I never…" she hesitated to use the word 'orgasm.'

Quinn looked back at Xandy for a long moment, shocked.

"Never?" Quinn asked, sounding as stunned as she looked.

"Nope," Xandy shrugged.

"That's just wrong," Quinn said, disgusted for the men who'd failed the girl so miserably. "What about emotionally? How was that?"

Xandy looked unhappy as she sighed softly. "I just felt like I was just there," she said, "like no real passion or anything, and sometimes barely even affection for the guy."

"So you don't feel like you loved them?"

"No, I mean, I guess not. I really just thought that maybe it was me, and that I was just closed off or that I just didn't know how love was supposed to feel."

Quinn winced a little at her description, imaging terms like 'frigid' and 'ice queen' had been hurled at her by guys who couldn't get her to respond to them.

"Well," Quinn said, "I can tell you that while I've never been in love with anyone, I have loved some of the women I've dated, and you know it when you feel it."

"What's the difference between being in love and loving someone?" Xandy asked, having heard people say things like that before, but never understanding what they meant.

"Well, to me," Quinn said, pulling out another cigarette and lighting it, "being in love is the end all and be all… the 'everything.' Loving someone means that you care about them, and what affects them affects you, but it's not as deep. Does that make sense?" she asked, feeling ill-equipped to describe love.

"Do you love Valerie?"

They'd talked about whether or not Valerie loved her, but never really got to the point of discussing if Quinn loved Valerie.

"No," Quinn said honestly, "she's fun, when she's not being a pain, but sometimes those times are way too few and far between."

Xandy nodded, noting that she felt relieved by that statement, which made her grimace again.

"Wot?"

Xandy looked immediately contrite. "I, uh…" she stammered, shaking her head in dismay, "I'm glad you don't love her."

"Why?" Quinn asked surprised by the admission.

"I guess because she just seems like she…" she began, but hesitated.

Quinn canted her head slightly, taking another drag off her cigarette waiting for Xandy to finish the thought.

Xandy blew her pent up breath in a rush. "She just doesn't seem like she's a very nice person."

Quinn grinned, finding Xandy's admission both amusing and telling.

"You're probably right about that," Quinn said.

Xandy shrugged, looking a bit forlorn, her eyes trained on the ground.

"It's okay that you don't like her," Quinn said, her green eyes sparkling in amusement. "I told you, I don't like her half the time either."

Xandy laughed at that, appreciating Quinn's effort to lighten up the conversation.

After a few moments of silence, Quinn leaned back again, crossing one knee over the other, assessing Xandy.

"I think that maybe you need to explore this," Quinn said.

"The possibility of being gay?"

"Yeah."

Xandy nodded, but looked uncertain. She started to say something, but then stopped, twisting the napkin in her lap again.

Quinn canted her head. "Wot?"

Xandy bit her lip, looking both apologetic and tragic at the same time.

"When we were on the ride the other day," she said, her eyes on the ground in front of her. "I did kind of look around at the women in the group." She looked up at Quinn. "But all I saw was you."

Quinn drew in a deep breath, blowing it out slowly, her look resigned. Then she gave Xandy a somber look.

"You know," Quinn said, her tone conciliatory, "that it's fairly natural for you to harbor some sort of feeling for me. It comes from the fact that I'm protecting you."

Xandy looked immediately rebellious at the idea, shaking her head.

"It's kind of the damsel in distress meets the white knight syndrome, you see me as some kind of protector," Quinn said.

"I didn't see Jason as a protector," Xandy pointed out.

Quinn hesitated, considering that statement, then shook her head. "I dunno, I'm just saying it's possible, it's happened before."

"To you?"

Quinn nodded.

"Was the client gay?"

Quinn's lips twitched, and she nodded. "Yeah, she was."

Xandy just nodded, not saying anything else. Shortly after that they cleared off the table and went into the house. On this night, Xandy went into her room. Quinn went to the room next door. It was less than an hour before Quinn heard Xandy call out, but Xandy's voice was pure terror.

Quinn jumped up, running quickly to Xandy's room.

"What is it?!"

Xandy pointed at the window, her hand shaking. "There was someone out there."

Quinn nodded her head, then beckoned Xandy forward. Taking the girl by the arm, Quinn strode back into her room. Reaching into the nightstand, she drew out a nasty looking gun, checking the safety and pulled back the slide to chamber a round.

"Come on," she said, taking Xandy's arm again, gently leading her to the front door, and turning she looked down at the girl. "Lock the door behind me, don't open it until I come back, okay?"

Xandy looked terrified, her lips trembling and tears gathering in her eyes. Quinn leaned down, kissed her quickly on the cheek, and pulled back to look down at her. "It'll be okay, I promise." With that she was out the door and Xandy did as Quinn had said and locked it.

It was ten nerve-racking minutes later when Quinn rapped on the door. Xandy opened it quickly. Quinn walked inside, shaking her head.

"Didn't see anyone," she said.

"I swear I saw someone," Xandy began.

"I'm not saying you didn't, Xan," Quinn assured her. "There just wasn't anyone there by the time I got out there."

Xandy nodded, accepting what Quinn was saying.

Quinn walked back down the hall to her room. Standing by the bed, she pressed the clip release on the gun, removing the ammunition clip. Then she drew the slide back, dropping the bullet from the chamber. Setting the gun aside, she picked up the bullet and placed it back in the gun clip, then slid the clip back into the gun with a snap. She then clicked the safety on, and placed it back into the nightstand drawer.

Xandy watched all of this from the doorway, once again she found herself entranced by Quinn's movements. There was just nothing this woman could do that didn't fascinate her. She had no idea what to do with everything she was feeling.

When Quinn turned back toward the door, she saw Xandy watching her. Canting her head to the side, she gave Xandy an assessing look. Then she walked toward the door, nodding her head toward Xandy's room.

"Come on," Quinn said, as she walked past the girl, "we're going to end up here anyway."

In Xandy's bedroom, Quinn moved to sit on the bed, holding her arm out to Xandy. Xandy laughed softly and moved to lie against Quinn. Within minutes she fell asleep.

A few days after the meeting at BJ's house, Quinn got a call from Devin inviting her and Xandy to her and Skyler's for dinner that Friday. She asked Quinn to make sure that Xandy brought her laptop.

Three days later, Quinn drove up to the address in Malibu that Devin had given her. Getting out of the car, she shouldered the laptop case, and walked around to open Xandy's door. Xandy had finally gotten used to her gallant habit, and had stopped reaching for the door handle herself.

Devin answered the door. She wore a purple silk tank top, and black capris. The top was the same shade as the purple in her hair, and it matched her makeup and jewelry too. Quinn thought once again, that Skyler Boché was a lucky woman. Devin was beautiful, but with a quirky edge to her.

"I love that top!" Xandy told Devin.

"Thanks. I gotta say I'm jealous of yours," Devin told the girl. "Is that the new Dolce?" she asked, as she motioned them into the house.

"Yeah," Xandy said, grimacing slightly.

"I didn't think that one was even out yet."

"It just came out, I had it on order. I know it was crazy, but I just loved it so much when I saw it. It's probably way too much for dinner, but I just got it," Xandy said, looking somewhat embarrassed suddenly. She was pleased that she had someone to share her very first high fashion purchase with though.

Devin admired the beautiful silk top; it was white with a colorful print in golds and blues, flared feminine sleeves and a handkerchief hemline. It looked beautiful on Xandy and she'd paired it perfectly with a pair of blue capris that picked up the colors, and a matching leather dauphine shopper style bag. Devin knew she was looking at well over $4,000 worth of outfit. Xandy definitely had good taste.

"It's gorgeous! That's never a bad thing," Devin enthused. "And of course you look great in it too."

Quinn was dressed much more casually; her sleeveless black shirt showing off her tattoos in all their glory. Paired with her black jeans and biker boots, it definitely painted a 'wild side' picture that Devin hadn't previously detected. Quinn had been wearing long sleeves at BJs house, even the tattoo on her neck had been covered that night.

Quinn inclined her head to Devin, then handed her the laptop case.

"Aw, perfect, thank you," Devin said.

Quinn whistled low as her eyes scanned the house.

Skyler is out back smoking," she said to Quinn, pointing to the back door. "Go on out; I need to take a look at Xandy's computer and I need her for that."

"I heard what I needed," Quinn said. She pulled her lighter out of her pocket, brandishing it lightly, and walked toward the back sliding door.

Quinn stepped out in the backyard, and was immediately greeted by a husky pup bounding up to her.

"Benny, sit!" Skyler called.

The pup's butt immediately plunked down on the ground, his light blue eyes staring up at the newcomer expectantly.

Quinn knelt down, giving him a good rub.

"There's a good dog," she told the puppy.

Moving to stand, Quinn looked over at Skyler who was sitting on a lounge chair a few yards away.

"He's beautiful," she said, giving the dog another pat on the head before turning to walk over to where Skyler sat.

She caught sight of the ocean at that point and stood staring. "Holy shite…"

"Yeah, it's pretty awesome, isn't it?" Skyler said, looking out over the view of the sea, with the cliffs of Malibu on either side of them.

"You're tellin' me," Quinn said, sitting in the chair next to Skyler and pulling out a cigarette. She lit the end and took a deep drag

"I had pretty much the same reaction the first time I saw it."

Quinn nodded, understanding.

Benny, who had followed Quinn over, moved to lay in front of Skyler, his eyes looking up at her, and then lay his head down on his paws.

"How old is he?" Quinn asked, looking down at Benny.

"About eight months," Skyler said, grinning down at the dog who wagged his tail slightly as if he knew he was being talked about.

"Why Benny?" Quinn asked.

"He's named after a member of my crew that died in Iraq," Skyler said, her tone somewhat subdued as she looked down at the dog.

"Oh, I'm sorry."

Skyler nodded, still looking affected. She looked at Quinn then. "You serve?"

Quinn nodded.

"Combat?" Skyler asked.

"Yeah, two years, in Syria peace keeping," Quinn said, her look wry.

"See much peace?"

"Nope. I saw a lot of good men killed though."

Skyler nodded, knowing what Quinn meant.

The two were quiet for a while, each smoking and lost in their own thoughts.

Inside the house, Devin was standing at the kitchen island with Xandy working on the laptop. "So Quinn seems pretty intense," she said conversationally.

"She is sometimes," Xandy said, smiling.

"But not always?" Devin asked, as she moved the mouse, clicking and then beginning to type again.

"No, she's actually really great."

"Intense can be pretty great," Devin said, winking at the girl.

Xandy looked at Devin surprised, but then nodded, biting her lip unconsciously.

"How long have you and Skyler been together?" Xandy asked.

"Almost two years now."

"Is Skyler intense?"

"Oh yeah," Devin said, rolling her eyes.

"And that's a good thing?" Xandy asked, very curious about the couple.

Devin grimaced. "It wasn't always."

"Why?" Xandy asked, hoping she wasn't being too nosy.

"Skyler's been through a lot in her life. Sometimes it backs up on her."

"But she has you."

"Yeah, she does. And I have her."

Xandy smiled wistfully. Devin noticed it, but said nothing. "So how did you meet her?" Xandy then asked.

"She came to a party here at the house, and the minute I saw her..." Devin said, shaking her head at the memory.

"What?" Xandy asked, wanting to hear the story.

"Oh, man, I really didn't know what had hit me," Devin said, turning to look toward the back yard. "I literally stood over there watching her from the back slider, just mesmerized by her. I had no idea what was drawing me to her, but I knew I needed to find out."

"Wow... what ended up happening? I mean, how long until you two got together?"

"Oh we ended up sleeping together that first night. It was afterwards that she tried to run."

"Really?" Xandy asked, surprised because the two seemed so deeply connected. She couldn't fathom that it hadn't been the case from the very first moment.

"Yeah, she tried. I pursued her, even when she tried to push me away."

"But it worked out."

"It did, but it wasn't easy at all. I just knew that I loved her, and that I wanted to be there for her in whatever way I could."

Xandy nodded feeling a bit envious that Devin was so sure about what she wanted, and knew how to get it.

Devin closed the laptop. "Okay I've got what I need to do some investigating. Do you want some wine or anything?"

"I'm okay," Xandy said, smiling.

Just then the doorbell rang.

"That must be Jams," Devin said, "I'll be right back."

A couple of minutes later, she came back with a man trailing behind her. The man was tall, with blond hair and blue eyes. He smiled warmly at Xandy.

"Xandy, this is Jams. He's Skyler's best friend, and copilot at the LAFD, and in Iraq too."

Xandy nodded, smiling, and extending her hand to him. "It's good to meet you."

"You too," he said, smiling again.

Jams looked over at Devin then. "She out there?"

Devin nodded, moving to the fridge and handing Jams a couple of beers.

"Good plan," he said, "it was a bit of a rough one today."

"She told me," Devin said, nodding.

"Well, that's headed in the right direction, right?" Jams said.

"Definitely," Devin said. "We'll be out in a minute. Hey, wait…" She reached into the fridge again and added a third beer to Jams' load.

"Quinn might want one too," she said, smiling over at Xandy.

Jams nodded. "Got it."

Devin watched Jams go and looked over at Xandy.

"Let me put this away, and then we can join them," Devin told her, picking up her laptop and walking away.

Xandy nodded. As she waited for Devin to return, she walked over to the slider and looked outside, seeing Quinn sitting next to Skyler. She was thinking about what Devin had said about being mesmerized by Skyler. The trouble was, Xandy didn't have either the courage or the confidence that Devin James seemed to have oozing out of every pore in her body. Xandy wished she could be that comfortable in her own skin, like this whole group seemed to be. It was intimidating.

"Let's go," Devin said, coming up behind her.

The two women walked out into the backyard just as Quinn was midway through telling a story.

"Wait, there were two of them?" Skyler asked, looking dumbfounded. She held her hand out to Devin as she approached, who took it and sat on her lap.

"That's what I'm sayin'!" Quinn said, her face animated. Seeing Xandy with Devin, she stood to give up her chair for her, without missing a beat. "There were two of the fuckers! Er, oh, sorry," she said, looking embarrassed to have cussed in front of the ladies.

Devin found the consideration and old world manners incredibly endearing. Devin shook her head, grinning. "Around these two, I hear worse."

Quinn glanced at Xandy who just shook her head smiling.

"So what happened?" Jams asked from his place in a chair across from them.

"I told 'em," Quinn said, hooking her foot around another chair and pulling it closer to sit down next to Xandy, "that I hoped they liked hospital food. That's when the charge went off, hard te beat, I tell ya."

Jams and Skyler laughed nodding their heads.

Music was playing in the backyard, and Xandy noticed it was an interesting mixture of rock and dance music. A particularly techno pop song came on, and Skyler scowled up at Devin,

"Really?" she asked, her tone accusing even as she grinned.

"Hey, you said you liked this song," Devin said, holding out her hands as if in futility.

Skyler picked up the iPod that rested it on the table in front of her, glancing at Quinn. "Who do you like?"

"Disturbed is good," Quin said, grinning.

"Oh, I do like you," Skyler said, smiling widely as she found a song by Disturbed.

The title track to Disturbed's album "Immortalized" pumped through the speakers.

Both women and Jams nodded their heads to the beat. Devin and Xandy exchanged a look and grinned at each other.

When that song ended, another one began, and Xandy saw Skyler's head drop back, and Devin and Jams wince.

The song had a kind of haunting beginning, and then a heavy beat. After the first few words, Skyler excused herself, standing up and gently setting Devin on her feet. Picking up her cigarettes and lighter, she walked over to the retaining wall a few yards away. Devin's eyes followed her, then she glanced at Jams. He nodded to her, and gestured with his head toward Skyler. Devin nodded in silent agreement, then looked at Xandy and Quinn, who were watching the scene in surprise.

"I'm sorry, I'll be right back," Devin said, and walked off toward Skyler, who was now smoking with Benny right by her side, her hand on his head.

Quinn looked over at Jams. "She okay?"

Jams shrugged. "This song reminds her of Benny; he loved Breaking Benjamin, that's why we gave him that nickname. We were called 'Hell's Angels.' Benny was one of the members of our helicopter crew that died when we went down in Iraq. This song, 'Angels Fall' came out after the crash."

"She mentioned the crash earlier," Quinn said, looking mournful for this woman she'd recently met, but already respected.

Jams nodded, looking surprised. "That's good. She wouldn't talk about it at all for the longest time."

"What actually happened?" Quinn asked.

"We took fire," Jams said. "It took out our tail rotor, we went down hot."

Quinn winced, knowing what that kind of crash looked like and that most people didn't survive it.

"You two went through that?" Xandy asked, her voice sympathetic.

"Yeah," Jams said.

"I'm so sorry," Xandy said, shaking her head sadly, tears shining in her eyes.

Quinn had a feeling Xandy was thinking of her family. She reached over, taking Xandy's hand in hers, squeezing it gently. Xandy returned the squeeze, looking over at Quinn and smiling softly.

"How many did you lose?" Quinn asked Jams, her tone respectful.

"We lost two men, Benny and Radar," Jams said, his tone grave.

The song played on; the chorus "when angels fall with broken wings" seemed to go right through all three of them.

Xandy looked over at where Skyler and Devin stood, watching as Devin looked up at Skyler, and then leant her head against her arm. Skyler put her arm around Devin's shoulder, and hugged her close. Devin's arms went around Skyler's waist. After a few minutes the two came back to the table and the group stood in response.

"Sorry guys," Skyler said, still looking a bit haunted.

"All good," Quinn said, extending her hand to Skyler.

Skyler smiled gratefully, grasping the other woman's hand and nodding.

Xandy stepped forward to hug Skyler. Skyler accepted the hug, though her face reflected surprise at such a kind gesture.

"Thank you for your service and your sacrifice," Xandy said, her voice muffled by Skyler's shirt.

She turned and looked at Jams. "Both of you."

Jams smiled, looking affected by the moment too.

Devin watched the scene with tears in her eyes. She knew Skyler would appreciate such heartfelt gratitude and understanding, and she instantly loved Xandy and Quinn for it.

Dinner was an interesting affair, with Skyler, Quinn and Jams arguing over the best way to barbeque steaks. Xandy and Devin hid out in the kitchen and prepared the side dishes. Before they sat down to dinner, they all stood around the dining room table to toast. Skyler held her bottle of beer, Jams followed suit, and then everyone else did.

"Angels fall," Skyler said.

"Angles fall," Jams repeated, clinking the bottom of his bottle to Skyler's.

Everyone else follow suit and drank to the fallen angels.

During dinner there were discussions of all sorts. At one point Skyler and Quinn were discussing the merits of service in their respective Army units.

"How long ago did you get out?" Skyler asked Quinn.

"Two years ago," Quinn said.

"How'd you get into bodyguard work?"

"What else is an ex-Army ranger gonna do? Besides, it's good money," Quinn said with a wink.

"You were special forces?" Jams asked.

Quinn nodded. "Hand to hand, weapons, explosives, you name it."

Jams and Skyler exchanged a look. "I think we chose the wrong path."

"Damned right," Skyler said, grinning.

"Excuse me," Devin put in, having tuned into their conversation, "Your path saved my ass, thank you very much."

Skyler grinned, dropping her head, looking embarrassed.

"Say what again?" Quinn asked, her interest piqued.

"She saved my life, literally," Devin said, shooting Skyler a look of both admiration and love.

"She took on a mudslide on Highway 1," Skyler said, winking at Devin, even as she took her hand.

"And you actually rescued her?" Xandy asked, astonished.

"In the rescue helicopter no less," Jams put in, grinning at his partner's obvious discomfort.

"Wow…" Xandy said, her eyes bright with awe. "That's true love for you."

"Well, it is that," Skyler said, looking at Devin.

"It definitely is," Devin said, smiling at Skyler.

Two hours later, on the drive back to Brentwood, Xandy was still enchanted with Devin and Skyler's story.

"I have to say that I like Devin and Skyler even more after tonight," she told Quinn. "It's really sad that Skyler went through what she did."

"Yeah, it really sucks," Quinn agreed. She thought about Xandy losing her entire family; did she realize how tragic it made her life seem to others? It definitely wasn't in the girl to wear her pain on her sleeve.

"When you were in the Army, did you have anything like that happen?"

"Sure, people were killed," Quinn said, "but never anyone in my unit. We had some injuries, but that was all. Nothing like Skyler's incident."

Xandy nodded, relieved. After a long silence, she looked over at Quinn. "What they have… that's what I want and I don't care if I find it with a man or with a woman." Her voice was determined on the last.

Quinn grinned, liking that the girl had at least started making some decisions about her life instead of letting it just happen to her.

"Yeah, but what they have is like unicorn stuff."

"Unicorn stuff?" Xandy repeated.

"You know, almost impossible to find, and almost impossible to capture."

Xandy grinned at the meaning. "Well, then I want a unicorn."

Quinn chuckled, nodding her head.

"And whether you'll admit it or not," Xandy said, reaching over to tap on the ring with the Viking Runes on it, "you do too."

Quinn looked over at her, her eyes reflecting surprise, then she shrugged. "It'll happen, when it happens. If it ever happens at all."

Xandy was surprised by the statement, but didn't comment.

"Quinn?" she queried tentatively.

"Hmm?" Quinn murmured, lost in her own thoughts for a moment.

"Would you take me to some of the areas of town where I could explore the lesbian culture, like you suggested the other day?"

Quinn considered the idea. "Think you'd be okay if your picture shows up out there?"

Xandy shrugged. "Doesn't matter to me."

"Alright, we can do that.

Chapter 5

True to her word, Quinn took Xandy to West Hollywood the next day. They walked around the shops and ate lunch at Alma, a fairly well-known restaurant in what is called WeHo, short for West Hollywood. There were plenty of pictures taken. Most of the pictures featured Xandy front and center, but with Quinn always just a couple of steps from her, her eyes constantly looking around.

At lunch they talked about the different people walking by.

"She's a lesbian?" Xandy asked, in hushed tones, looking at a woman that had walked by them, giving Quinn the eye. Quinn responded by winking and smiling.

"I hope so."

When Xandy grimaced, Quinn laughed out loud. "She was, don't worry."

"That's mean," Xandy told Quinn, giving her best pouty look, but spoiling it with a grin.

"Uh-huh," Quinn said, winking.

That was the picture that Valerie Henning received from a number of her friends the very next morning. One of her friends sent it with the caption, *Is this where Quinn's been lately?* That had Valerie flinging her phone across the room.

Less than an hour later, she showed up at Xandy's front door.

When Xandy answered the door, having seen who it was, Valerie was in what Quinn would call "full star trip mode." She wore black leather pants that were skin tight, and a cropped tank top that exposed a fair amount of tanned and toned skin, as well as her tattoo of a panther ready to pounce; it said a lot about Valerie's current mood.

"Hi," Xandy said, unaware of Valerie's current frame of mind, "you're Valerie, right?"

"Where's Quinn?" Valerie demanded.

Xandy's eyes widened at Valerie's tone and rudeness. It took her a minute to respond.

"Um," Xandy stammered, "she's in her room."

"Yours?" Valerie practically spat.

"What?" Xandy said, both stunned and terrified by the question.

Surely Valerie couldn't know that she had a thing for Quinn...

When Xandy didn't respond further, Valerie made a rude sound in the back of her throat, and stormed by the girl and into the house. She looked around, then strode down the hallway, her dark hair flying behind her. Xandy followed at what she considered a safe distance.

Valerie stuck her head in the first open door she came to and saw Quinn sitting on the bed there. The sound of Valerie's boot heels on the hardwood floor had alerted Quinn.

"Jesus Val, what're you doin' here?" Quinn asked.

Valerie walked straight over to the bed climbing onto it, and straddling Quinn's outstretched legs. Leaning forward she kissed Quinn passionately. At first, Quinn responded to the kiss, her hands grasping at Valerie's bare midriff. Then she recalled herself and pulled her head back, disengaging Valerie's mouth from hers.

"Val, I can't," Quinn said, moving her hands from Val's back to her shoulders to gently push her away.

Before Quinn could react, Valerie's hand grabbed her by the throat; her nails that were always filed to points, bit into her skin and drew blood.

"You're fucking her, aren't you?" Valerie growled.

Quinn had to contain the instinct that would have had her doing some serious damage to Valerie. Instead she narrowed her eyes dangerously.

"Move your fucking hand, Val," she growled, "or you won't be using it for a month."

"Tell me if you're fucking her," Valerie responded, eyes blazing.

Quinn reached up between them, putting her thumb around Valerie's wrist and began to apply pressure.

"Don't think for a second that I can't break it," Quinn said, her voice still low.

Valerie held on as long as she could, but had to let go of Quinn's throat or she knew Quinn would do exactly what she was threatening. Yanking her hand out of Quinn's hand, she rubbed her wrist, shooting daggers at Quinn, but moving off of her and kneeling on the bed next to where Quinn sat.

Quinn reached up and gingerly touched the punctures on her neck. As she pulled back her fingers and saw the blood, she threw a nasty look at Valerie.

"Are you fucking crazy?!" she yelled, her green eyes points of fire.

Valerie looked immediately contrite, but she still had a bone to pick and she wasn't letting it go that easily. Pulling out her phone, she pulled up the picture that was burned into her brain, then shoved the phone in Quinn's face.

"What the fuck is this?" Valerie asked accusing.

Quinn had to pull her head back to keep from having the iPhone smacked her in the face, then she narrowed her eyes to look at the picture.

"Oh, Jesus fecking Christ, is this what's got you all hepped up?" Quinn asked, disbelieving.

"That's not you?"

"Oh Jesus Val, wind yer neck in here, we were having lunch, she was doing shopping. I am her fecking bodyguard, I go where she goes."

"And she just happened to go to WeHo?"

"It's a restaurant Val, not a brothel."

Valerie looked back at Quinn, her look fierce. Quinn looked back at her, passively. There were a few long minutes where the two stared at each other. Finally the fight left Valerie, and she dropped her head, shaking it.

"I'm sorry," she said, sounding miserable.

Quinn said nothing, her expression telling Valerie that she should be sorry.

"It's just that I haven't seen you for like two weeks," Valerie said, tears in her eyes, "and I've missed you so much, and then I saw these pictures. All my friends were asking where you've been… and then I see this… and…"

Quinn watched the performance unmoved. Valerie was an actress, and Quinn knew she could turn on the water works on command.

Valerie noted that Quinn wasn't responding, so she moved forward, taking Quinn's face in her hands.

"I just love you so much..." Valerie said, moving to kiss Quinn.

She found Quinn's lips a lot less welcoming this time.

Sitting back her eyes searched Quinn's. "Please come to dinner tonight at my place. So we can talk, okay?"

Quinn knew she needed to get Valerie out of there, hopefully before there was a big ugly scene between her and Xandy.

Blowing her breath out she said, "Fine, I'll see you tonight."

Valerie's smile was brilliant. "Great!" she said, moving to stand. "Let's say eight o'clock?"

"Okay," Quinn said.

Valerie nodded, then turned to leave. Quinn watched her go, and just shook her head.

Valerie didn't notice Xandy who stood in the doorway to her room as she left. Xandy had heard everything though. Xandy waited until she heard the front door close and then went to lock the door. Then she turned around, seeing Quinn walk across the hall to the bathroom. Xandy walked down the hall after her. When she got to the bathroom she could see that Quinn was looking at the marks on her neck from Valerie's nails. She heard Quinn mutter, "Bitch..."

"Quinn?" Xandy queried from the doorway.

Quinn glanced up at her in the mirror, then turned around. That's when Xandy could see the wounds on Quinn's neck.

"Oh my God…" Xandy said, walking forward, her eyes on Quinn's neck.

"It's okay."

Xandy looked pained, but nodded her head.

"Look, I'm gonna have Mackie come by tonight," Quinn said, turning back to the mirror and wetting a washcloth to wipe the blood off her neck. "I need to go to Val's. Is that okay?"

Xandy nodded. "Okay."

Later that evening, Xandy had to fight to contain her jealous feelings when Quinn walked out of her bedroom, wearing all black, including a long sleeve button up shirt and Harley Davidson boots. She looked really good. *But she's going to go have sex with Valerie, you idiot,* her mind told her.

"You look great," Xandy said, smiling up at Quinn as she stood in front of her. *And oh my God you smell amazing!* her brain wanted to add.

"Thanks. Okay, so Mackie is outside. If you need anything just let him know. He'll come in to check on you every hour or so, okay?" She handed Xandy a piece of paper. "That's Mackie's cell phone. If you need him, you call him… if you need me, you call, okay?"

Xandy nodded, thinking, *Could you just not go in the first place?* But she knew she couldn't say that, so she said, "Have fun," mentally rolling her eyes at her overly cheery tone.

Quinn grinned. "I may not be back until late."

Don't go, said Xandy's heart. "Okay," her mouth said instead.

Three hours later, Xandy was surprised to hear Quinn's boot heels on the wood floor in the hallway. Xandy was in her bed reading. She waited to see if Quinn would come in, but she didn't. Finally, Xandy couldn't stand it anymore, so she got out of bed, walked out of her room, and cautiously stuck her head into Quinn's room. She was surprised to see Quinn sitting on her bed. Her boots and shirt were on the floor, but otherwise she was still dressed. She had her knees up toward her chest and her arms draped over her knees, her head was leaned back against the headboard of the bed, her eyes were closed.

"Quinn?" Xandy queried softly.

Quinn's head dropped to look at her. "Hey."

"I thought you were going to be late…" Xandy said, moving a little bit closer.

Quinn gave a short soft laugh. "We broke up."

Xandy stepped closer and that's when she saw the bloody nail tracks from Quinn's neck to her chest.

"Oh my God!" Xandy said, moving to sit next to Quinn, her eyes on the marks on her neck.

Her blue eyes went to Quinn's. "She did that?"

"You're surprised?" Quinn asked with a raised eyebrow.

"Sadly, no, I'm not."

"Told you lesbian break-ups are rough."

"Well, I hope she's got some marks to show for it too then," Xandy snapped in a rare show of anger.

Quinn's eyes widened, even as she began to grin. "Tell me how you really feel…"

"I really hate her," Xandy said, as she reached over and picked up a discarded rag and dipped it in a glass of water on the nightstand, and then turning to Quinn.

Quinn grinned as she straightened her legs. Xandy straddled her lap, touching the wet rag to the bloody scratches. Quinn jumped slightly in response, her hands grasping at Xandy's waist.

"Sorry."

"S'okay."

"I really can't believe she did this to you…" Xandy said, shaking her head in disbelief.

"She's a passionate girl."

"She's a mean bitch."

Quinn laughed. "Wow, I guess you've made up your mind about that, huh?"

Xandy stopped blotting at the scratches and looked at Quinn. "Yes I have. I don't like her, she doesn't treat you right, and she doesn't deserve you."

Quinn rolled her head around, then side to side, stretching her neck wincing as she stretched too far pulling at the scratches.

"Stop," Xandy said, taking Quinn's face in her hands, "you'll make them bleed again."

When their eyes connected they both held their breath. Slowly, Quinn reached up to touch Xandy's cheek, she drew Xandy's face to hers and their lips met. Xandy's hands grasped Quinn's shoulders as the kiss began tentatively.

Xandy's soft moan caused Quinn's breath to catch and she deepened the kiss. Quinn slid her hands around Xandy's waist, pulling her close, her arms folding around her, to hold her there. Xandy reveled in the sensations coursing through her. She slid her hands from Quinn's shoulders to her head, but accidentally brushed the scratches left by Valerie's nails.

Quinn jumped and the sharp pain brought her to her senses. Pulling back, she closed her eyes against the assault of her own body screaming at her for stopping.

"Xan, wait," Quinn said, shaking her head. "We can't... I can't... I'm sorry, I can't."

Xandy felt like the air had just been sucked out of the room. "What? Why?" she asked, breathless.

"It's not right. If I do this, I'm no better than Jason."

"Jason tried to force me," Xandy said, her eyes welling with tears. "I want this."

Quinn grimaced, her looking mournful. "I'm sorry, I shouldn't have started this, I'm sorry...." Her voice trailed off as she shook her head, feeling horrible.

She didn't see the devastated look in Xandy's eyes. Xandy quickly got up, then turned to walk out of the room.

"Xandy?" Quinn queried, knowing that she needed to explain herself. "Wait, we need to talk. Please?"

Xandy stopped, but didn't turn around. She didn't want Quinn to see the tears in her eyes.

"It's okay, we can talk about it tomorrow."

Quinn pressed her lips together, knowing she didn't have any right to push Xandy on this. It had been her decision to start the kiss and her decision to end it. If Xandy didn't want to hear her explanation, what right did she have to force her?

Xandy left the room. Quinn banged her head on the headboard a few times, knowing she'd just done something incredibly stupid. The problem was, she couldn't decide if it was stupid to start it or to stop it. She sat on her bed for a while, and was surprised when she heard the bathroom door shut. A few minutes later she heard the shower start. Sitting there her mind started working, she'd thought that Xandy was already in bed when she'd come in.

Getting off the bed, Quinn walked to Xandy's room, and saw that the bed covers were set aside, like Xandy had gotten out of bed to come in to see her.

Then why is she taking a shower now? she asked herself.

Something inside her clicked, and she strode to the bathroom door, knocking on it.

"Xan?" she called, loud enough to be heard over the shower.

No answer.

"Xandy!" she repeated louder but still with no response. She tried the door, it was locked.

"Xandy, answer me, damnit!" Quinn yelled, her voice strident with her rising fear.

"It's okay," Xandy called from the bathroom, "it'll be okay…"

The tone of Xandy's voice made the hair on the back of her neck stand up. Without hesitation Quinn stepped back and kicked the bathroom door open. The scene in front of her would stay with her for years afterwards; Xandy was sitting on the floor, a pool of blood on her left, staining her blue lounge pants, her head was down, and Quinn caught a flash of metal in her hand.

"Xandy! No!" Quinn yelled, striding forward and slapping the razor blade out of Xandy's hand.

Because Xandy had looked up at Quinn's exclamation, the razor blade and tilted upward, and sliced through Quinn's hand as she dislodged it from Xandy's grip.

"Fucking son of a bitch!" Quinn growled, gritting her teeth against the pain that shot through her.

She grabbed a towel off the sink and used it to wrap up Xandy's heavily-bleeding wrist.

"Fuck, fuck, fuck," Quinn chanted, as she did her best to hold the towel firmly. She reached into her pocket for her cell phone with her now heavily-bleeding hand.

She had a hard time using the touch screen because it kept getting smeared with her own blood, but she finally dialed 911, and hit the speaker phone, dropping the phone to reach for a towel for herself.

When the dispatcher answered, Quinn gave them Xandy's address and said that there'd been an accident. She knew that 911 calls were recorded; she'd be damned if she was going to allow that call to end up on some stupid tabloid show. She told the dispatcher that Xandy had been cut accidentally, that she was losing a lot of blood, and that they needed an ambulance right away.

Quinn stayed on the phone, but pulled Xandy into her lap, holding the towel at her wrist. Xandy was in and out of consciousness.

"Xan, stay with me, come on babe, open your eyes."

Xandy slowly opened her eyes, but Quinn could tell she was very out of it.

"There ya go," Quinn said, smiling weakly, "come on, stay with me." To the dispatcher she yelled, "Where the fuck are these guys?"

"They're coming, they'll be there in about two minutes," responded the dispatcher.

Quinn moved to stand, picking Xandy up as she did. She was hit with a wave of dizziness and had to lean against the sink to keep from passing out. She knew her own blood loss was getting a little too high. She gripped the towel on her hand tighter, gritting her teeth against the sharp pains.

She walked out of the bathroom, leaving her bloodied phone on the floor and walked to the front door to unlock it. She heard the sirens then, and waited for the paramedics. When they took Xandy out of her arms, they saw her bloodied hand and moved to tend it, she yanked her hand away from the paramedic.

"Help her! I'm fine," she yelled, even as her vision blurred a bit.

"My partner has your girl," the paramedic explained calmly, "but you're losing a lot of blood too, and you're as white as a ghost, so how about you let me help you too?"

The fight left Quinn then, and she nodded, moving to sit down on the step in the front of Xandy's house.

An hour and a half later, BJ Sparks hit the doors of the emergency room at a dead run. Quinn had called him to tell him that Xandy was in the hospital. BJ strode up to the counter, looking at the faces behind the nurses station.

"Em!" he called, recognizing one of the nurses.

"BJ!" she called, nodding understandingly. "That's right she's one of yours. She's not conscious yet, but the doctor is with her. He should be out soon. Her bodyguard is being particularly difficult with us," she said, knowing how BJ handled his people and knowing if anyone could get Quinn Kavanaugh to cooperate, it would be BJ.

"Where is she?" BJ asked.

"Out in the courtyard smoking like a train," Emily answered.

"Thanks beautiful," BJ said winking at the nurse.

Turning, he walked out into the courtyard. He spotted Quinn across the square; she was leaning against a wall, one knee bent, her booted foot on the wall behind her. Her head was down, but BJ noted the blood-soaked bandage on her shaking hand as she lifted the cigarette to her lips.

BJ walked toward Quinn. Hearing his boots on the pavement, she lifted her head. BJ immediately saw the devastation on her face. If he hadn't already heard from the nurse that Xandy wasn't dead, he would have thought she was from the look of distress on Quinn's face.

Without a word, BJ walked up, took Quinn into his arms and hugged her.

"Don't do this to yourself," he told her, knowing that no matter what had happened, Quinn would blame herself as Xandy's bodyguard.

Quinn gritted her teeth, not wanting to cry. She did, however step out of the hug BJ was giving her, pulling her head up as she did. BJ nodded, understanding that she wasn't willing to take any comfort at this point.

"What happened?" BJ asked, devoid of accusation.

Quinn shook her head. "I fucked up… I fucked up and Xandy hurt herself because of it."

BJ winced, he'd been afraid of this. "Quinn…" he began, but Quinn shook her head.

"No, don't," Quinn said, making a cutting gesture with her hand, her eyes narrowed.

BJ looked back at her and shook his head, she wasn't in a place to listen to him now.

The doctor walked out into the courtyard at that moment. BJ and Quinn walked over to talk to him.

"How is she doc?" BJ asked.

"She's going to be just fine," he said. "She's going to need some rest, and I'm going to prescribe an anti-depressant for her. She lost a lot of blood," the doctor said, but then looked at Quinn, "but your quick thinking saved her life."

Quinn looked like she wanted to argue, but didn't.

"Now, you need to let us take a look at that," the doctor said, pointing to Quinn's hand.

"It's fine."

"And it's going to get looked at," BJ said, his tone stern.

"BJ, it's fine."

"That's great," BJ said, his smile wintery, "but since you don't have a medical degree, the man that does is going to look at it."

Quinn looked back at BJ with narrowed eyes.

"Don't test me on this one, Quinn," BJ said, with a sigh.

Quinn's lips twitched, but finally she nodded.

Two hours later, Quinn sat next to the hospital bed Xandy lay in. She had one elbow up on the bed, her head resting on her fist. Her now bandaged hand rested on the bed. She was watching the girl sleep. Xandy's left wrist was bandaged, her color had improved with the infusion of blood she'd been given.

Xandy stirred, opening her eyes slowly. She looked up at the ceiling for a long moment, then a devastated look crossed her face, as she started to come to terms with what had happened. Quinn reached out and touched her shoulder. Xandy turned her head, looking at Quinn, shock reflected in her eyes.

"Wot?" Quinn asked softly.

"You're here," Xandy said quietly.

"Where else would I be?"

Xandy didn't answer, her lavender-blue eyes searching Quinn's, then her eyes dropped to Quinn's bandaged hand.

"Did I do that?"

"I did that."

"How?"

"Blade removal gone wrong."

Xandy breathed out audibly, near tears.

"Hey…" Quinn said, her voice imploring. "I'm okay, you don't need to worry about this, okay?"

"But I hurt you…" Xandy said. "I didn't want to hurt you…"

Quinn moved to sit on the bed next to Xandy, moving to put her head on the same level as Xandy's, her eyes searching Xandy's.

"No," Quinn said, gently, "you wanted to hurt you."

Xandy swallowed convulsively, but then nodded.

"Can you tell me why?" Quinn asked.

Xandy didn't answer at first, her face showing that she was trying to gather her thoughts.

"I guess I just couldn't handle things."

"What things?" Quinn asked.

Xandy shook her head, moving back from Quinn.

"Okay, okay," Quinn said gently, sensing that she was pushing too hard. "We don't have to talk about that now," she said, reaching up to touch Xandy's face softly. "So, BJ and I have been talking…"

"BJ is here?" Xandy asked, suddenly afraid.

"It's okay," Quinn said, her tone reassuring. "We both think that you need to get away from here for a little bit."

Once again Xandy's eyes became round with fear. "You're sending me away?"

"No, Xan, no, listen to me, will you?" Quinn said, her voice still soft.

Xandy nodded her head, but was biting her lip in worry.

"I want to take you home," Quinn said.

"Home?" Xandy repeated, shocked. "I can't go home, I don't have anyone in Kansas, not my family," she said, shaking her head, and in her upset moving to sit up.

"Xan!" Quinn said, her voice sharper than she meant it to be in her worry that Xandy would get up too quickly and pass out or get hurt. "Will you listen?" she repeated, her voice calming. "I meant my home."

"Belfast?" Xandy asked, breathless.

"That's where I'm from," Quinn said with a grin.

Xandy looked like it was Christmas morning and Quinn couldn't help but be heartened by that.

Three days later they touched down at Belfast International airport at ten o'clock at night, local time. BJ had sent them in his private jet. Xandy had slept for some of the trip, but had been too excited to sleep for long. Quinn had purposely kept any and all conversations light, not wanting to upset Xandy again.

Quinn gestured for Xandy to precede her down the stairs from the plane, having picked up Xandy's overnight bag, knowing the plane's crew would offload their luggage. When they got off the plane a man was waiting on the tarmac for them. Quinn led Xandy over to the man who stood beside a black Mercedes E-Class.

"Kavanaugh," the man queried.

"That's me," Quinn said, nodding.

"For you," the man said, handing her a key and a clipboard for her to sign on.

"Thanks," Quinn said, nodding at the crew who were already loading the bags in the trunk of the car.

Glancing over at Xandy, Quinn grinned. "Looks like BJ's reach is far and wide."

Xandy smiled. "I guess."

Xandy was in sensory overload. The night air smelled so clean and crisp, and it was cool. She knew just beyond the airport there was so much to see, but it was dark so she knew she wouldn't be seeing it that night. Regardless, she knew she was in Northern Ireland, and it felt a little bit surreal.

When they got into the car, Xandy had to adjust to Quinn sitting on the opposite side to normal. Quinn noticed her discomfort and grinned, giving her a wink. With that, Quinn drove out of the private terminal area and got onto the road to take them 'home.'

Xandy hadn't wanted to ask too many questions about the trip, not wanting to seem ungrateful for this gift that Quinn and BJ were bestowing on her. She felt a lot of guilt about everything that had happened, but she continued to push that away in her mind.

The two lane road that Quinn drove onto, going what Xandy perceived as the wrong way, was more like where she'd grown up in Kansas, than Los Angeles. There were no street lights, only reflectors and occasional decorative lights when they passed a house. Even the houses were few and far between. After about twenty minutes they came upon a lit-up store and a few other commercial buildings.

"This area is called Templepatrick," Quinn told Xandy.

Xandy nodded, trying to take in everything she could see in the lights of the area. Quinn continued to drive. Within three minutes they were through the town and back in the country again. They went through another area that Quinn said was called Newtonabbey. There were street lights in this area, and Xandy could see the tidy little one story brick houses that lined the road they were on. This area was bigger and it took them longer to get through the town, but then they were back out in the country.

At one point, Quinn pulled up to a light. There were street lights on across the road, and Xandy could see water.

"Is that the ocean?" Xandy asked pointing across the street.

"That's the Belfast Lough," Quinn said, pronouncing the last word "lock."

"The Titanic actually followed this lough up out of Belfast on her way to start her maiden voyage."

The light turned green, and Quinn turned left onto the road that ran alongside the lough. Xandy stared past Quinn, trying desperately to see the lough, but in the dark it was impossible.

"Relax, we'll see everything," Quinn assured Xandy.

They passed a few lit areas, including a car dealership and even a KFC, much to Xandy's surprise, then Quinn took a right. Within a minute she was stopping, not in front of a hotel, but in front of a house. It was a two story brick house, with large picture windows and lights burning warmly inside. There were double front doors that were a pristine white.

Quinn looked over at her. "Ready?"

"To what?" Xandy asked, her eyes wide.

"To meet my family?" Quinn asked, grinning.

"This is your family's home?" Xandy asked, shocked.

Quinn nodded grinning, as an outside light turned on. She got out of the car and walked around to open the door for Xandy, putting her hand out to help Xandy out of the car. As Xandy got out of the car, the front door of the house opened and two screaming women came out, yelling Quinn's name.

Quinn let go of Xandy quickly enough to keep her from being bowled over by the two red heads barreling toward her. Quinn grabbed up both women, one in each arm. There was much laughing and squealing from the younger women. When Quinn finally put the women down, she turned them toward Xandy. Xandy noticed that the women looked exactly alike, they were twins.

"Xan, this is Ida and Maggie," Quinn said, motioning to each woman in turn, "my two younger sisters."

Xandy smiled, extending her hand to them in turn. They both smiled, each taking Xandy's hand and smiling sweetly.

"It's great to meet ya," Ida said, smiling brightly, her accent thick.

"It is very lovely to meet you, Xandy," said Maggie.

"Come on, let's get inside," Quinn said, nodding toward the house, "it's getting cold out here."

"Has your blood thinned so in California?" Ida asked, poking a finger at her sister.

"Feck off," Quinn countered, grinning.

The house inside was beautiful with rich wood wainscoting, and beautiful colors on the walls. Xandy was overwhelmed looking around her, as they wandered through to the living room.

"And this must be my lovely gel?" an older woman asked as she walked into the room, wiping her hands on a towel.

"Ma," Quinn said, smiling as she walked over to her mother, giving her a big hug.

"Och, you're still too thin!" said the woman, swatting Quinn on the butt, smiling all the same.

"Fightin' weight, Ma, just fightin' weight," Quinn replied.

"Away on that!" the woman replied.

Quinn turned to Xandy, holding her hand out to the girl. Xandy walked forward taking Quinn's hand.

"Ma, this is Xandy, my friend," Quinn said. "Xan, this is my mom, Brann Kavanaugh, the true head of the Kavanaugh clan."

"Don't be sayin' that 'round yer da," Brann said, laughing even as she stepped forward to hug Xandy.

"It's lovely to meet ya," Brann said to Xandy after a quick hug.

"You too," Xandy said, smiling warmly.

To Quinn, Brann said, "Cara nó leannán?"

"Cara mháthair," Quinn replied, glancing at Xandy.

Brann looked at her daughter, her look very skeptical.

"Where's da?" Quinn asked then trying to get off the topic that had just been brought up, knowing her father would be out there to greet them already if he was home.

"Still at university," Brann said rolling her eyes, "he's deep in exams."

"Aw, yeah," Quinn said, nodding her head.

Quinn reached up to scratch her nose, which pushed her sleeve up enough to expose the bandage on her hand.

"What happened, Quinn?" Brann said, instantly concerned.

Xandy grimaced, still feeling a lot of guilt about the injury to Quinn's hand.

"I'm fine, ma," Quinn said, catching Xandy's grimace, "all good."

Quinn stifled a yawn; she'd been up for the past twenty-four hours and was starting to feel it. There'd been a lot of preparation to make sure Xandy would be safe in Northern Ireland. BJ had pre-released some songs from her upcoming album and they'd flown up the charts. Xandy Blue was about to be a very busy girl. It also meant that there were extra precautions to take, plus getting a passport rushed for Xandy.

"Ma we need to hit the four post inn," Quinn said, telling her mom that she and Xandy needed to go to bed.

"Right you are," Brann said, nodding. "I put you in your old room."

Quinn nodded, looking at Xandy and held out her hand.

"I'll be back down in a minute," she told them.

Quinn lead Xandy to her old bedroom, opening the door and realizing that not much had changed in her room. Her mother had hung more pictures, but the bed was the same, as was the rest of the furniture. Fortunately, she'd had a queen sized bed before she'd left home.

"Okay, you get settled," she told Xandy. "I'll get the bags."

"Quinn, I can help you," Xandy said, worried. "What if you open your hand up again?"

Quinn had already pulled the stitches in her hand twice in the last three days. She wasn't used to being hindered.

"I'll be fine," Quinn said.

With that she turned and left the room.

An hour later, Quinn lay on her bed on her stomach watching Xandy who was wandering around the room looking at things. Quinn glanced at the bedside clock, it was just past midnight.

"Xan…" Quinn said, her voice pleading, "you need to get some sleep."

"I can't," Xandy said, glancing over her shoulder at Quinn and smiling. "I'm just way too keyed up. I'm dying to see this place in the day time."

"Babe, it's gonna be day time in like five hours," Quinn said. "You need to sleep, because if you don't you're gonna be jet lagged the whole time we're here…"

Xandy sighed. "Okay," then she turned to the bed, and hesitated. "Is this going to be okay? I mean…"

"Xandy Blue Hayes," Quinn said, her voice firm, "get in this bed right now."

"How do you know my full name?" Xandy asked, moving to get into the bed all the same.

"Magic"

Xandy lay down, but Quinn could see that she was trying to stay back from her. Making an annoyed sound in the back of her throat, Quinn slid her arm under Xandy's neck, and pulled her close. Regardless of her original hesitation, Xandy immediately relaxed against Quinn.

"What your mom said to you earlier," Xandy said, looking up at Quinn. "That was Gaelic, wasn't it?"

"Yeah, it was."

"What did she ask you?"

"She asked if you were a friend or a lover."

"And you told her I'm a friend?"

"Yes."

"But she didn't believe you, did she?"

Quinn smiled. "No."

"Why?" Xandy asked.

"'Cause she knows I have a thing for pretty girls."

"Uh-huh," Xandy said, sounding unconvinced.

"Might be because I've never brought a girl home before either." Quinn said, her tone so off-handed that Xandy almost missed what she said.

"You haven't?"

Quinn shook her head. "Not my thing."

"To bring girls home to your parents?"

"Yeah, I have too much respect for them, to do that."

"What do you mean?"

"I don't bring random people home to meet my family, least of all girls," Quinn said.

"Well, yeah, but in this case there's a different reason for you bringing me here," Xandy reasoned.

"Is there?"

Xandy looked back at Quinn, unable to think of a response.

"Xan, I could have taken you anywhere," Quinn said, her eyes looking down into Xandy's. "I wanted to bring you here."

Xandy blinked a couple of times. Quinn could see her mind working.

"Because I said I wanted to see Ireland," Xandy offered softly.

"Because I wanted to show you my homeland," Quinn said, "because I wanted you to meet my family, because I wanted you here."

"But…" Xandy began, but her voice trailed off as she shook her head.

"Look," Quinn said, her finger reaching up to touch Xandy's lips, as if to still not only her words, but her mind. "I know that night I said that I couldn't do this with you, but then… what you did…" Quinn said, with a pained look. "It wasn't that I didn't want you, it was that I didn't want to compromise my ability to do my job, to protect you."

Her fingers moved to touch Xandy's cheek, her eyes searching Xandy's face. "But what you did…" she said, her voice trailing off as she shook her head, her eyes never leaving Xandy's face. "I can't let that happen again, I can't take that chance." Xandy's eyes reflected tears at the sadness in Quinn's voice. "So, now I need figure out how to do my job and be with you at the same time."

Again Xandy had to pause to take in what Quinn had just said. She'd already made up her mind that Quinn just didn't want her in that way, and had used her job to try to keep from hurting her feelings. But now she was saying she wanted to be with her? Was that possible? Was she really hearing this?

"Xan?" Quinn queried, seeing so many questions in Xandy's eyes, but seeing that the girl was clearly shocked.

"I…" Xandy began, clearly searching for the right words to say.

Quinn pulled Xandy toward her, lowering her head, and kissed Xandy gently. She felt Xandy sigh softly, and Quinn gathered her even closer, moving her hand to the back of Xandy's head, to kiss her deeper. Xandy's hand came up, grasping Quinn's shoulder almost desperately. Quinn pulled back, looking down into Xandy's eyes, and reached up to take the hand that was on her shoulder. She held it between them, her thumb rubbing near the bandage on Xandy's wrist.

"I need to know that you aren't going to do this to me again," Quinn said, her look beseeching.

Xandy pressed her lips together, tears in her eyes suddenly.

"I can't lose you, not like that," Quinn told her, her expression so mournful, Xandy reached up to touch Quinn's face.

"I'm sorry," Xandy said. "I just… everything just came down on me."

"Can you tell me what you were thinking?" Quinn asked tenderly.

Xandy looked reflective and then said, "That I was never going to find my place here."

"Here?"

"In this world," Xandy said, her voice reflecting the hopelessness she must have been feeling that night.

"You thought you'd found it with me?" Quinn asked; her voice held no judgment.

"Is that stupid?"

"No, you're still trying to find out who you are, Xan."

"I thought I knew. But so much changed, so much happened…"

Quinn knew Xandy was talking about both the past and the present. She pinned her with a look.

"This isn't the first time, is it?" Quinn asked sadly.

Xandy looked back at Quinn, her face reflecting first surprise, then resignation as she nodded, dropping her eyes from Quinn's. Quinn lifted her chin back up to meet her eyes again.

"Tell me," Quinn said simply, her eyes saying much more.

Xandy looked uncomfortable, but Quinn could see that she was trying to pull herself together.

"When I was a little kid," Xandy said, "when things would get hard, I would run and hide in the barn. I'd sit there and wait for someone to come find me, and when they didn't, I started to think that maybe no one really cared if I was around." Xandy's hand was on Quinn's arm, her thumb rubbing over Quinn's tattoo, her eyes unfocused as she stared straight ahead. "I think that's where it started, but then when I came to California, I just never felt like I fit in. All the girls there are so self-involved and competitive."

"But you were on shows and things, weren't you?" Quinn asked, remembering that from the bio she'd read.

"Yes, but that didn't mean any of those girls liked me, or were friends with me," Xandy said.

Quinn nodded, waiting for Xandy to continue.

"I guess the first time I thought about just giving up," her eyes flicked up to Quinn's, "you know… letting go, was when my mom left to go back home."

"She was with you when you came to LA right?"

"Yeah, she came and stayed with me for the first three years, but then it got too hard for her to be away so much, so she had to go home. I was seventeen when she left."

Quinn nodded, imaging that must have been very hard for a very young Xandy. "So you thought about it then?"

Xandy nodded. "I just figured that it would be less worry for the people who loved me, they wouldn't have to worry about coming to see me, or if I was okay."

Quinn grimaced at that thought, not able to imagine believing that being dead was more favorable than being alive.

"You had to know that it would have devastated them," Quinn said, her tone still gentle, not wanting Xandy to feel judged.

"I think I did and that's what stopped me then."

"But there were other times?"

Xandy nodded, breathing her breath out audibly, her look pained. "I married Tommy because I was lonely, and I thought I loved him. He didn't scare me the way other men did sometimes… but he was so caught up in the Hollywood scene that he just didn't seem to care that much about me. I thought there must be something wrong with me, because I'd had that trouble with other boys too. Like they couldn't really care about me, I never felt like they did, anyway. Not like you," she said, looking up at Quinn.

Quinn looked curious. "How do you mean? Like me? What's different that I do?"

Xandy chewed on the inside of her lip in thought. "You just seem to sense when I need you, like you're connected enough to me to feel my pain. Like that day at BJ's, when you put your hand out for me to hold it, because you knew BJ terrified me. The way you protected me that day from his anger, you could have lost your job, he even threatened you with that, and you stood up against him anyway. No one's ever done something like that for me." She could see Quinn's look and inserted, "And don't say it's because it's your job," she said her look narrowed, "you could have lost your job, but your job wasn't your priority at that moment."

"You were," Quinn said.

Xandy nodded. "And I felt that. And that's what I mean."

Quinn inhaled slowly, breathing out as she nodded.

"But Tommy didn't care about me, not even when my family was killed. I mean, he pretended like he was upset, he said all the right things, even went with me to the funeral, but... I could sense that he wasn't really being honest. He wanted to get back to LA the next day, because he had "things going on." The night of the funeral I locked myself in the bathroom, and I really thought that was it."

There were tears in her eyes then, and one look at Quinn's pained expression, and the tears spilled over. Quinn pulled her into an embrace, feeling so desperately sad for what Xandy had been through and so angry at the man who'd been so callous with her. Xandy clung to Quinn, feelings overwhelming her as she cried.

After a few minutes she calmed down, but stayed within Quinn's arms, taking comfort from their strength.

"I took a bottle of pills that night," she said.

Quinn closed her eyes, feeling absolutely sickened by the thought.

"Fortunately, that's when I found out I have a strong gag reflex and threw them up not too long after," Xandy said, shaking her head ruefully. "Tommy never even came to check on me."

"He had to have heard you throwing up," Quinn said, appalled.

"I'm sure he did," Xandy said, shrugging, "he just didn't care enough to find out why."

"Oh Xan…" Quinn said, shaking her head. "I'm so sorry that you went through that, especially when you needed that son of a bitch most."

Xandy took heart from Quinn's obvious anger at the situation and she nodded. "Even so, I stayed with him. I had no one else at that point. But the sex tape thing, that was just too much."

Quinn nodded, understanding that completely.

"When I signed on with BJ," Xandy said, her voice changing again, becoming more serious, "I was going through the divorce with Tommy and it was getting nasty, so BJ wanted me to be protected. That's when he brought in Jason…"

Quinn closed her eyes, knowing she wasn't going to like what was to come.

"He was okay at first," Xandy said, her eyes narrowing, "but after about three months, he started making comments about how he could take care of me in a way that Tommy hadn't… you know?"

Quinn curled her lips in disgust, knowing that Jason had meant sexually. *'Cause that's all a woman needs, right? A good fucking,* she thought derisively. To Xandy she nodded that she did understand what Jason meant.

"I never really said anything, but I guess because I never outright said that I wasn't interested, he decided I must really be."

Quinn stared at her open mouthed for a moment. "If you don't say no, it must mean yes?"

She knew that Navy Seals were trained to have more respect for women than that. On the other hand, for many men who were considered elite, their ego would tell them that if I woman really meant no, she'd say it, and that if she didn't, then she just wanted to be pursued harder. She wondered if this had been the case here.

"What happened?" Quinn asked, her tone cautious because she wasn't altogether sure she wanted to know.

"He started making a point of touching me whenever he could," Xandy said, looking dismayed. "He'd run his hand down my arm, or touch my waist to 'guide' me, but would leave his hand there longer than he needed to…" she said, breathing a sigh. "At first I thought I was just imagining things, but then he would try to pull me close in small areas, like elevators or waiting areas."

"Did you ever say anything to him about it?" Quinn asked, wanting to confirm her thoughts about the guy.

"I tried to move away from him, and at first he'd let me, but then he got more insistent. But no, I didn't know what I could say," Xandy said, looking embarrassed.

"Xan," Quinn said, touching her face, "it wasn't your job to tell him to stop. He should have known better. I was just asking because I'm trying to get a read on him."

Xandy nodded, looking relieved. Then she looked resolved, and began to talk again.

"*That* night," she said, making Quinn know that she was about to hear what had really happened, "I had just gotten back to the apartment from a small show that I'd done. He always went into the apartment with me and checked it before leaving for the night. He did that as normal... but then he didn't leave. He was telling me how great the show was, and how sexy I looked. I tried to tell him that I was really tired, and that I'd see him the next day, but he wasn't listening. Then he said that he thought he and I would be good together. I asked him what he meant, and he said 'let me show you.' That's when he grabbed me kissing me. I tried to shove him away, but he was so strong, I couldn't budge him. He had his hands all over me," she said, looking sick now. "I couldn't make him stop..."

Quinn clenched her teeth, desperately trying to hold onto the anger that wanted to explode. The guy wasn't there, and Xandy didn't deserve to deal with Quinn's impotent fury.

Xandy could see the fury in Quinn's eyes; part of her was grateful for it, but the other part was a bit afraid and she shrunk back from Quinn a little.

"Babe," Quinn said. The fury was instantly replaced with a mortified look, as the idea that she'd just scared this girl ripped through her.

She resisted the urge to grab Xandy, knowing that would be doing exactly as Jason had, and she wasn't about to do that.

Instead her voice was deeply apologetic and endlessly tender as she said, "I'm sorry, I'm not mad at you... please..." Her eyes begged Xandy to understand.

Xandy drew her breath in, unable to be afraid of someone that was willing to treat her so carefully and with so much concern.

"I know, I just… I guess I reacted to that look in your eyes," Xandy said, smiling softly as she moved closer to Quinn, her hand curling around Quinn's hand.

"I'll tell ya though, I could just fucking kill that guy and I'm hoping I get the chance," Quinn said, her look backing that statement up completely. Then her look softened. "You know that none of that was your fault, right?"

Xandy looked doubtful. "I could have told him I wasn't interested a lot sooner."

"No," Quinn said, regretting that she'd asked the question earlier on, thinking that it might have made Xandy think that she thought that too. "That man was trained and conditioned to control his emotions, he was trained to respect those that he protected. He broke his promise to protect you, and that's on him, not you."

Xandy looked back at her, considering, finally she nodded, accepting what Quinn was telling her.

"That's what you were afraid of, wasn't it?" Xandy asked then. "That you were breaking your promise to protect me."

Quinn nodded, her look sorrowful. "That didn't work out so well."

"What didn't?" Xandy asked, confused.

"Protecting you," Quinn whispered.

"You saved my life, Quinn, I know what I did was going to kill me," she said, her tone sure. "I knew exactly where to cut to cause the most blood loss…"

Quinn pulled her head back, a grimace on her face, like she couldn't handle what she was hearing. It was true, she was having a really hard time hearing it, but she knew Xandy needed to say it. She felt Xandy's hand on her cheek, and looked down at the girl.

"If you hadn't come to the door when you did, I would have finished the job," Xandy said, her voice soft, but strong. "If you hadn't kicked that door in, and stopped me," she said, reaching for Quinn's still bandaged hand, pained at the memory.

She had finally remembered what Quinn had done that night to cause the cut to her hand; slapping the razor out of Xandy's hand. She remembered Quinn screaming her name. She remembered the blade being slapped from her hand, and hearing Quinn yell, "Fucking son of a bitch!" and thinking hazily that Quinn's ma would be mad at her for saying "fuck." She also remembered Quinn's voice telling her to stay with her. It had been that plea that had made Xandy think that maybe she'd made a mistake, but it had been too late then and the world seemed to be fading in and out. The last thing she heard was Quinn yelling at the dispatcher.

"I would have been dead. You had no way of knowing about my past, my thoughts… I've never told anyone about any of that. There was no way to know…"

She paused, watching Quinn's reaction.

"Please, Quinn," Xandy said, seeing that Quinn clearly still felt like she'd caused Xandy's suicide attempt. She reached up to touch Quinn's face. "You have to know that the only reason I'm still here is because of you and not just because you stopped me, but because you asked me to stay with you…" Her voice trailed off as her eyes searched Quinn's. "I wanted to stay with you."

"I'm glad you did," Quinn replied, her voice so heartfelt that it brought tears to Xandy's eyes again.

Quinn leaned in, kissing Xandy again, her lips were so tender, with just a note of the heat that they'd both experienced that night they'd first kissed.

They ended up falling asleep facing each other, Quinn's arms wrapped tightly around Xandy.

Chapter 6

Quinn woke the next morning as the sun shone into the room, hitting her square in the eye. Glancing down, she saw that Xandy was still asleep. Moving carefully, so as not to disturb her, Quinn got up. She was wearing her usual sleeping attire, sweat pants and a tank top. She pulled on a sweat jacket and put on some tennis shoes. Grabbing her cigarettes, she walked downstairs. Glancing at the clock on the wall, she saw that it was only six o'clock Belfast time. She knew she'd only slept for about four hours, but it didn't matter, she'd gotten Xandy to talk to her about her state of mind. That was definitely worth a few hours of lost sleep. Her mother, the saint that she was, had coffee made already. Quinn poured herself a cup.

She made her way to her parents' conservatory; a sun room enclosed with glass, with windows open to the morning air. Sitting down on one of the wicker couches, she pulled out a cigarette, still sipping at her coffee. Lighting her cigarette was made difficult by the bandage on her hand and the stiffness of the stitched cut underneath. She finally managed it and leaned back and inhaled deeply. She listened to the sound of the ocean and breathed in the salty air.

It always felt good to come home, she always felt at peace there. Having Xandy there to share it seemed to make it even more enchanted than it had always been to her. Quinn knew that Xandy would appreciate Northern Ireland, and that she would see Belfast, the way that Quinn had always seen it and loved it.

Bryan Kavanaugh stood just inside the house watching his daughter for a few minutes. He saw the fond smile she made and the way she inhaled the morning air deeply, looking blissfully happy. Quinn had always been his wild child, but she had also always been one of his most respectful children, and he loved her endlessly. Knowing her as he did, he knew that the moment he opened the sunroom door she would sense it, and so he'd wanted to observe her before she knew she was being observed.

Brann had told him that Quinn had brought home a young lady. She also told him that while Quinn claimed the girl was only a friend, she'd seen something different in their daughter's eyes and that she thought this girl was far from just a friend. Seeing Quinn's serene expression, Bryan tended to agree with his wife's assessment.

He stepped out into the sunroom, carrying his own coffee.

"And there she is…" he said affectionately.

"Da!" Quinn said, getting up immediately and setting her cigarette and coffee aside, so she could reach up and hug him.

"Mar a tha mo nighean?" he queried, asking, "how is my daughter?" in Gaelic, always testing his children to ensure they remembered their native language.

"Tha mi mòr athair," Quinn responded, saying, "I'm great Dad."

"That's grand, lovey," Bryan replied, smiling down at his daughter, and gesturing for her to sit again.

He took a seat across from her, assessing her as he sipped his coffee.

"How's it happening in the west?" he asked Quinn then.

Quinn nodded, as she took another drag on her cigarette. "Good, da, fine."

"What happened to yer hand?" Bryan asked, gesturing to the bandage.

"Got cut," Quinn answered simply, "it's fine though. How is work going?" she asked, wanting to steer the conversation away from her being hurt on the job; it always worried her parents. "Ma said you were late last night with exams?"

Bryan knew full well he was being led away from the topic, so he made a note to ask further questions later. "Aye, they're a sight, I'll tell ya."

Quinn nodded, grinning.

"So your ma tells me you brought a girl home with ya," Bryan said, his eyes belying the casual tone.

Quinn grinned unrepentantly, knowing it had been the first thing her father had wanted to ask, but he'd waited.

"Yes, I did," Quinn said, smiling broadly.

"Your ma said you told her she was only a friend, but it's clear from the sun on your dial there that she's more than that."

Quinn grinned at her father's use of the word "dial," meaning her face, he was forever picking up slang from his students.

She inclined her head. "She is, yes."

"So why not tell your ma that?" Bryan asked, looking perplexed, Quinn wasn't usually very secretive.

Quinn grimaced. "It's kind of complicated."

"How?"

"Well," Quinn said, stubbing out her first cigarette and pulling out another one and lighting it, "I'm her bodyguard."

"You think it's a conflict of interest?"

"Exactly," Quinn said, knowing her father would understand the concern.

"But she's here with you," Bryan said, his blue eyes narrowed slightly as he worked through the problem in his mind, "so something's changed."

Quinn chuckled, her father was always trying to solve puzzles, and this was just another one for him.

"Yes, something did change."

"And what is that?" Bryan asked; it was obvious Quinn wasn't going to elaborate without a push.

Quinn inhaled deeply on her cigarette as she tried to decide how much she wanted to tell her father. She normally wouldn't hold information back from her parents, but she also didn't want them thinking that Xandy was somehow unstable. She wanted, needed, her family to like Xandy. Her family was her entire life, and if they didn't like the woman she was so deeply involved with, it wouldn't bode well for the relationship. What her family thought was everything to Quinn, it always had been.

Bryan waited patiently for his daughter to decide what to tell him. He could easily see that she was conflicted, and he didn't want to push her into closing up. Quinn had learned her patience and how to wait people out from her father; he was the very best at it, often waiting hours or even days to get an answer from someone when it was important.

"Recently," Quinn said cautiously, which told Bryan he wasn't about to hear the whole story, but a version of it, "my job got in the way of my relationship with her, and it had very serious consequences. I can't let that happen again."

Bryan looked back at his daughter, his eyes falling on the bandage on her hand, wondering if her injury had something to do with those consequences. He could see that Quinn had very deep feelings for this girl, and that she was having to adjust her very disciplined work ethic to maintain a relationship with her. It said a lot to Bryan about this girl Quinn had brought home; she must be very special indeed to have so thoroughly captured his wild daughter's heart.

Bryan and Brann Kavanaugh had always known that Quinn was different from the other girls in the family. Quinn had never been interested in boys, other than as playmates. They'd been through the boy-crazy phase with their older daughter Fallon, who was four years older than Quinn. So when Quinn had gotten to that age, they expected her to suddenly see boys for more than just playmates. When that never happened, they talked for a long time about the possibility that Quinn just wasn't made that way. Then there'd been her very definite interest in the O'Shay girl down the way and when that didn't seem to fade quickly, they were sure that Quinn was gay.

It took Quinn until she was twenty to finally admit it to them, but since they already knew, it was no shock at all. They loved their daughter, and they fully accepted that she was still the same person they'd always known. It had actually hurt their hearts to see her struggle with telling them the truth, so they'd done their best to make it easy for her.

Looking at his daughter now, Bryan was once again grateful for the way that they'd handled Quinn's sexuality. It meant that he got to see his daughter's face the way it was at that moment, as she talked about this girl that meant so much to her. If he and Brann had handled it the way they knew other parents handled their children being gay, disowning them, shaming them, even physically attacking them, Quinn would have left home and never returned. That, to Bryan and Brann, was a fate worse than death.

As if she knew she was being talked about, Xandy wandered out onto the porch. She'd been looking for Quinn for a few minutes at that point.

"Hey…" Quinn said, smiling and moving to stand, as did Bryan.

Xandy smiled softly, then glanced at Bryan.

"Xandy, this is my father, Bryan Kavanaugh, head of clan Kavanaugh," Quinn said, smiling. "Da, this is Xandy Blue Hayes."

Bryan executed a half bow, inclining his head to Xandy.

"A pleasure, miss," he said, his tone very proper.

"It's very nice to meet you," Xandy replied shyly.

Quinn held her arms out to Xandy, who walked over and into them. Quinn hugged her gently, leaning down to kiss the side of her head.

"Good morning," she said softly to Xandy.

"Good morning," Xandy replied glancing up at Quinn.

Quinn moved to sit, gesturing for Xandy to sit with her. As she did, she saw that Xandy was shivering, she was wearing short sleeves. Quinn unzipped her jacket and began to take it off.

"No," Xandy said, holding her hand up to forestall Quinn's movement, "I'm fine."

Quinn shook her head, and took the jacket off, putting it around Xandy's shoulders. Xandy smiled shyly. "Thank you."

Bryan winked at Xandy. "Chivalrous one, isn't she?"

Xandy nodded. "She always is."

"That's because she was raised proper," Bryan said, grinning at his daughter.

"Oh yeah," Quinn agreed, smiling at her father.

"Xan, did you want some coffee?" Quinn asked.

"I'm okay," Xandy said, sliding her arms into Quinn's jacket and pulling the sides close around her.

Quinn detected that Xandy was feeling very shy. She hoped her father would sense it too and not be his usual boisterous self. She glanced over at him, giving a friendly warning that he should go easy on Xandy. He gave a small, quick nod in response.

"So, Quinn, what are your plans while you're here?" Bryan asked, directing his questions at Quinn, rather than Xandy so as not to scare the girl.

Quinn grinned, nodding at her father by way of a thank you.

"Well," Quinn said, looking over at Xandy, "Xandy's never been to Norn Iron, so today I was thinking we'd drive The Causeway."

Bryan nodded enthusiastically. "A brilliant idea."

"Norn Iron?" Xandy repeated, causing Quinn to grin, she'd known that the girl couldn't resist asking for clarification, her insatiable curiosity overriding her bashfulness.

"It's slang for Northern Ireland," Bryan put in, his voice low.

"Oh," Xandy said, nodding, looking a bit abashed, "I'm always driving Quinn crazy with my questions."

Quinn smiled warmly. "No, you don't drive me crazy, I like that you're interested."

"Quinn can definitely give you a lesson, she learned from the best," Bryan said, winking at his daughter.

"That I have," Quinn said nodding. "My da's a professor of history at St. Mary's College."

"Oh," Xandy said, "that's why you know so much about it."

"Oh yeah," Quinn said.

"Quinn has been telling me a lot about her homeland," Xandy told Bryan, now feeling more comfortable with him.

Bryan nodded, looking proud. "She does know her history. Our Quinn has always been a quick study. We're very proud."

Xandy nodded.

They were all quiet for a few minutes. Xandy breathed in deeply smiling as she did.

"It smells so good here!" she said to no one in particular.

Quinn and Bryan chuckled. "That is does," Bryan said, agreeing.

A couple of hours later, Quinn and Xandy were back in the car.

"I thought we'd have some breakfast first," Quinn said, glancing over at Xandy, "and then head over to Carrickfergus Castle. Sound good?"

"Sounds perfect."

They ended up at Delacey's, a bakery not too far from the castle. Xandy got her first taste of Irish hospitality. The waitress was very sweet, as were the patrons who smiled and nodded at the two.

Quinn let Xandy peruse the menu, while she just sat back waiting, she'd already ordered coffee. The waitress had asked "Irish?"

"Yeah, but for the whiskey," she said, with a grin.

"Not as fun that way," the waitress said, winking at Quinn.

"Oh, I know," Quinn said.

"You don't need a menu?" Xandy asked.

"Nope, I already know what I'm getting."

Xandy put her menu down, and said, "Okay, I'll get what you get."

"Alright," Quinn said, grinning at her plucky little attitude.

Quinn nodded at the waitress who came over.

"What'll ya have, love?" she asked Quinn, as she set her coffee down.

"Two Ulster Fries," Quinn replied.

"Slim or soda?" the waitress asked.

"Slim," Quinn said, glancing at Xandy and seeing that she was completely lost. "Do you want coffee or tea?" she asked Xandy.

"Um, tea," Xandy said, surprised by the question.

"Got it, love," the waitress said, smiling at both of them, then bustled away.

"Okay," Xandy said, "what am I having for breakfast?"

Quinn chuckled. "Afraid you're gonna end up with haggis or something?"

"Um, yeah?"

"Well, haggis is Scottish, so you're safe."

"Oh my God, brat!" Xandy said throwing her napkin at Quinn.

Quinn chuckled as she caught the napkin, and handed it back to Xandy. "Ulster fry is basically your standard breakfast: eggs, bacon, sausage and fried either soda bread or potato bread."

"What's slim?"

"It's potato bread."

"Oh. That sounds pretty good actually."

"Well, we'll see," Quinn said, "when we head south the breakfasts change a bit."

"South?" Xandy asked.

"Yeah, you know, to Dublin and all that," Quinn said.

Xandy bit her lip, thrilled beyond words that Quinn was going to take her exploring.

"You did want to see more than my hometown, didn't you?"

"Of course! I just didn't know if that was going to be possible."

"Why wouldn't it?"

Xandy shrugged. "I guess I didn't know if you were willing to drag me all over."

"Drag you?" Quinn repeated. "Xan, I want to show you everything."

Xandy smiled, Quinn always said the exact right thing that made her feel so special.

After breakfast they made their way over to the castle. Xandy couldn't believe that she was actually standing in front of a castle that was over eight hundred years old. Xandy took in the towers and the embattlements on the top. Walking through the archway of the front gates, there were areas with canons pointed out to sea. There were statues that were standing on the overlooks of the walls, pointing rifles down toward would-be enemies attacking the castle. There was an area where prisoners were held. There was a statue of a man with a bandage over his hand with fingers missing and only his ring finger and pinky showing.

"That's something interesting," Quinn said, pointing at the statue. "Legend has it that back around the fourteenth century, when they'd capture long bowmen, the French would remove their index and middle fingers so that they could no longer operate their bows."

"Yikes!" Xandy said, grimacing.

"Yeah, so the gesture that the uncaptured fighters would make would be to hold up their two fingers to the other soldiers and wiggle them."

"So kind of like an FU to the soldiers."

"Pretty much," Quinn said.

"Wow, that's wild."

They spent a couple of hours wandering through the castle. Quinn told her more things about its history, and showed her where she'd played as a kid. Xandy was fascinated.

Their next stop was Ballycarry Cemetery, a cemetery that had been in existence for centuries. There were the ruins of a medieval church that was later the site of the first Presbyterian church in Ireland. The gravestones in the church were carved stone; some so old the carvings had been worn away by rain and the sea air. Walking through the cemetery Xandy found it hard to believe she was in a place so much older than anywhere in America.

The countryside they'd driven through was everything she'd ever heard about Ireland. It was lush and rich green. Standing at the edge of the cemetery, Xandy could see sheep in the field just below, one sheep in particular stood stock still and stared right back at her.

"Are you making eyes at that sheep?" Quinn asked her, coming up behind her.

Xandy laughed. "What makes you think he's not making eyes at me?"

Quinn slid her arms around Xandy's waist, leaning down to put her head on Xandy's shoulder, staring at the same sheep for a long minute.

"I think you're right, he's making eyes at you. Feck away, you wooly bastard!" she called to the sheep.

Xandy laughed, shaking her head.

Their next stop was an area called the Giant's Causeway. It was a series of interlocking columns that rose up out of the sea, and extended hundreds of feet in the air. The tops of the columns were flat, so they made up what seemed like stepping stones that went from the foot of the cliffs and disappeared into the sea.

"What are they?" Xandy asked Quinn as they walked along the shore, watching people climbing up and down the stones.

"Well, this set of stones actually extends under the sea and there's another set of them over on the Scottish shore. They think they're from an ancient volcanic eruption but there's a much better legend about them," she said with a twinkle in her eye.

"Tell me!" Xandy said.

Quinn led her over to some of the stones that were at a low level, and they sat on them. As Quinn told the story she gestured out to the sea.

"So the story goes that there are these two giants, one named Fionn, he's Irish, and the other was Benandonner, he's Scottish. Fionn challenges Benandonner to a fight and Benandonner accepts. So Fionn builds the Giant's Causeway so they can meet in the middle to fight. As the story goes, Fionn ventures over the causeway to check out his opponent and sees that Benandonner is much bigger than him, so he goes back home. Well, when Benandonner shows up to fight, Fionn freaks, his fast thinking wife Oonagh disguises him as their baby, putting him in the cradle with a blanket, pacifier and bonnet."

Xandy was laughing by this time at the picture Quinn was painting, Quinn was grinning as well.

"So, when Oonagh shows the giant that her husband isn't home, only she and her baby, Benandonner takes a look at the baby. He sees that the baby is really large, and thinks if that's the baby, how big is the father? So Benandonner decides to make a hasty retreat and he uses his massive club to break down the Causeway stones between Ireland and Scotland so that Fionn can't come beat him up."

"Oh my God!" Xandy said, clapping her hands together, "I definitely like that one better!"

Quinn chuckled. "I thought you might."

When they left the Giant's Causeway, the sun was starting to sink in the sky, so Quinn decided to save the rest for later. They were both fairly tired by that time. Driving back took a couple of hours. During that time Quinn had her iPod plugged in for music. When one song came on, she looked over at Xandy.

"You should listen to this song," she said.

Xandy nodded, listening as the song began. She saw on stereo display that it was called "The Light" by Disturbed, a band Quinn seemed to really like. Xandy found she liked them too; the lead singer, David Draiman, had an incredible voice.

The words were so haunting, Xandy listened to every one of them. The chorus of the song resonated deeply in Xandy. It said that she should never think that everything wasn't forsaken even when she thought it was. That sometimes being in such a dark place could show her the way.

When the song ended, Xandy looked over at Quinn. "So are you saying that you think some of the bad things that have happened in my life, have been for a reason?" she asked, wanting to understand.

Quinn looked over at her, not wanting to make light of the tragedies in her life, but feeling like she needed to help her get through them in whatever way she could.

"I think that there's a reason you weren't in Kansas when that tornado took your family," Quinn said gently.

Xandy nodded, her face reflecting pain, but trying to understand what Quinn was saying.

"What do you think that reason was?" Xandy asked.

"I don't know, I just think that everything in this life happens for a reason."

Xandy considered that thought, then glanced at Quinn again. "Like you becoming my bodyguard?" she asked. "And being there when I almost succeeded in taking my own life?"

Quinn flinched at the last part, but nodded, glancing at Xandy again to see how she took that.

Xandy nodded, her look considering. "But what was the reason for my family? For Tommy?"

Quinn shrugged. "I don't know, babe, but I think you need to let things happen so you can find out. And maybe Tommy was in your life to show you what you didn't want from a relationship."

"So I could appreciate the one with you?"

"Maybe, but you know that my being your bodyguard and being there when you… did what you did… maybe it's not just that I was there to save you. Maybe you were there to save me too."

Xandy looked over at Quinn, surprised by the statement. "Save you?" she asked, clearly confused. "How?"

Quinn shrugged. "From a life without love."

Xandy bit her lip, tears springing to her eyes. "Oh Quinn…"

Quinn looked over at her, thinking she had probably just gotten through. It was a good day.

That night they had dinner with some of Quinn's family. Ida and Maggie were there, as well as two of Quinn's older brothers, Garran and Hagan. Xandy thoroughly enjoyed the family atmosphere in the Kavanaugh household. The siblings all seemed get along really well and there were lots of stories.

"No, it wasn't Quinn, it was Liam that did that!" insisted Garran, his green eyes, much like Quinn's, rolling in annoyance.

"It was Quinn!" Hagan insisted, looking to his younger sister, Hagan was five years Quinn's senior. "It was you, wasn't it?"

Quinn looked back at her brother, her look unreadable as she chewed the steak she'd just put in her mouth. Xandy looked between the two, sensing that this was a matter of a sibling feud.

When Quinn swallowed, she grinned. "Liam actually helped, he was the one that picked me up off the ground when I hit."

"Feck clean off, I tell you!" Garran crowed, gesturing at Hagan.

"No!" Hagan protested. "I thought it was Liam that went off the roof!"

"Obviously," Quinn said, grinning and winking at Xandy who was shaking her head. "But no, it was me. I was going to try and see if I could land it."

"Broke an arm that time," Brann said, shaking her head at her daughter.

"I thought it was my ankle that time," Quinn said.

"Nah," Brann said, "you broke yer ankle when you jumped into the lough and ran into a piling down in the water."

Quinn looked considering for a minute, then began to nod. "Yeah, okay, I remember that now."

Xandy looked horrified by the list of injuries piling up.

"So the 'hooligan' shirt really was true," Xandy said, looking astounded.

"I said it was," Quinn said, chuckling at Xandy's look.

"Quinn wasn't a hooligan," Hagan said, "she was an adventurer!"

"I think she's probably the bravest of us all," Garran said.

"I think Finn's got me beat," Quinn said. Looking at Xandy she said, "He's with the Belfast Fire Brigade, a fire fighter, plus he has medical training."

"Oh," Xandy said nodding, "sounds handy."

"Oh yeah," Quinn said, grinning, "he's the oldest out of all of us too, he's forty-five."

"And there's still…" Xandy said, trying desperately to remember all the names of Quinn's other siblings.

Quinn laughed. "You're going to make yer head explode if you try to remember everyone without even meeting them, babe. There's still Liam and Miles as well as Fallon, and you obviously haven't met Finn yet."

Xandy nodded, looking relieved. She looked at Garran.

"Quinn said you're a history teacher? Like your dad here?" she said, smiling at Bryan.

"Well, Da is a professor and the head of his department at the college, but I'm a teacher at secondary school, yes." Garran said.

Xandy looked at Quinn, a question in her eyes.

"Secondary school is like your junior high and high school, we start it at eleven," Quinn explained, knowing that was what had tripped Xandy up.

"Yes, and Maggie teaches music at the primary school," Garran supplied, nodding toward his sister, "the younger babbys."

"I teach ages eight to nine," Maggie put in.

"So three teachers," Xandy said, looking at Bryan, "you must be very proud."

Bryan nodded. "I'm proud of all my little uns."

"Liam's in the Army like I was," Quinn told Xandy.

"He's not Ranger Wing though, like Quinny was," Hagan put in, winking at Quinn.

"Ranger Wing is more difficult isn't it?" Xandy asked, looking at Quinn.

"Yeah, there's about a hundred and fifty of the Rangers, out of about seventy-five hundred defense forces," Hagan said, obviously very proud of his sister's ranking in the military and knowing that Quinn wouldn't brag for herself.

"Wow," Xandy said, knowing that American Army Rangers were considered the best of the best, but it seemed like the Irish version was just as elite if not more so.

"How much extra training did you go through, Quinn?" Hagan asked, prodding his sister to blow her own horn a bit.

"A lot," Quinn replied simply, not playing along.

"Quinn's not a braggart," Hagan said, giving his sister foul look, "but trust me, she's deadly if she needs to be."

Xandy looked at Quinn, who was staring at her brother, her lips twitching slightly when he referred to her being deadly. She asked Quinn about it later.

They were lying in bed, with Xandy in her usual position with her head in the hollow of Quinn's shoulder, except that she was lying face up, instead of her side. Quinn's arm was under Xandy's neck and their right hands were intertwined as much as was possible with Quinn's bandaged hand.

"You really don't like to talk about your skills do you?" Xandy asked, glancing up and back at Quinn.

Quinn shrugged. "I know what I'm capable of. I don't need to talk about it for it to be true."

Xandy smiled at Quinn's logic.

"But most people like you, you know, that were in such elite groups, like to talk about it don't they? I mean, brag a little."

Quinn considered the thought for a minute, then shrugged again. "I'm sure some do, but I'd rather prove than talk."

Xandy let go of Quinn's hand, moving to sit up and look down at her bodyguard-turned friend-turned possible lover. Quinn was wearing a black tank top and black sweatpants; with her tattoos and short hair she looked very rough indeed. It was impossible to see the woman that Xandy knew from the rough looking exterior, the one that had been so kind to her and who had saved her life. It was easy, however, to believe that this woman with the lean fighter's build, could be dangerous. Xandy just wasn't sure how dangerous. She found out, the next night.

They'd spent the following day meandering south toward Belfast. They'd stopped at shops and churches and sometimes just to look out at the sea. They'd gone to the Titanic museum in Belfast when they'd gotten to the city. By the time they were done there, they decided to go find someplace to have dinner.

Quinn parked the car on a side street and they walked to a local seafood restaurant. They had a nice dinner, but by the time they were done, it was dark and the clubs were just starting to get going. As they walked by one club, there were people standing outside waiting to get in. Someone recognized Xandy, who had apparently had another sudden jump in popularity.

"You're Xandy Blue!" someone yelled, and many heads turned.

A couple of guys stepped out of the line to approach Xandy. Quinn immediately went on high alert, standing between Xandy and the guys approaching her, her arm extended slightly to motion Xandy to stay back.

"Okay, guys, leave off," Quinn said, all business.

"We just wanna chinwag…" said one of the men, his speech slightly slurred.

"Yeah, she's a lash," the other man said, referring to Xandy as a 'hot girl.'

"She's with me, and we're leaving," Quinn said, her tone no-nonsense, as she moved to step around one of the men.

"No hold on…" the first man, closest to Quinn said, putting his arm out, and touching Quinn's shoulder.

Quinn's look was icy as she dropped her eyes to the man's hand, then looked up at him.

"You'll want to remove that," Quinn told the man, her voice as icy as her expression.

"Are ye startin'?" the man said, his look amazed.

"I don't start, I only finish," Quinn replied, reaching up to take the man's wrist, twisting it towards her and making the man go down to his knees immediately.

She let go just as quickly as she'd grabbed him. Glancing down at him, she said merely, "Now get lost."

Reaching back, Quinn took Xandy's hand and began to lead her away from the bar. The second guy caught up to them, ready to protect his friend's manhood.

Quinn heard him approach and turned to face the man, pulling Xandy behind her, and then pushing her back away from her.

"I'll knack yer ballix in!" the man said, moving to throw a punch. Quinn ducked the punch, and came up with one of her own, landing it square in the man's midsection, causing him to double over.

Quinn quickly stepped back, knowing that the man wasn't done yet. She was right; he got angrier and charged her. Jumping aside, she brought her fist up to punch him in the face on his way past. He stumbled, almost falling, but spun with surprising agility for his size. He was at least a half a foot taller than Quinn's five eight frame, and he looked like he weighed about fifty pounds more.

When he turned, he came at Quinn directly, and there was nowhere for her to back up to, or she'd run into Xandy. The two stood facing each other. People who had been in the club queue were now walking toward them, always interested in a good old-fashioned street fight. Quinn could tell by the set of the man's jaw that he had no intention of letting a woman best him, especially not in front of all these people. She knew she was going to have to fight this one through.

Blowing her breath out slowly, Quinn brought her hands up, her legs parted in a fighter's stance. With her finger tips she motioned for the man to come at her. He did with surprising speed, his fist seeking to shatter her jaw, catching Quinn in the shoulder as she pulled back at the last second.

"Quinn!" Xandy screamed as she watched Quinn get hit.

Quinn glanced back at Xandy, afraid that someone else was approaching her, and that's when the man charged her, knocking her to the ground. She felt her gun at the small of her back, but had no intention of using it, her sense of fair play firmly intact. She always carried one just in case, though rarely had to use it. If things went badly and she needed to shoot the guy to protect Xandy, she would, but not yet.

Grabbing the man's shoulder with her right hand, she felt a burning pain shoot up her arm as her stitches on that hand reopened. She used all her strength to shove him away from her. He hadn't expected a woman to be that strong, no matter how masculine she looked, so he fell heavily away from Quinn. She leapt to her feet and turned to kick him in the mid-section to do her best to keep him down. Someone else grabbed her from behind, she had no idea if it was the first guy she'd fought with, or someone new. What she did know was that they were male and strong, with arms like vices holding her fast.

She could see the guy on the ground getting up, a malicious smile on his face, he intended to use her disadvantage to do her some damage. Quinn felt the man's breath behind her, so she knew his face was close, ramming her head backwards she caught him square in the face. He let go of her then, and Quinn turned punching him in the face as hard as she could, and he went down.

That's when the other guy grabbed her arm; she turned to scuffle with him, even as she heard the police siren in the distance. The man grabbed her by the throat, doing his best to use his brute strength against her. Quinn twisted out of his grasp, and holding onto the arm he'd used to try to grab her, she yanked him over her shoulder, throwing him to the ground.

He lay still for a few moments, and Quinn stood breathing heavily, thinking that she was in the clear. She was just turning to scan the area when she was caught in the back of the head with something extremely hard. She heard Xandy scream, and saw stars before dropping to the ground unconscious.

She woke a few minutes later as two people were helping her to a chair outside the club. As they sat her down, she became fully conscious.

"Fucking son of a bitch!" she snarled as her head exploded in pain. Grabbing her head, she leaned over, every cell in her body concentrating on not throwing up from the pain. "Fuck, fuck, fuck," she chanted, as she tried to get a handle on the pain in her head.

Her legs were spread in a wide stance and her elbows rested on her knees, her head in her hands and down between her knees. Her legs bounced as she tried to force the pain to go away.

"Lousy fuckin cheats…" Quinn said to no one in particular, she didn't care about anything at that moment, but then it clicked, *Xandy!*

Her head snapped up, even as she grimaced at the movement, she quickly located Xandy who was standing in front of her, looking worried.

"You okay?" Quinn asked.

"I'm not the one who's currently bleeding..." Xandy said her tone flabbergasted.

Quinn blew her breath out audibly as the temporary ebb in the pain, having been replaced with fear momentarily, fell away. Someone handed her a bottle of Guinness and she took it gratefully, downing half its contents in one long swig. As she took a cigarette out of her jacket pocket, she noticed that her hand was bleeding from under the bandage.

"Son of a...." she muttered, reaching for her lighter and lighting a cigarette with her left hand.

A police officer walked over then, with one of the guys in cuffs. His three friends were sitting on the curb with another officer, also in cuffs.

"Can you tell me what happened??" the officer asked Quinn.

"One of those bastards jumped me from behind. Which one was it?" Quinn asked, glancing back at Xandy.

Xandy pointed to the man that stood with the officer.

Quinn stood up, getting a proper look at the guy. He was no taller than Quinn and quite skinny. Her look was murderous, so much so that the man tried to back up. She stabbed him in the chest with her finger, holding her cigarette just under his nose as she did, her eyes narrowed.

"This one, yeah," Quinn told the officer. "Next time, fucking come at me if you got the balls for it."

"You'll need to come down and make a formal statement, if you want to pursue this further," the officer said.

Quinn gestured to her still slightly bleeding head and hand, and said, "Can I do it tomorrow?"

The officer nodded. "Just come down to the station."

"You got it," Quinn said, nodding and grimacing at she did because it hurt her head.

"You want medical attention?" the officer asked.

Quinn shook her head, moving to sit back down in the chair and continued to smoke her cigarette.

The officer led the man off and put him in a police car. The other three were released, Quinn presumed just cautioned.

Xandy looked horrified. "Quinn, you should go to the hospital," she said, still completely horror-struck at what had happened in front of her.

Part of her had been amazed and impressed with Quinn's fighting ability, but she'd also been terrified that she'd see Quinn killed before her eyes. Especially when the man had come running up with the pipe in his hands, she hadn't even had time to scream to warn Quinn; he'd come out of nowhere. Seeing Quinn get hit and go down had scared her beyond belief.

Fortunately, that had been when the people in the crowd had enough of the unfair odds Quinn was fighting against and had stepped in to grab the man with the pipe and the other man who was still trying to get up to fight back. The police had shown up shortly thereafter and people had helped Quinn up and to the chair.

Now Xandy was further worried that Quinn was refusing medical help.

Quinn shook her head in answer to Xandy's question. "No point," she said, stubbing out her cigarette in the ashtray on the table.

"What do you mean 'no point'?" Xandy asked, stunned. "You could have a skull fracture!"

Quinn grinned. "I don't."

"And you know this how?"

Quinn shrugged. "I'm fine, Xan."

Xandy sat down heavily in the chair across from Quinn. "There's no way you can know that."

"I do," Quinn said, when she saw that Xandy was still unsettled she said. "Look, that guy weighed about a hundred pounds, hell, I weigh more than he probably does. He hit me hard, but trust me when I say, I've been hit harder and there was no fracture. I have a really hard head."

"She does, she definitely does," said a man standing next to them suddenly.

Quinn glanced up and dropped her head back blowing out her breath. "Damnit…"

"Oh, the hell you say," the man said, rolling his eyes, then he looked at Xandy. "Hi, I'm Liam, Quinn's brother."

Xandy looked over at Quinn, who nodded as she grinned, reaching for the bottle of Guinness again. "And that's Miles," she said, gesturing to the man behind Liam. "What're you two doing here?" she asked suspiciously.

"Pub crawl," Miles said, moving forward to shake Xandy's hand and look at his sister. "Yer bleedin' ya know," he said, his tone matter of fact.

"I know," Quinn said, grinning as she finished off the Guinness, setting it on the table and reaching for another cigarette.

"Ya do that a lot when you're home," Liam commented.

"Feck ya," Quinn said, grinning.

Someone walked up then, handing Quinn another Guinness and saying, "Good on ya," with a nod of respect.

"Slàinte," Quinn said, and raised the bottle, taking a long swig.

"So, you don't think you have a fractured skull, but you could still go to the hospital to get checked out, maybe they could at least give you some pain killers," Xandy said, still trying to reason Quinn into going to the hospital.

Quinn laughed out loud at that, and Liam and Miles shook their heads.

"Not a good idea," Liam said.

"Very bad idea," Miles agreed.

Quinn took another long swig of the Guinness and looked over at Xandy. "I'm allergic to pretty much every pain med there is."

"How allergic?" Xandy asked.

"She could die," Liam said, his tone mild.

Xandy's eyes widened as she looked at Quinn. "Seriously?"

Quinn nodded, taking another drag off of her cigarette. "Almost did when I was seven, heart actually stopped. That's when they figured it out."

"Wow," Xandy said, "I had no idea."

"Well, I wasn't expecting some guy to try and cave my head in after dinner," Quinn said, with a grin.

"Some touch," said a young man who handed Quinn a shot glass full of an amber liquid.

Quinn took it, held it up to the guy's glass and clinked it, then downed the shot. "Thanks," she said, nodding as she handed back the glass.

"Some touch?" Xandy asked.

"Means like 'good job,' " Quinn said.

"Hey, you're on YouTube!" some girl said to Quinn.

"Are you fecking kidding me?" Quinn said, her tone far from amused.

The girl held up her phone. It was a video of the fight.

"Fucking technology…." Quinn said, her tone low, she looked at Xandy. "Think BJ has YouTube?"

Just as she said it, her phone started ringing.

"You have got to be fucking kidding me right now!" Quinn raged, as she saw from the display that it was BJ calling.

"Want me to answer it?" Xandy asked.

"Nah, I got it, it's my head he wants to bite off," Quinn said, swiping the answer button for the speaker phone with a bloody finger that she then tried to wipe off on her jeans. "Hi Beege," she said, wincing as her head started pounding again.

"So ya havin' a good night?" BJ asked, his tone falsely jovial.

"Well, I was, till about an hour ago," Quinn said, her accent thick.

"Yeah, so I saw…" BJ said, letting his voice trail off ominously.

"They jumped us, Beege," Quinn said, her tone by no means apologetic.

"Yeah, I saw that too," BJ said, "and I also saw why I hired you to protect her."

Quinn looked over at Xandy, seeing her proud smile and warmed by it.

"Thanks," Quinn said simply.

"Xandy's okay, right?"

"I'm fine, BJ," Xandy answered.

"Good," BJ said, "heal up, I still need you in the game."

"I'm on it," Quinn said.

"Have a Guinness on me," BJ said, grinning at his end.

"I'm on that too," Quinn said with a grin of her own.

They hung up then. The club they were in front of was a dance club, so the music they were playing wasn't really to Quinn's liking.

"Jesus, do you think I can put in a request?" Quinn queried to no one in particular.

Liam stepped up. "What ya want sis?"

"Bushmills single malt, bottle, and some fuckin' rock," she said, though not really expecting results.

She forgot how charming her younger brother could be. The next thing she heard was from the DJ, "This is for Quinn, our knight in shining armor out front, protecting the lovely and quite talented lass, miss Xandy Blue! Good on ya Quinn! Slàinte!"

Liam arrived with the bottle of Bushmills then. Quinn held it up in a salute to the DJ and took an extremely long swig.

Then the song "The Vengeful One" by Disturbed started. Quinn guessed that Liam had requested Disturbed because he knew Quinn loved the band's music. The song choice also seemed to fit Quinn.

The line in the chorus, "I'm the hand of God, I'm the dark messiah, I'm the vengeful one, look inside and see what you're becoming," seemed to fit Quinn fairly well at that moment. Someone in the crowd outside obviously thought so, because they took video of Quinn singing along with the song as she smoked her cigarette and drank the bottle of Bushmills.

A bit later that night the four of them piled into a cab to go back to their parents' home. By this time, Quinn was quite drunk, and needed help getting into the house, although not the slobbering drunk most people became. She certainly was in much less pain as a result, for which Xandy was grateful.

Brann and Bryan waited for their arrival, and Brann had the boys help Quinn to a chair in the kitchen where she examined the cut on Quinn's head. Quinn closed her eyes as her mother pulled back her hair to reveal the cut, jumping slightly as her mother touched a spot that pulled at the now drying blood. Xandy sat down in a chair right next to Quinn, moving close so she could hold of her hand, her eyes watching Quinn's face with deep concern.

"Okay, this is going to hurt a bit wee one," Brann said, looking at Xandy.

Xandy put her other hand around Quinn's hand, holding it tightly as Brann used a wet cloth to try and clean away some of the blood. Quinn jumped slightly a few times, her hand tightening in Xandy's grip. Xandy winced every time Quinn did. The men in the family glanced at each other, grinning, happy that Quinn seemed to have found someone that wanted to take care of her.

After a few minutes, Brann had cleaned enough of the cut to see the depth.

"Aye, this doesn't look bad a'tall," Brann said, then she reached down to pick up Quinn's right arm. "Now this…" she said, shaking her head. Quinn yanked it away, gasping at the pain from it being touched.

Brann pursed her lips and shook her head, glancing at her husband. "Well, then, we'll just leave that be for now," she said, her tone cautious. "Boys, help your sister upstairs, will you?" As they complied, Brann leaned in to Xandy. "I don't like the way that arm looks," she told her confidentially, "I'm going to have Finn come by in the morn to take a look."

Xandy nodded, remembering that Finn had medical training. "Is she really okay? I mean her head?"

Brann smiled, nodding. "She's hurt it worse over the years."

"Our Quinny has a hard bloody head," Bryan said, winking at Xandy.

She was immediately relieved, if Quinn's family wasn't worried about her or freaked out, then she felt like things were okay. She made her way upstairs, Liam and Miles were waiting for her in the bedroom. They'd helped Quinn to sit down on the bed.

"We're gonna go now," Liam said. "We'll come by tomorrow."

"Okay, thanks guys," Xandy said, smiling.

Quinn was looking very tired, so Xandy did her best to help her get comfortable. She hung up her jacket, and helped her change into her usual bed clothes. By this time Quinn was moving to lie down and Xandy let her. She spent most of the night checking on Quinn off and on to make sure she was still breathing.

Chapter 7

The next morning Xandy was up before Quinn, which usually never happened. It was a testament to how drunk Quinn had been the night before. Xandy made herself busy by taking a shower and getting dressed. She then returned to the room to keep an eye on Quinn. She could see a couple of bruises already on Quinn's arms which were extended in front of her as she slept on her side. Xandy imagined there'd be more.

Xandy sat on the bed, trying not to disturb Quinn; she had a book to read that she'd bought on Irish history, one that Bryan had suggested. At one point, Quinn stirred and turned over to face her. Glancing up with bleary eyes, she moved to lie on her stomach putting her head in Xandy's lap, and wrapping her arms around her waist. Xandy smiled fondly down at her, reaching down to stroke her hair, careful to avoid the area that had been injured.

Around nine o'clock there was the lightest tap on the partially-open bedroom door. A man with dark red hair and green eyes exactly like Quinn's stuck his head in the door smiling at her.

"Good morning," he murmured softly.

"Hi," Xandy said smiling.

"I'm Finn," he told her, looking down at his sister who still lay with her head in Xandy's lap. "She's gotten more ink since I saw her last," he remarked, leaning a knee on the bed to try and get near Quinn's head to take a look.

Even though Finn moved with the utmost care, Quinn sensed it and opened one eye, the one closest to Finn.

"Morning Finn," she murmured tiredly.

"Morning baby sis," Finn said affectionately. "I heard you saw some action last night."

"Check YouTube, you can see it," Quinn growled.

Finn chuckled, as he continued checking the wound to Quinn's head.

"Your head hurt?" Finn asked.

"Can't tell where the bangin' ends and the hangover begins," Quinn said.

"I hear you're thoroughly medicated though," Finn said.

"S'not my fault that people were buying me drinks," Quinn said.

"True, if they're paid for, you legally have to drink them," Finn said, winking at Xandy. "Okay," he said, moving off the bed, "gonna need ya to turn over, sis. Ma's worried about that hand."

Quinn groaned loudly as she moved to turn over. Xandy got off the bed and went to get Quinn some aspirin and water. Walking back over to the bed, she handed the pills to Quinn, then went to hand her the water. Quinn shook her head, putting the pills in her mouth and swallowing them. She winced as Finn pulled the bloodied bandage off her hand. The cut, extending from the heel of Quinn's hand to just under thumb, looked angry and sore.

"Oh…" Finn exhaled in surprise, "what did you do to yourself baby sis?"

"My hand met a sharp object," Quinn said simply.

Xandy could see that Finn was waiting for more of an answer, and Quinn didn't look like she was going to be forthcoming, so she spoke up.

"It was a razor blade," Xandy said, frowning. "She was slapping it out of my hand."

Finn looked at Xandy for a long moment, blinking a couple of times, then looked back at Quinn.

"Always the white knight, huh baby sis?" he asked, his tone affectionate.

"Yeah… that's me," Quinn muttered looking uncomfortable.

Her discomfort had Finn chuckling again. "Never good at taking compliments either," he added.

Quinn flinched when he touched close to the cut.

"That hurt?" Finn asked.

Quinn nodded.

"Yeah, feels hot too," he said, placing his hand gently over the cut. "Probably should be on some antibiotics just in case. And these stitches need to come out." He gave his sister an apologetic look.

Quinn nodded, looking like she was steeling herself. Xandy moved to sit on the bed next to Quinn, reaching out to take her other hand.

"I'm gonna spray it with Lidocaine," Finn said, "but it's still gonna hurt a bit."

"S'okay, do it." Quinn said.

As he worked, Quinn started asking questions to distract herself.

"How's the new baby?" she asked.

"He's good," Finn replied, but there was a look that crossed his face that Quinn easily recognized.

"You and Ginny having problems again?" Quinn asked.

"Yeah," Finn said, looking unhappy.

"Want me to talk to her?" Quinn asked, wincing as he snipped a stitch and grazed too close to the surface of the skin.

"Sorry sis. Well, you are her favorite sister-in-law," he said, his tone hopeful.

"No problem," Quinn said, "I'll see what I can do."

"Thanks," Finn said, smiling.

When the job was finished, Finn could see that Quinn was tired. Leaning down he kissed her on the cheek.

"We'll be by later tonight, so you can see your nephew," he said to her.

"Thanks Finn," Quinn said, nodding tiredly, "love you."

"Love you, baby sis," he said smiling. "Xandy we'll see you later too?"

"Of course," Xandy said smiling as she walked with him to the bedroom door. "Is her hand going to be okay?" she asked him out in the hallway.

Finn smiled, liking that this girl was so concerned about his sister. He and Quinn were a full ten years apart in age, but they'd always been close. He'd always called her "baby sis" even though he had younger sisters. He'd seen her go through a lot to become who she was now and

173

he hoped that maybe she'd found the right woman to share her life with.

Quinn bringing Xandy home was a source of much discussion in the family. Finn knew better than anyone how much the family meant to Quinn; she'd give up anything for them. The fact that she'd brought Xandy not only to Belfast, but to the family home spoke volumes about this girl and Quinn's feelings for her. Finn just hoped those feelings were well placed, but it was the consensus among the Kavanaugh children that Xandy seemed to be a good fit for their wild sibling. From what Finn had seen, Xandy definitely cared about Quinn's well-being.

"It looks bad right now," he told Xandy in answer to her question, "but I think it'll do better now. She'd strained some of the stitches, but the butterfly closures will be a little better for the kind of person my sister is."

"What does that mean?" Xandy asked, looking surprised.

"My sister can't stop using her hands, it's who she is," Finn said.

"Oh," Xandy said, nodding.

Finn looked back at Xandy for a long moment. "Our Quinn is very special," he said, his tone cautious.

Xandy nodded. "She's very special to me too," she said. "She's saved my life quite possibly twice now and has quickly become the best friend that I have ever had."

Finn found that he very much liked this American's honesty, it was refreshing.

"Then hold on to her with both hands," he told her, winking.

"I'll try," Xandy said, nodding.

After Finn left, Xandy went back into the bedroom to check on Quinn, who was, once again, asleep. Xandy decided to go downstairs and see if she could get some coffee. When she got downstairs she found that Liam and Miles were there already. They were sitting at the dining room table with Brann.

"Good morning," Xandy said smiling at the three.

Brann got up immediately. "Would you like some coffee? Or tea?"

"Coffee would be great," Xandy said, smiling.

"Cream or sugar?" Brann asked.

"Both, please" Xandy said.

Brann brought a cup over, gesturing for Xandy to sit down.

"How's Quinn feeling?" Miles asked, knowing that Quinn had to be hungover.

"She's kind of miserable," Xandy said, sighing. "I gave her some aspirin earlier, hopefully that will help. She's asleep right now."

"Good," Brann said, nodding, "she seems to take her job very seriously when it comes to you."

Xandy smiled softly. "Quinn takes everything she does seriously."

The three members of Quinn's family nodded in agreement to that.

"So, where in America are you from?" Brann asked conversationally.

"I'm from Kansas, it's in the Midwest," Xandy replied.

"Kansas," Brann repeated, "what's there?" she asked, her tone quizzical.

"Um," Xandy began, unable to think of a good response, "basically wheat and dust, and tornadoes."

Brann blinked a couple of times. "Tornadoes? Those nasty twisty things?"

Xandy grinned at the description. "Yes, those."

"Terrifying looking, those are!" Brann said.

"They're pretty scary up close too," Xandy said, her tone more serious.

"You've seen one?" Liam asked, interested.

Xandy nodded. "More than one," she said, her voice changing slightly.

"Are they as scary as they look in the movies?" Liam asked.

"They're worse," Xandy said, her voice tremulous, "much, much worse."

Brann recognized that somehow this was a difficult topic for the girl and with a quick look at Liam, decided to steer the conversation in a new direction.

"Quinn tells us you're a singer?" Brann said.

"Ma, she's not just a singer," Liam said, shaking his head.

Pulling out his phone, Liam pulled up the song that had been released by Badlands from Xandy's upcoming album. Handing the phone to his mother, he reached over and hit play.

The chords for the song started out simple enough, and Xandy's voice was so clear and bright it filled the room. Brann looked quite impressed as the song went on. The song was nearly acapella with only piano as an accompaniment. As the song faded, and Xandy's haunting last note seemed to drift in the air.

"That was beautiful dear," Brann said, looking affected by the song.

"Thank you," Xandy said, smiling demurely.

"And humble, as well, I see," Brann said, her tone approving. "That's a beautiful thing too, my dear," she said, winking at Xandy.

The conversation moved onto other things after that.

A couple of hours later, Xandy went up to the bedroom to check on Quinn and found her awake in bed. Moving to sit down on the bed, she smiled down at Quinn.

"How are you feeling?" Xandy asked.

"I'm alright," Quinn said, grinning as she moved to sit up.

Xandy gasped at the bruises she saw. Quinn had bruises on her throat, and the lower half of her upper arms, where one of the men had tried to restrain her. Then there was another nasty bruise on her shoulder where one of the men had missed her face and hit her shoulder.

Quinn glanced down at the bruises and then back at Xandy. "S'okay," she said, "they'll fade."

"Still," Xandy said, reaching out to touch the bruise on Quinn's neck gently, her face reflecting her distress.

"Hey…" Quinn said, reaching up to touch Xandy's cheek, anxious to remove the concern from her face. "I'm okay. This is nothing."

Xandy didn't look comforted by that statement, so Quinn pulled Xandy into her arms, hugging her. Quinn leaned back against the headboard, letting Xandy lean against her. They stayed that way for a while, each of them thinking their own thoughts.

"So is my family torturing you down there?" Quinn asked, grinning.

"Of course not," Xandy said, "actually your brother pulled up one of my songs for your mom to hear."

Quinn grinned, betting her mother was very much impressed with Xandy's talent.

"Oh, and you should know…" Xandy said, letting her voice trail off as she looked at Quinn, her grin a bit abashed.

"Wot?" Quinn asked suspiciously, warned by the twinkle in Xandy's eyes.

"You're kinda famous right now," Xandy said.

"Why?" Quinn asked, looking horrified at the thought.

"Well, not only was a video of the fight posted to YouTube, but someone also took a video of you singing to "The Vengeful One," and that's kind of gone viral too."

"Oh, Jesus fecking Christ!" Quinn said, rolling her eyes. "I think it's about time we get out of Belfast. Let's head south into Ireland."

"South?" Xandy asked.

"Yeah, to Dublin and down in that area."

"Okay, if you're up to it."

"Let me make some arrangements," Quinn said, "and we can go tomorrow."

"Okay," Xandy said.

That night, Xandy got to meet Finn's wife, Ginny and their infant son. She also found out that Ginny and Quinn had been in secondary school together and that's how Quinn knew her. At one point Quinn and Ginny disappeared, and Xandy saw them out in the conservatory talking. When they came back in, Ginny walked over to Finn and hugged him, he looked over at Quinn and nodded to her in obvious appreciation.

"What did you tell her?" Xandy asked Quinn, who'd just picked up a bottle of Guinness and taken a swig.

"Nothing much," Quinn said. "I just talked."

"So we should add family therapist to your growing list of talents," Xandy said, smiling.

"Uh, no," Quinn said, rolling her eyes.

By this time, everyone in the family had seen the video of Quinn fighting in Belfast the night before, as well as the video of her singing outside the club. She'd become some kind of urban hero, it embarrassed her completely. It was obviously being noticed in America as well, since Xandy had gotten an email from Devin telling her that Quinn was quite the hit in LA. When Xandy had informed Quinn she'd shaken her head and gone out to the porch to smoke. She definitely didn't like the idea of fame.

The next morning, they drove to Dublin. They toured the city for several hours before checking into a hotel. Quinn had made reservations at a hotel in Dún Laoghaire called The Royal Marine. Quinn had already been recognized a number of times, as had Xandy. They were becoming quite the sensation in Ireland too.

In their hotel room, Xandy had gone into the bathroom to put away her toiletries. When she emerged, she found Quinn relaxing.

She was sitting on the bed in jeans and a tank top. Her feet were planted on the bed, her knees bent with her arms resting on them. She was the picture of sexy in Xandy's mind. With her red hair falling across her forehead, and her bright green eyes, her prominent cheekbones and very kissable looking lips. Xandy realized how very attracted she was to this woman, yet again. Not that the feeling had ever really tapered off, but she'd been more circumspect about it while staying in Quinn's parents' house. She'd known, without being told, that nothing really sexual could happen at the Kavanaugh family home. To Xandy's way of thinking, that was just simple respect and she knew Quinn would feel the same.

Now standing at the foot of the bed, watching Quinn chuckle, Xandy felt drawn to her. Setting aside the bottle in her hand, Xandy got bold. Crawling onto the bed, her eyes intent on Quinn's, Xandy moved to position herself between Quinn's knees. Quinn's grin indicated pleased surprise.

"Now what are you on about?" Quinn asked, sounding very Irish.

Xandy didn't say a word, she simply lowered her head, her lips capturing Quinn's in a kiss. Quinn groaned slightly against Xandy's lips, her hands sliding around Xandy's back to gather her closer. Quinn slid her legs down to rest on the bed, as she lifted Xandy onto her lap, their lips never parting.

Xandy felt her body tingling everywhere, heat flowing through her body as she pressed herself against Quinn. Xandy was wearing cotton capris pants and a tank top so there wasn't a lot of material between her and the jeans Quinn wore. She found that the feel of this combination was quite exciting.

As Quinn's lips deepened the kiss, she pulled Xandy closer, pressing that very sensitive part of Xandy's body even harder to her. Xandy felt her body ignite in a kind of slow burn. Every move Quinn made aroused Xandy more, so when Quinn's thumb brushed upward, just grazing her nipple through her shirt, Xandy cried out. She grasped at Quinn's shoulders, not noticing Quinn wince in pain, as the throes of the orgasm rocked through her.

Afterwards she lay against Quinn, gasping for breath. The myriad of sensations making her shudder slightly every so often. Quinn held Xandy against her, stroking her hair and grinning. The girl certainly didn't have any qualms about having sex with a lesbian, was her thought. It had been Quinn's experience that some women thought they were interested in other women, but when it came to the actual act of sex with one, they shied away. Xandy had definitely not done that, at least not yet.

When she'd finally caught her breath, Xandy leaned back, looking at Quinn. "Wow," she said simply, causing Quinn to grin again.

"That was…" Xandy began, her voice trailing off as she shook her head. "I mean, we both still have our clothes on!"

This exclamation elicited an outright laugh from Quinn.

"Well, we can fix that," Quinn said, grinning.

"Can we?" Xandy asked, her eyes alight.

Quinn nodded, leaning in to kiss her again, and sliding her hands up Xandy's sides, taking her shirt off and reaching back to unclip Xandy's bra deftly. Lifting Xandy slightly, Quinn shifted them both so she could lay Xandy on her back sideways across the bed, sliding her pants and underwear off. Quinn moved to lie on her side next to Xandy, her hand caressing Xandy's stomach.

"Well, that just makes one of us naked," Xandy said, her look expectant.

"And that's a problem?"

"A very definite problem, yes," Xandy replied.

Quinn nodded. She stood up, as Xandy watched, and removed her tank top, along with the sports bra, her eyes fixed on Xandy's. Then she unbuttoned her jeans and slid them off, leaving only black boxer briefs with the word "Tomboy" on the waistband. As Quinn removed those, Xandy noticed that not only were there other tattoos she hadn't seen before, but that Quinn had the most amazingly toned, leanly muscled body she'd ever seen in her life. Every move Quinn made had sinewy muscles rippling.

As Quinn climbed onto the bed, her body like a panther's, Xandy drew in a deep breath; her heart was beating madly in her chest. Quinn moved over Xandy, one hand on either side of her head, as she leaned down capturing Xandy's lips again. The fire in Xandy's body reignited instantly as she wound her arms around Quinn's neck, trying to press her body up and against Quinn's, but Quinn held her body firm. She continued to kiss Xandy, moving expertly; pulling back, their lips just touching, then pressing in again almost teasingly, and making Xandy more desperate for contact with Quinn's skin.

Quinn's lips left Xandy's, first kissing her neck, and then moving further down to the hollow of her shoulder. Xandy gasped with pleasure as Quinn moved lower, her lips touching Xandy's extremely hard and sensitive nipples, but pulling back right as Xandy would have reached her release. This was repeated a few times, driving Xandy insane.

When Xandy was sure she couldn't take anymore, Quinn lowered her body, pressing against Xandy and within moments they were both moaning and grasping at each other as they came. Afterwards, Quinn rolled to her side, taking Xandy with her so that Xandy was slightly over her. Xandy laid her head against Quinn's shoulder, still trying to calm her breathing.

"Wow, doesn't even begin to cover that," Xandy said, her voice breathless.

Quinn, who was less winded, but definitely still affected, nodded. "Agreed."

They both lay there awhile, enjoying the feel of the other's skin. Xandy's fingers traced the tattoo that was on Quinn's right hip. It was a sunburst with an eight pointed star and the words "Óglaigh na hÉireann" in a circle band in the center, with two Fs in script in the very center.

"What is this one?" Xandy asked, her fingers still brushing the tattoo.

Quinn glanced down. "It's the badge of the Irish Defense Forces."

"The Army?" Xandy asked.

"The forces as a whole," Quinn replied. "There are a lot of parts to the forces, like the Army and the Navy. For us, Defense Forces is like your armed forces."

"Oh," Xandy said nodding. "So what's this phrase?"

"Óglaigh na hÉireann," Quinn pronounced, it sounded like "oogly na herrin."

"And what does it mean?"

Quinn grinned, Xandy never got tired of learning this kind of thing.

"It basically means Irish volunteers, or Irish warriors."

Xandy nodded. "Which is what you are."

"Uh-huh," Quinn murmured, rolling her eyes.

"And this part?" Xandy said. "The FF?"

"It stands for Fianna Fail," Quinn said, "which is basically Celtic army and destiny."

Xandy glanced up at Quinn, moving to lever herself up on her elbow.

"Maybe that's what's happening here?" Xandy asked.

"Wot?" Quinn asked, her eyes searching Xandy's. "Destiny?"

"Maybe this is the light I needed to see," Xandy replied.

"Or maybe it's just that you needed to feel close to someone again," Quinn replied, not wanting Xandy to think that she was some kind of answer.

Xandy nodded, looking slightly deflated.

"Hey," Quinn said, reaching out to touch Xandy under the chin to guide her eyes back to hers again. "I'm not saying this doesn't mean anything, Xan," she said, her voice soft. "I just think that your destiny is much bigger than this."

Later that night they went down to one of the hotel restaurants to have dinner. It was a beautiful restaurant with large black multi-tiered chandeliers and elegantly appointed tables and booths. Quinn asked for a table near the windows and was greeted with great deference, which she was apparently unaccustomed to, judging by her reaction. Their waitress made it clear why she was being treated with such respect.

"You're famous," the waitress told Quinn.

"I think you mean her," Quinn said, pointing to Xandy.

The waitress' eyes went to Xandy then back to Quinn. "Of course we know Ms. Xandy Blue," she said, smiling brightly, "but what you did standing up to those guys like that… you're a hero."

Quinn widened her eyes at Xandy, who hid her grin behind her hand.

"Well, ah, thanks," Quinn said, having no idea what to say.

The waitress nodded emphatically.

After they'd ordered, and Quinn's Guinness arrived, Quinn looked over at Xandy. "So I was thinking…" she began, not sure how she really wanted to broach the subject on her mind.

Xandy bit the inside of her cheek, worried about what Quinn was about to say.

"Now, I want you to hear me out, okay?" Quinn said, her look cautionary.

Xandy looked even more worried, but nodded agreement.

"You need to consider how much you want this," Quinn said, indicating the two of them, "to get out."

"You mean, us being together?" Xandy asked, her look already recalcitrant.

"Yeah," Quinn said, "for your reputation, and your sales."

"No," Xandy said, shaking her head. "I'm not going to hide you."

"I'm not asking you to hide me, Xan. I'm just saying that this might not be something you want to advertise openly."

"No."

"Xan, listen to me," Quinn said, knowing she needed to make the girl understand. "You and I both know that sex is what sells in this world, and that's what BJ is selling with you."

"I don't care," Xandy said, sitting back and folding her arms in front of her.

Quinn sighed, knowing that this was going to be difficult.

"I just want you to think about it, okay? 'Cause I can tell you that BJ is going to be pissed about this. This is not what he bought when he signed you."

"Well, too bad," Xandy said, her lower lip jutting forward in her determination, "this is too important to me to just pretend it hasn't happened."

Quinn couldn't help grin at her defiant tone and it did feel good that someone wanted to be with her above all else, but she was still worried.

"Xan, what you and I have isn't reduced by the idea of no one knowing about it."

"And you'd be okay with us hiding it?"

"It doesn't matter to me," Quinn said, shrugging,

"How can it not?" Xandy asked, surprised.

"Because my relationships and how I feel about someone has nothing to do with how many people know about it," Quinn said, her voice calm and reasonable.

Xandy looked back at Quinn for a long moment, thinking about what she'd said. On the one hand, she liked that Quinn was more interested in being with her than her fame. It was a nice change from Tommy; she knew Quinn wasn't looking to get anything out of her fame. On the other hand, Xandy wasn't sure she really cared enough about her career to hide something this important to her.

Finally, she nodded. "Okay, I'll think about being discreet. But I'm not out-and-out hiding it, if someone asks, they're getting the truth."

Quinn grinned at her vehemence, but nodded seriously. "Okay then."

They spent a few more days in the Republic of Ireland, checking out Dublin and even made their way to Camp Curragh where Quinn had done most of her military training. However, they were only able to see very limited parts of the camp.

Back in Belfast, on the last evening before they flew back to Los Angeles, Quinn's family came together. Xandy finally met Quinn's oldest sister, Fionna. She also found out why she hadn't heard much about Fionna during her time with the family. Fionna had married an English businessman, who seemed to disdain anything Irish. Fionna also seemed to disdain her family. And she definitely didn't approve of Quinn, her sexual orientation, the tattoos, the short hair, or anything else about her life.

Fortunately for everyone, Fionna's visit was very short, and it seemed everyone in the family relaxed after she left. Xandy asked Quinn about it later that night. "Fionna doesn't like you, does she?" she asked, as she lay in Quinn's arms.

Quinn grinned into the darkness, she was lying on her back, and Xandy was, as always, snuggled up next to her.

"Fionna changed a lot when she married Winslow," Quinn said, shrugging.

"Were you two close before that?" Xandy asked, glancing up at Quinn.

"Not really, no. She was almost a teenager when I was born, and we never really had anything in common growing up. Since I spent most of my time with the boys, she had no real use for me."

"But you love her…" Xandy said.

"Of course I do," Quinn said. "I just don't really know her, especially now."

"She doesn't approve of you, does she?"

"What makes you say that?" Quinn asked.

"The way she looked at you. I noticed that you wore sleeves tonight, but she still made a comment about the tattoo on your neck."

"Oh, yeah, she just doesn't get the tattoo thing at all. I covered most of them for my mother's sake, not hers."

"What do you mean?" Xandy asked, surprised by the comment.

"My mother likes for us kids to get along. Fionna doesn't hold back when she doesn't like something, so she'd start with me about the tatts and I'd go right back at her, and it would upset my mother. So I don't give Fionna too much of a reason to bitch at me."

Xandy moved to lever up on her arms, looking down at Quinn.

"Is that why you didn't respond to her?" Xandy asked.

Quinn nodded.

"You'd do anything for them." Xandy said.

"I'd die for them, even Fionna."

Xandy looked back at Quinn, surprised by the statement, but realizing that she shouldn't be. It had been obvious to her from the moment she'd met Quinn's family. Xandy knew that Quinn was important to them, and that they were her world.

Reaching out, she touched the family crest on Quinn's neck.

"Family," Xandy said.

"Above all else," Quinn added.

Xandy nodded understanding completely. Her family had been her world, before they'd been snatched away from her. Lying back down, she snuggled against Quinn and they fell asleep.

The next morning, Quinn was up before Xandy, and she was sitting out in the sunroom, smoking and drinking her coffee when her mother walked out.

"G'mornin' Ma," Quinn said, smiling at her mother and immediately stubbing out her cigarette.

Brann leaned down kissing her daughter on the cheek, then moved to sit down.

"So you're leaving today?" Brann asked.

Quinn nodded. "Xandy needs to get back to put some finishing touches on her album."

"She's a very sweet girl, Quinn," Brann said, her eyes shining.

"She is indeed," Quinn said, nodding.

"There's kind of a shadow about her, though, isn't there?"

"She's been through a lot."

"But she's so young!" Brann replied, sounding shocked.

"She lost her entire family, ma," Quinn said, her tone grave.

"Was it a tornado?" Brann asked, remembering how haunted Xandy had seemed when they talked about tornadoes.

"Yeah," Quinn said, looking quizzically at her mother.

"She got a bit upset one day when your brothers asked about tornadoes."

"Oh," Quinn said, nodding. "She's still not sure why she's still here when they're all gone."

"Oh the poor lamb…" Brann said, shaking her head sadly.

Quinn nodded, looking sad as well.

"Perhaps you are meant to help her with this," Brann said.

"Maybe."

"The good lord never gives us more than we can handle, but he does send angels to help us sometimes," Brann said, winking at her daughter.

It was those words that Quinn carried home with her as they flew back to America in BJ's jet.

Chapter 8

Back in California, they arrived to a balmy day in Los Angeles. They also arrived to the good news that Devin had traced the threatening emails back to Tommy Shay, which truly surprised no one. The police made a visit to Tommy's house and confiscated his computer and laptop. The evidence was quickly found on the computers and Tommy was arrested under the stalker laws. He pleaded guilty and was sent to jail for three months, and was fined $1,000. Quinn hoped it would give Xandy some peace of mind, and it did for the most part, but Xandy was worried and it showed.

They were driving to a celebratory lunch date with Devin and Skyler. Quinn noted that Xandy was particularly quiet. At first she chalked it up to jet lag as they'd only been back for three days, and it had been a difficult adjustment for Xandy. Quinn had gone back home often enough that her body adjusted easily to the time changes.

During lunch with Skyler and Devin, they met Sebastian, Skyler's brother. Sebastian was a handsome young man, and was very impressed with Xandy, so he spent much of the lunch chatting with her. At one point, Xandy's hand reached for Quinn's under the table. Quinn, who was engaged in a deep conversation with Skyler about cars, didn't sense Xandy's hand reaching for hers as she usually would, so she didn't take it. She didn't catch the sad expression on Xandy's face either.

Later back at Xandy's house, Quinn noticed that Xandy went straight to her room. It made Quinn's mental antennae go up. She gave Xandy a few minutes to come back out, but she stayed in the doorway of the room she'd been using, keeping her senses on alert. Xandy hadn't closed her bedroom door, which was the only reason Quinn gave her any time at all to come back out. However, when Xandy didn't reappear, Quinn moved to the doorway to Xandy's bedroom.

Xandy was lying on her side on the bed, her back to the door, her knees up to her chest, with her arms wrapped around them. Quinn walked over to the bed and without saying a word, lay down behind Xandy and curled herself around the smaller girl. She felt Xandy jump when her arms wrapped around her, but then she felt her relax and almost melt into her. Quinn's lips were at her temple, kissing Xandy softly.

"Xan, what's wrong?" Quinn asked gently.

"You're going to leave now, aren't you?" Xandy said, her voice filled with tears.

"Babe..." Quinn said, her voice strident, "no... why do you think that?"

Xandy shrugged. "Your job is done."

"Yeah, my job as your bodyguard is done," Quinn said, kissing Xandy's temple again, and pulling at Xandy to get her to turn over and face her.

After a few moments Xandy complied. Quinn touched her cheek gently. "Xan, unless you're sick of my ass, I'm not going anywhere."

Xandy's eyes searched Quinn's, as if she was looking for signs of deceit.

"You're going to stay?" Xandy asked, her voice full of wonder.

"Yeah, now I just get to be your girlfriend," Quinn said, quirking her lips sardonically.

Xandy looked so relieved it was almost painful. Quinn leaned down, kissing Xandy's lips softly and Xandy melted into her. Within minutes they were making love and afterwards lay in each other's arms. Xandy lay against Quinn, and Quinn held her close, stroking her hair.

"I'm not going anywhere, Xan. I love you."

Xandy turned to look up at Quinn, her eyes wide. "You do?"

"Yeah, pretty much," she said, her eyes twinkling with amusement at Xandy's shocked expression.

Xandy reached her hand up, touching Quinn's face. "I love you. I have since the moment I met you… my heart just didn't know what to call it."

"Well, it does now, so you're not going anywhere, not without me." Quinn's look pinned Xandy knowingly.

Quinn knew that Xandy had started a backward slide into depression after feeling rejected at lunch, and from the look that Quinn gave her, Xandy knew that Quinn knew it too.

"Will you do something for me?" Quinn asked.

"What?" Xandy asked, looking cautious.

"Will you think about finding someone to talk to?"

"I have you," Xandy said, her look guarded.

"Xan," Quinn said seriously, "you know what I'm talking about."

Xandy nodded.

"I'm worried about you," Quinn said, reaching out to touch Xandy's cheek gently. "I need to know that you're going to be okay."

"What do you mean?"

"I mean, that if I hadn't come after you tonight, you might have done it, right?"

Xandy looked back at Quinn for a long moment, surprised that Quinn was actually addressing the issue directly. No one had ever cared enough about her to even try. Finally, she nodded, slowly.

"Xan, I know I can't make you believe me when I say that I'm not going anywhere," Quinn said, her thumb smoothing over Xandy's cheek. "Only time is going to prove that. But what if I hadn't been here tonight? What if I'm gone on a job and you get to thinking like you did…"

Xandy looked back at Quinn, still unable to really comprehend someone loving her, not like this. She chewed on the inside of her cheek, trying to reconcile what Quinn was saying.

"It's not your fault," Xandy said, finally. "My state of mind… it's not…"

"I know that, babe," Quinn said, "it's the fault of life, and fate, and whatever god you may or may not believe in. And it's the fault of those two bastards that hurt you, and the storm that took your family away from you." Quinn looked deep into Xandy's eyes, trying to drive home her point. "But that stuff is never going to go away, Xan, and your mind is going to try to get you to see things from that side, and you've got to learn a new way to think, to perceive things."

Xandy nodded slowly, starting to understand what Quinn was saying.

"I need to know you're going to be okay," Quinn repeated.

"In case you're not here."

Quinn looked back at her, hoping she was getting through. "In case I'm gone on a job, Xan, or for when you go on tour, or whatever work stuff separates us."

Xandy nodded, having heard the assurances she needed. "I'll talk to someone."

"Thank you," Quinn said, smiling.

They spent the rest of the night lying together and talking about whatever came to mind.

They decided that they needed a project to focus Xandy's energies on. So, the next day they began working on Xandy's house. Xandy also got in touch with a counselor and had appointment within a week. They spent hours driving to antique shops, and picking out paint colors. Quinn contacted some of her friends that were contractors and got them to give a bid for redoing the bathrooms and the kitchen. Within a month the little house was as beautiful inside as it was outside.

BJ had taken the news that his latest star was now dating her female bodyguard surprisingly well. He'd long suspected that Xandy had a lot of emotional baggage from the trauma she'd been through in her short life. He'd also suspected that she suffered from depression and the suicide attempt had confirmed that. It had been the reason he hadn't let Quinn blame herself for Xandy's condition. It was also the reason why he'd not only suggested a trip to get Xandy away from the world, but had happily footed the bill for it.

In truth, he was eternally grateful to Quinn for saving Xandy and getting her into counseling. To show her his appreciation, he'd paid her a handsome $50,000 bonus for the "great job" she'd done. He was also planning to throw her as much work as she was willing to take. To BJ, she'd proven herself, and once you were in with BJ Sparks, you were in for good.

During her counseling sessions, the counselor had said she thought Quinn was an excellent support person for Xandy and even asked to meet her. Quinn and the counselor had talked and found that they were definitely on the same page when it came to Xandy's mental health. After a few sessions, Xandy decided to give some antidepressant medication a try to see if it would help stabilize her mood. It had been very successful thus far.

Xandy had also asked Quinn if she wanted to move into her house, since Quinn never really left, unless Xandy was with her. Quinn shocked everyone that knew her by giving up her apartment in Santa Monica to move in with Xandy. It told everyone everything they needed to know about their relationship; it was definitely the real thing.

Devin and Skyler were very happy for them. Quinn and Xandy had invited the couple to their house for dinner. For dinner they barbequed and had salads and Margaritas. Afterwards, Xandy and Devin took the dishes inside, while Quinn and Skyler smoked.

"Things seem to be going well with you two," Skyler commented, pointing at the house and Xandy inside.

Quinn nodded. "Yeah," she said, then shook her head in wonder. "I'd never have imagined this working out like it has."

Skyler canted her head. "Why do you say that?"

Quinn looked considering, taking a drag off her cigarette. "I guess because I've never been with someone like her."

Skyler raised an eyebrow at Quinn. "Was she even gay when you met her?"

Quinn couldn't help the grin that spread on her lips, she knew it was a source of endless gossip in her circle of friends. She'd been called everything from a stud to a god. It was kind of funny to Quinn, since she'd never set out to capture Xandy's heart in the first place.

"So, no," Skyler said, her light blue-green eyes sparkling in amusement.

"No, but I wasn't looking to turn her," Quinn said in her defense.

Skyler laughed outright at that. "I take it you're hearing a lot of shit about it?"

"Hell yeah! They're talking like I'm some kind of lesbian god or something. I wasn't trying here…"

Skyler shook her head. "That just makes it worse, Quinn. I wouldn't lead with that one."

Quinn just chuckled and shook her head.

Inside Devin and Xandy worked in the kitchen making more margaritas and talking.

"You and Quinn make a good couple," Devin said, smiling. "I always thought you would."

Xandy looked at her surprised. "You did?"

"Oh, yeah," Devin said, "I was telling Sky that, the same day we met you."

"How did you know?"

"I could see the way you were with her. It was obvious that you two were bonding, the way she held her hand out to you when BJ was going ballistic. It was very sweet, and I don't know anyone who can resist that level of gallantry."

Xandy bit her lip, happy once again to have Devin to talk to about this kind of thing.

"I've never had anyone treat me like she does," Xandy said honestly.

"That's good," Devin said, nodding. "Though, it doesn't always happen that way."

Xandy considered that statement. "Well, I know it never worked that way with the men I dated. I thought maybe women were different."

Devin nodded. "Yeah, some are. I think women are more capable of being empathetic to another woman's needs. But believe me, all women are not like Quinn or even Skyler. I've dated a few women that were as bad, if not worse than men."

"Really?" Xandy asked.

"Oh yeah," Devin said, rolling her eyes. "One woman I dated was so into football that I wasn't even allowed to see her on Sundays during football season. And God help me if I interrupted her game, I caught hell."

"Why did you stay?"

"At first I thought it would get better, that I could change her. I learned really quickly that people don't change if they don't feel the need to. So I left," Devin said, shrugging.

Xandy nodded, thinking that someone as beautiful as Devin would have her pick of women. "I feel pretty lucky," Xandy said. "It seems like a lot of women are interested in Quinn."

"Well, you're the one that counts," Devin said, winking at her as Skyler and Quinn walked into the house.

"Who, what, where?" Skyler asked, grinning at her partner.

"I was just telling Xandy that she's a special girl," Devin said, winking at Xandy.

"Uh-huh," Skyler said, her eyes narrowing slightly in suspicion.

Devin just smiled back at Skyler unfazed by Skyler's suspicious look.

The four ended up in the living room with the newly installed wide-screen TV, watching a movie that wasn't even out in theaters yet; a perk of being friends with BJ and Ramsey. Quinn and Xandy sat on the lounge part of the couch; Quinn's knees were bent, and Xandy sat between them, leaning back against Quinn's chest. Devin and Skyler sat on the other part of the couch, with Devin lying with her head in Skyler's lap.

When the movie was over, the news came on. There was a report about an F4 tornado in Kansas. Quinn glanced down at Xandy, sensing her tension immediately.

"Is that close?" Quinn asked Xandy.

Xandy nodded. "It's about twenty miles east."

"Is that near where you lived?" Devin asked, moving to sit up.

Quinn looked askance at Xandy. Xandy looked back at her, then looked over at Devin and Skyler.

"My family was killed by a tornado three years ago," she said, her tone grave.

"Jesus..." Skyler breathed.

"Oh honey, I'm so sorry," Devin said, her eyes reflecting tears instantly.

Xandy nodded appreciating Devin's concern.

Later that night, Quinn was sitting on the bed, when Xandy came in from the bathroom. Quinn's knees were, as always up to her chest, her arms draped over them. It was obvious she'd been deep in thought before Xandy had walked in. Xandy moved to the bed, her look searching Quinn's face.

"What were you thinking about?" Xandy asked, remembering what her counselor had told her about asking questions, instead of assuming what someone was thinking.

Quinn's emerald-green eyes stared back at her for a long moment, then she put her hand out to Xandy pulling her into her arms. Xandy happily moved into them, sighing against Quinn's chest. She felt Quinn's hand stroking her hair. She knew that was something Quinn did to soothe her, and she knew she needed to wait patiently her answer.

"I think we need to go to Kansas," Quinn said, her voice reflective and soft.

Xandy sat up, looking at Quinn, her expression apprehensive. "Why?"

Quinn reached up smoothing her thumb over Xandy's cheek, as if trying to smooth the look of concern out of her eyes.

"The news reporter was saying that some people have lost everything," Quinn said, "and that the Red Cross is highly depleted of funds because of the record tornado season they've been having back there."

"Okay…" Xandy said, cautiously.

Quinn pinned her with a look. "I think you could do those people a lot of good."

"How?"

"What do you think of doing a benefit concert?"

Xandy looked surprised, but then the idea settled on her, and Quinn could see her mind examining the possibilities.

"It could help to generate donations if you were there and maybe you could even share your story…" Quinn said, her voice purposely gentle on the last part, knowing the idea was likely to scare Xandy a little bit.

Predictably Xandy's eyes widened at the idea of sharing her story, but looking into Quinn's eyes she could see that Quinn's sole concern was for her.

"Kind of like shock therapy?" Xandy asked, grinning.

Quinn grinned too, happy that Xandy was taking the suggestion well; it showed that she'd made progress.

"Yeah, kinda like that," Quinn said. "Honestly though babe, people know who you are now, and if you can pull enough heart strings, then it could help a lot of people from your hometown and around the area."

Xandy started to nod, understanding what Quinn was saying and liking the idea more and more.

"I'd have to talk to BJ," Xandy said. "I have no idea if he'd let me do this, or where to start to plan something like this. Would it take too long to plan?"

Quinn shrugged. "Beats me, babe, but let's start with talking to BJ."

The conversation with BJ went beyond well. He loved the idea, and was more than happy to assign her staff to contact people in the right places and get things set up.

Xandy ended up working with Tabitha Sparks-MacGregor, BJ's daughter who was married to the lead guitarist, Devlin MacGregor, of BJ's band, Sparks. Within twenty-four hours, Tabitha had made contact with the Red Cross to set up some tours of the devastated areas for Xandy and Quinn, who had no intention of letting Xandy handle this trip on her own. Tabitha had also booked time at the In Trust Bank Arena in Wichita, Kansas and had already set up advertising for the show that would be one week from that day.

It was a whirlwind for Xandy. Within forty eight hours of Quinn voicing the idea, they were landing at the airport in Wichita, once again in BJ's plane. Quinn sat next to her, having held her hand tight when they'd flown over the area that had recently been devastated. Quinn knew she needed to keep a close eye on Xandy during this time; it was likely to be very hard on her.

Once at the airport, they were met by a representative from the Red Cross. The woman was tall with blond hair pulled back into an efficient pony tail. She had a no-nonsense but gentle air about her.

"Ms. Blue, I'm Gina, and I can't begin to tell you how much this means to us," the woman told her, holding Xandy's hand in both of her own. "What you're doing will help so many people, it is so generous of you to do this."

Xandy smiled at the woman. "I'm really glad I can help."

"I understand you're from Kansas," Gina said, as they turned to walk out to a vehicle waiting at the curb.

Quinn picked up her duffle, swinging it over her shoulder and picked up Xandy's suitcase, shaking her head with a quick grin at the young man that started to help her. Quinn wanted to stay close to Xandy, to hear what she said, and how she said it.

"Yes," Xandy said, "I grew up in Wakefield."

Gina stopped dead in her tracks and turned to look at Xandy. "Does your family still live there?" she asked.

Xandy shook her head, her eyes glazing with tears. Quinn had handed the bags off to the man at the vehicle, so she moved to hold Xandy's shoulders from behind. It was her way of letting Xandy know she was there.

"Oh, Ms. Blue…" Gina said, tears in her own eyes. "I'm so sorry. Wakefield lost so many good people that day."

Quinn squeezed Xandy's shoulders, as Xandy nodded to the woman, grateful that she hadn't had to explain.

The tornado that had killed Xandy's family had devastated the town of Wakefield, and it was well-known by the Red Cross. Gina had personally worked the site, so she knew all too well how many people had lost their lives that day.

Xandy nodded, doing her best to reign in her emotions. She had known coming home was going to be hard. She drew strength from

Quinn standing behind her, and the kind, understanding look from Gina.

"We can take you right over to your hotel," Gina said. She glanced at her watch, knowing it was a deviation from their schedule, but thinking that maybe she needed to give Xandy some time to adjust.

Gina was all about her schedule; it was how she accomplished what she did for the Red Cross. As a coordinator, it took a lot of effort to get supplies and people to sites as quickly as humanly possible. She'd worked her way up from the bottom, and at forty-two, she was one of the best coordinators the Red Cross had. It made her feel good every day that she did as much as she could for her fellow man. In this case, though, she felt like she needed to be much more flexible than usual, and it surprised her small team.

Xandy took a deep breath, blowing it out slowly and shaking her head. She knew that she was scheduled for a site visit in a little over and hour, she didn't want to start this tour out with what she considered a "star trip" with needing to go to her hotel first.

"No, I'm okay," Xandy said, smiling at Gina.

Quinn lowered her head, putting her lips next to Xandy's ear. "Xan, are you sure?"

Quinn didn't notice the cameras that were rolling and snapping pictures, nor would she have cared if she had. Her focus was on Xandy and her well-being. Xandy lowered her head, tilting it to the side to touch the side of her head to Quinn's face, in a show of vulnerability. Quinn moved to stand closer, putting one arm around Xandy's shoulders, her lips pressing against the side of Xandy's head.

Xandy closed her eyes for a long moment, taking in the strength she felt from Quinn's actions.

It was the first picture of Xandy and Quinn to confirm their relationship, and it also was a definite testament to the connection they shared. It was a moment that captured people's hearts, gay or straight. It was paired with the tragic story of Xandy losing her family to a devastating tornado and Quinn and Xandy quickly became a media favorite.

At the first site visit, they toured the area. After seeing everyone working together to dig people out, Quinn decided to pitch in. She set aside her jacket and began helping to shift debris, working right alongside the rescue workers. This action was, of course, heavily photographed. But when reporters on site tried to talk to Quinn she waved them away, and pointed them back to the Red Cross as the true good Samaritans. Regardless, Quinn's previous title of "White Knight" coined on YouTube, came right back to haunt her. It was obvious to everyone that Quinn Kavanaugh wasn't interested in publicity. BJ Sparks, as her employer, was quoted as saying, "Quinn Kavanaugh is a rare combination of graceful metal under tension and downright bad assedness."

"Is that even a word?" Allexxiss asked BJ after the reporter took down every word.

"It will be now," BJ told her with a wink.

Allexxiss simply rolled her eyes at her husband. BJ was all too happy to have Quinn's good deeds come to light and he intended to make sure he gave her all the support he could.

After three site visits, Quinn was hot and tired. Her white tank top was filthy, as were her jeans and her boots. Xandy begged her to stop on the final site visit because it was obvious Quinn was overdoing it. Quinn had various cuts and bruises from encounters with debris and nails. Fortunately someone had handed her some work gloves at one point, which had at least saved her hands.

At the Hotel Ambassador, they were shown to a suite called the Rock Star Suite. It was the biggest hotel room Quinn or Xandy had ever seen. With 1,596 total square feet, it was bigger than Quinn's old apartment.

"Holy show...." Quinn muttered as the manager opened the double doors into the lavish suite.

"Compliments of Mr. Sparks," smiled the manager.

Quinn and Xandy looked at each other, their shock evident.

"This is crazy!" Xandy said, laughing as they walked inside.

The Rock Star Suite was a lavish one bedroom suite with all the amenities imaginable, including iPod docking stations, a Keurig coffee maker, its own fully-stocked bar, and a private dining room that could seat six. There were incredible views of downtown Wichita through the many windows in the room. The living room featured a fifty-five inch flat-screen TV and multiple couches from which to view it. The private bedroom had a king sized bed, a forty-two inch flat-screen TV and a huge master bathroom. The bathroom featured a Jacuzzi tub as well as a separate walk in shower. There were designer soaps and toiletries. Both Xandy and Quinn were bowled over by the amazing room.

After getting over the shock of the hotel room, Xandy ordered Quinn into the tub to soak her muscles while she ordered them dinner from room service. When the food arrived, Xandy walked into the bathroom, and found Quinn drying off. Xandy found herself admiring Quinn's body again, loving the way her muscles rippled as she moved. Her smooth skin, touched in places with tattoos, was extremely sexy to Xandy. Walking up, Xandy slid her hand from Quinn's neck down her back to her waist, leaning in to kiss her shoulder where a nail had cut Quinn's skin.

"Mmmm," Quinn murmured, turning to face Xandy and dropping the towel on the floor.

Sliding her arms around the smaller girl, she kissed Xandy's lips, pulling her closer. When things got heated, Xandy pulled back, shaking her head.

"Oh no, Ms. Kavanaugh, you're going to eat!"

Quinn grinned, reaching for her towel again. Xandy gave her a narrowed look, but then grinned too.

A few minutes later they were sitting down to dinner. The news was on, and there was a story about them. It was the first time they'd seen that they had suddenly become a media sensation in Kansas. The blond reporter who'd been at one of the devastated areas was talking about the couple's visit, while showing clips of Xandy talking to storm victims, and Quinn pitching in to help clear debris.

"Kansas-born Xandy Blue was in town today, touring the devastated areas, with her now-renowned bodyguard, Quinn Kavanaugh. Ms. Kavanaugh recently became an overnight sensation thanks to a couple of YouTube clips showing Ms. Kavanaugh doing her job as Xandy Blue's bodyguard and taking on no less than three men in Ms. Blue's defense. She's been dubbed the 'White Knight' by many viewers of the videos. While Xandy Blue spoke with Red Cross workers and victims of the

storms, making some people's days it seemed, Quinn Kavanaugh pitched in on the cleanup efforts.

"Xandy Blue is here in Kansas to do a benefit concert for the victims of last week's F four tornado that tore through three towns here in lower Clay County. When asked about the storms, Xandy Blue shocked this reporter when she stated that her family was killed by another F four tornado that ripped through the town of Wakefield three years ago. Many of you will remember the massive loss of life in that storm. When asked about Quinn Kavanaugh, Ms. Blue stated that she didn't know where she'd be without Quinn by her side. The two were caught in a very tender moment this morning at Wichita airport and it's obvious that Ms. Kavanaugh and Ms. Blue are closer than they say. Quinn Kavanaugh refused any interviews, but BJ Sparks, Ms. Kavanaugh's employer, has nothing but good things to say about the Belfast-born bodyguard, calling her a combination of graceful metal under tension and bad assedness. Looks like we'll need to watch these two very closely."

With that the story ended, and Quinn looked over at Xandy her eyes wide.

"Well, alright then," Quinn said, shaking her head. "I didn't even notice the cameras at the airport, did you?" Xandy said.

"Nope, but it looks like you're out now."

Xandy smiled at Quinn. "Good. It's where I wanted to be all along."

"Uh-huh," Quinn murmured, shaking her head.

"That 'White Knight' thing seems to really be sticking…" Xandy said, laughing as Quinn made a disgusted noise in the back of her throat.

"I was really hoping it wouldn't," Quinn said.

"I know, but it's pretty accurate."

"The hell you say," Quinn said, rolling her eyes.

"Quinn," Xandy said, reaching out to touch Quinn's hand, "how many people do you think would go out of their way to help these people? Like you did?"

"All of those volunteers, babe."

"Okay, but that's what they came to do, it isn't what you signed up for."

"I signed up to be here for you," Quinn said, her voice softening, "but if I can help out in the meantime, I'm going to do that." She winked at Xandy then. "You do what you're good at, and I'll do what I'm good at."

"I just don't want you to get hurt," Xandy said, her true concern coming to bare.

"I'm fine babe," Quinn said, "figure it's like gym time."

"Uh-huh," Xandy replied, her tone disbelieving.

Later that night they'd just climbed into bed when Xandy's phone rang. She reached over picking it up and looking at the display. It was BJ.

"Hi BJ," Xandy said, smiling. "I have to thank you for this room, it's insane!"

Quinn watched Xandy talk on the phone, only hearing her side of the conversation. She watched as the girl's mouth dropped open, and her eyes widen. She looked at Quinn her eyes alight with excitement.

"Oh my God, are you serious?"

Then Xandy nodded, as BJ must have affirmed that he was serious. When she hung up the phone she was practically dancing.

"Wot?" Quinn said, smiling at the excitement on Xandy's face.

"BJ said that both Jordan and Fast Lane are joining the benefit concert," she said, smiling widely. "And…" she said, biting her lip. "Sparks is going to play too."

"Holy crap!" Quinn said, knowing that these were serious powerhouse bands.

"I know! BJ is even talking about adding a second night! The first show is already sold out, and they're going to be clamoring in the streets when they hear about these bands!"

"That is fantastic babe," Quinn said, smiling as she reached over to hug Xandy.

"This is so great," Xandy said, snuggling into Quinn's arms, "and I have you to thank."

"Me? I'm not the one that got this together, Xan, and I'm definitely not the one with the talent to sell out an entire arena in less than a week. That's all you babe."

"But if you hadn't given me the idea, Quinn…" Xandy said, shaking her head.

"Okay, I'll take credit for that part," Quinn said, grinning.

"Good!"

They were asleep when the hotel phone rang. Quinn turned over on her back groaning loudly as her muscles protested. She reached blindly for the phone muttering curses in Gaelic as she picked it up.

"Yeah?" she answered her accent thick.

There was shocked silence on the other end of the phone.

"Ya woke me up and yer not gonna talk?" Quinn snapped.

Xandy, who'd also woken when the phone rang, reached across and took the phone gently.

"Hello?" she queried.

"Xandy?" came a woman's voice.

"Aunt Sarah?" Xandy replied, sounding surprised.

"Yes, yes," the woman said, "so glad I got you!"

"It's kind of late, Aunt Sarah," Xandy said, glancing down at Quinn who had a very definite look of shock on her face. "Can I call you in the morning?"

"I want you to come see us. We didn't know you were here till we saw you on the news…"

"I wasn't sure you'd want to see me," Xandy said, her eyes narrowing slightly.

"Of course we want to see you!" Sarah said.

Xandy paused, looking at Quinn again considering, and then she nodded.

"Okay, *we'll* come see you," she said, her emphasis on "we'll."

"Oh," Sarah said. "I see… you can't come, just you?"

"I don't go anywhere without my bodyguard," was Xandy's swift reply.

Quinn was surprised by not only the fact that Xandy apparently had a living relative still in Kansas, but how she was talking to her.

There was silence on the line for a long moment, Xandy waited, having learned the skill of waiting people out from Quinn. Quinn noted the technique and wondered further at it.

"Well, okay," Sarah finally said, sounding resigned.

"Great!" Xandy said, with false cheer. "I'll text you when I know when we can make it there. See you tomorrow."

Xandy disconnected the line then, moving to lie back down.

"Oh, hell no, you're not going to get away with not explaining this one," Quinn said, moving to sit up, wincing as her muscles screamed again.

"You're hurting aren't you?" Xandy said, instantly concerned.

"Oh, no," Quinn said, sounding very Irish, "you're not gettin' outta this one lassie. Talk."

"Okay, but first…" Xandy pulled at Quinn so she was sitting in front of her in a position where she could knead at the muscles in Quinn's back. Quinn moaned softly at the feel of the very sore muscles getting a soft massage.

Glancing back, she said, "Still not getting out of tellin' me."

Xandy sighed. "Yes, I have an aunt, she is… was… my mom's baby sister."

"Okay," Quinn said, grunting as a particularly tight muscle started to ease, "so why don't you like her?"

"I didn't say I don't like her," Xandy said, her look inscrutable.

"I heard the way you talked to her, love, you don't like her. Just tell me why."

Xandy was quiet for a few moments, then she shrugged. "She's always been religious, and I'm talking hard core. She told my mother that I shouldn't be using my God-given talent for money, that I should use it to serve God... that I was sinful for what I was doing..." Her voice trailed off, as she massaged a spot particularly hard.

Quinn jumped in response and moved to turn around and look at Xandy.

"And now you're sure she's going to really hate us being together, right?" Quinn guessed accurately.

Xandy nodded, her fingers picking at the bed covers and not looking at Quinn.

"And that's why you told her that *we* would come," Quinn further deduced.

Still Xandy wouldn't look at her, but she shrugged, nodding miserably.

"Xan..." Quinn said, reaching out to touch Xandy under the chin to get Xandy to look at her. "Are you thinking I'll be mad about this?"

"Are you?"

"No," Quinn said, shaking her head, "I'm more than happy to go with you to deal with this aunt of yours."

Chapter 9

The next day, Quinn and Xandy pulled up to a run down one story house. The whole block had definitely seen better days. They'd rented an SUV, for the drive, avoiding the media for a bit. Xandy led the way to the front door and knocked.

A young kid, who was about ten, answered the door.

"Cousin Xandy!" he exclaimed, opening the screen door and moving to hug her tightly.

"Oh my gosh you've grown so much!" Xandy said, smiling down at the boy hugging her. "Quinn, this is Bobby."

Bobby turned to Quinn and literally took a half step back, and uttered a, "Whoa," his eyes as wide as saucers.

Quinn's tattoos were on full display as she wore a sleeveless muscle tee with Harley Davidson on the front. Bobby looked Quinn up and down, in the open honest way that kids do. Quinn simply stood by awaiting his approval or otherwise. He snapped his fingers finally, nodding to himself.

"You're the bodyguard!" Bobby said, proud of himself for knowing that information.

Quinn nodded. "That I am."

"Where ya from?" Bobby asked, a little suspicious.

"Bobby!" Xandy exclaimed, not wanting Quinn to have to deal with too much from her family.

"S'okay, Xan," Quinn said, looking back at Bobby. "I'm from Northern Ireland."

"Cool," Bobby said, smiling and nodding.

"Xandy?" queried a woman from the door. She held on her hip a towheaded child who looked about six years of age.

Quinn stood back, observing the woman. The first thing she noticed was that the woman looked haggard. Quinn imagined that Sarah had been pretty at one time, but it looked like life had essentially killed her spirit. She was blond like Xandy, with eyes that seemed to be a dull grey. Her hair was pulled back into a messy pony tail and she wore no makeup. On her slight body she wore a grey t-shirt and jean shorts, her feet were bare.

"Aunt Sarah," Xandy said, smiling at her aunt weakly.

Sarah looked at Xandy, and then past her to Quinn, her eyes narrowed, her look assessing and not welcoming in the slightest. Quinn looked back at the woman, unfazed by the near hostility she saw in the other woman's eyes.

Xandy glanced between the two, and took a step back toward Quinn, unconsciously shielding Quinn from her aunt. Quinn reached out to touch the small of Xandy's back. A sign that she recognized Xandy's gesture was thanking her for the loyalty.

Sarah noted both gestures and it was obvious she didn't like either, by the way she sourly curled her lips. When she looked back at her niece and this other woman she saw that they were both looking at her with expectant and amused looks on their faces. Sarah was surprised; Xandy had always been such a sweet and obedient child.

What had this woman done to her niece? she thought, as she opened the screen door and gestured for them to enter the house.

Xandy walked in first, leaning down to kiss the little girl on the cheek.

"You've grown so much, Elly," she said to the child, who giggled.

Quinn stepped over the threshold and Elly's eyes widened. There was a tense moment where it was impossible to tell what the child was thinking. Elly shocked everyone by smiling brightly at Quinn. Quinn returned the smile and winked at the little girl.

"Aunt Sarah," Xandy said, reaching over to touch Quinn's arm, "this is Quinn."

Sarah nodded at Quinn, her look now even more sour. "I know, the bodyguard," she said, dismissively.

Quinn looked at Xandy with a sardonic grin, her green eyes sparkling mischievously, but she said nothing. It was obvious Xandy was about to correct her aunt, and Quinn shook her head slightly; it would be playing into Sarah's hands. Sarah wanted Xandy on the defensive but Quinn didn't want Xandy to give her that gift.

Xandy, having caught the shake of Quinn's head, turned to look around the house. Quinn, noticing Sarah's confusion at the silent conversation, had to hide her grin behind her hand.

"Where's Erin?" Xandy asked, looking around for signs of her eldest cousin.

As if Xandy had just insulted her, Sarah's eyes flashed in quick anger. "She's not here."

Quinn's eyebrows shot up as she looked over at Xandy, there was obviously something going on there.

"Oh," Xandy said, nodding, as if she hadn't even heard the tone in her aunt's voice. "Maybe I'll get a chance to see her later," she added moving into the room.

In truth Xandy was dying to get away from her very hostile aunt. Sarah had once been a very happy person; Xandy remembered back to her childhood when life and a cheating husband hadn't beaten her aunt down. Now it just seemed that Sarah was bitter and angry at everyone. Part of her wanted to ask her aunt exactly why she'd wanted to see her, but she knew that would only anger her aunt more. It was obvious Quinn didn't want her to get into a confrontation with her aunt, so she was doing her best to keep things light, hoping they could get out of there quickly.

Sarah put Elly down, and moved to sit down. Elly immediately walked over to Quinn, staring up at her in what appeared to be awe. Quinn knelt down, putting herself closer to the child's level. It was obvious Elly was surprised by this action as her big blue eyes, widened dramatically.

Xandy moved to sit down in the chair across from her aunt and nearest to Quinn. Quinn turned her head to look at Xandy, and suddenly felt a tiny finger on her neck. Elly was touching the tattoo on Quinn's neck, her eyes blinking as she rubbed her finger across it then looked at her finger. It seemed like she expected the ink to come off.

"It doesn't come off, little one," Quinn said softly, her accent clear.

Elly's eyes went to Quinn's face again with the sound of her accent.

"Sound funny," Elly said, her tiny little voice the only sound in the room.

Quinn chuckled softly. "I hear that a lot."

Elly nodded, as if confirming that Quinn should hear that a lot. Quinn laughed, her laughter rich and causing Elly to smile brightly again. Elly's reaction made Xandy wonder if she heard laughter very often from the adults in her life, it made her a bit sad to think probably not.

"She's not used to people with them tattoos all over 'em," Sarah said, her tone snide and meant to be insulting.

Quinn's emerald eyes glanced over at Sarah, her look amused, but she said nothing. It was obvious that Sarah was doing anything she could think of to pick a fight.

"Aunt Sarah," Xandy began, glancing at Quinn. She knew she was giving into Sarah's tactics, but she was already tired of the palpable animosity in the room and wanted to get away from it. "Was there a reason you wanted to see me?"

Sarah looked over at Xandy, surprised, then a mask of condescension descended on Sarah's face. Quinn knew that Xandy had just walked right into the woman's trap.

"That's what family does, Xandy Blue Hayes," Sarah said, her tone preachy. "They don't just come to town and not see their relatives."

Xandy's face reflected her annoyance at being talked to like she was a recalcitrant child. She glanced down at Quinn as she felt Quinn's hand giving her leg a reassuring squeeze. Sarah watched the exchange, clearly not liking what she was seeing. Xandy responded by giving her aunt a wintry smile. "Well, with this lovely reception, why wouldn't I want to come see you?" Xandy asked, her tone wry.

"Cousin Xandy!" Bobby exclaimed, walking into the middle of the tableau without even realizing it.

He walked toward Xandy, a toy car in his hand.

"This is my new car!" he said, shoving the toy at her.

"That's really cool," Xandy said, happy for the distraction, "what kind of car is that?"

"Guess!" Bobby challenged as he grinned, looking confident.

Xandy contemplated the car for a few long moments, her eyes skipped to Quinn who was grinning.

Bobby caught the look and looked at Quinn.

"Can you guess?" Bobby asked Quinn, his look still cheeky.

"I can," Quinn said, inclining her head.

"What is it?" Bobby asked smugly, sure that this girl wouldn't know.

"It's a nineteen seventy-five Chevy Camaro," Quinn told him. "The first of the Camaros to have a catalytic converter installed."

Bobby looked stunned. "How..." he stammered, "how'd you know?"

Quinn grinned, glancing at Xandy. "I kinda like cars. I drive a sixty-nine Mach one. Do you know what that is?"

Bobby thought about it for a long minute. "It's a Mustang, right?"

Quinn smiled nodding. "Very good."

"What's it look like?" Bobby asked.

By this time, Elly had moved to sit down, her hand on Quinn's leg, still looking up at this person with the strange voice. Quinn reached into her back pocket pulling out her phone and pulling up a picture of her Mach and handing the phone to Bobby.

"Cool!" Bobby exclaimed, turning to show his mother the picture. "Look Mom, isn't that the coolest car you've ever seen?"

Sarah tried not to be affected by her son's excitement, but she had to smile. This Quinn definitely had been a hit with her kids, and it bugged her no end.

"Yes, it's a lovely car," Sarah said mildly, her eyes on her niece.

Quinn raised an eyebrow at the term "lovely." Her phone chose that moment to ring in Bobby's hands.

It was extremely ironic; Quinn had recently been cajoled into changing her ringtone from Queensryche's "Walk in the Shadows" to Disturbed's "The Vengeful One," since that's what she'd become famous for on YouTube.

The lyrics that talked about being the hand of God rang out clearly in the room. Bobby turned as Quinn stood and handed her the phone. Quinn excused herself and walked toward the back door of the house as she answered the call.

Sarah looked aghast by the lyrics, her eyes following Quinn out the door, then she wheeled to look back at Xandy.

"What is wrong with you?!" Sarah practically spat.

"Oh, for God's sake," Xandy said, rolling her eyes and shaking her head.

Sarah put her hand to her throat as if Xandy was choking her physically, as she gasped, "Do not take the Lord's name in vein in front of my children!"

Xandy looked back at her aunt, surprised that she'd managed to forget just how crazy her aunt really was with the religious rhetoric. Xandy's immediate family had been Christians, but they'd never been crazed about it, not like her Aunt's family. They attended church and prayed at meals, but that had been most of it. They had never judged people, not like her aunt had begun to after her life had turned so bad.

"Your parents would be ashamed of you," Sarah said, even as she watched her daughter get up from the floor and walked to the back door, standing at the window watching Quinn through it.

Xandy could hear Elly saying, "Kin, Kin..." over and over, like a chant that would bring Quinn back into the house.

Bobby had sat down and was playing with his car. It looked to Xandy like he was purposely ignoring the exchange, and it was obvious to her that he had heard his mother act like this before.

Xandy's eyes touched on both of Sarah's children pointedly, the look on her face holding the irony she was feeling. Neither child seemed affected by anything, other than Quinn's absence in Elly's case. Then she looked back at her aunt, shaking her head.

"You don't care?" Sarah exclaimed, looking shocked again, she'd really expected that barb to find its home.

Xandy looked back at her aunt for a long moment, indicating her disbelief that her aunt was actually pursuing the subject.

"My parents would be happy that I'm happy, Aunt Sarah, like you should be."

"I can't condone that abomination!" Sarah said, gesturing toward the backyard.

"You're calling Quinn an abomination?" Xandy asked, moving to stand in her need to exert her defiance of such an accusation.

"I'm saying all of this," Sarah said, moving to stand as well, her gesture taking in the space where Quinn had been and where Xandy stood. "This relationship you're so proud of that is all over the news... besmirching our good name... flaunting such an abhorrent sin!"

"Okay, yeah, I've heard enough," Xandy said, moving to walk toward the backyard.

Walking out into the backyard she saw that Quinn was leaning against a wall, smoking a cigarette, an ashtray on a small table next to her. She had music playing on her phone and was singing to the song that was on.

Sarah had followed Xandy into the backyard and once again gasped in shock.

"I don't allow smoking around my children!" she exclaimed, outright hostile at Quinn now.

Quinn raised her head, lifting her cigarette to her lips and taking a long drag as she looked around her, and then back to Sarah.

"That's why I'm doing it in the yard, where your children aren't," Quinn said mildly. Then she looked around, her eyes pointedly settling on the cigarette butts all over the ground in various areas. "It doesn't look like I'm the first to smoke out here."

Sarah's eyes flared in anger at what she considered an accusation. "This is my house! And no matter how you were obviously raised, you will respect my wishes in my house!"

Quinn looked back at the woman as if she were insane, taking yet another drag on her cigarette, her look considering through the smoke she blew out a couple of moments later. Her emerald-green eyes glanced around her again, then clenching her cigarette between her teeth she spread her hands.

"Technically, I'm not in the house," Quinn said, raising an eyebrow at the woman, an amused grin on her lips. "However…" she said, taking one last drag on the cigarette and then stubbing it out pointedly in the ashtray, her eyes on the butts on the ground again. Then she turned back to look at Sarah as she put a booted foot up on the wall behind her, crossing her arms in front of her chest as if to ask, *are you happy now?*

Sarah's eyes fell on the cell phone lying on the table, still playing rock music. "I don't allow my children to listen to that Satan worship either!"

Quinn's eyes touched on Xandy's for a moment, then they trailed around the yard again, the yard still devoid of said children. Then she reached down and turned the music pointedly off without a word.

"You obviously don't respect anything or anyone!" Sarah railed, her voice strident in her need to assert herself in the face of Quinn's calm acceptance of every edict she made.

Quinn simply looked back at the woman with her lips pursed slightly, then she looked at Xandy.

"You ready to go, babe?" Quinn asked Xandy.

"Definitely!" Xandy said, relief clear in her voice.

After a very unhappy Elly was pulled away from Quinn's leg, Xandy and Quinn made their exit. Quinn flipped Bobby a quick wave, but it was obvious the boy was afraid to make an exhibition of himself like his little sister was, even though he looked extremely unhappy too that Quinn and Xandy were leaving. Sarah stood at the door watching them leave and doing her best to quell Elly's cries.

On the way back to the hotel, Xandy looked over at Quinn. "I'm so sorry!" she said, shaking her head.

Quinn smiled mildly. "For what, babe?"

"For that, for having to put up with my aunt's bullshit."

Quinn chuckled. "Babe, she's not the first Bible-banger I've dealt with in my time."

Xandy looked over at her. "But how do you keep from losing your temper with them?"

Quinn shrugged. "Nothing I'm gonna say is going to change how they think, so why bother?"

"I can't believe she acted like that."

"She seems like she's very unhappy, babe."

"Well, that's no excuse," Xandy said angrily, "she's got no right to treat you like that."

Quinn grinned, shaking her head.

"What?" Xandy asked, seeing that Quinn didn't see it the way she did.

"Babe, she's afraid for you," Quinn told her.

"Afraid for me?"

"She thinks that you're doing something that's wrong, and she probably thinks I'm the one that led you down this path. That's why she's leveling all that hate at my head."

Xandy folded her arms in front of her chest. "Well, it's not okay, and I'm done."

Quinn grimaced, shaking her head again. "You can't do that babe."

"What do you mean?" Xandy asked, trying to understand, but afraid she was never going to catch up in this conversation.

Xandy had expected Quinn to be furious with her aunt for the way she'd acted and she'd fully expected Quinn to take it out on her since Sarah was her family member. But Quinn wasn't acting angry in the slightest and now she was saying that Xandy couldn't cut Sarah off?

"I mean," Quinn said, reaching over to touch Xandy's hand, "that she's the only family you have, her and your cousins."

Xandy shook her head, not willing to accept that answer. Quinn glanced over at the younger girl, her look searching.

"Babe," Quinn said, her tone beseeching, "you can't expect her to change her mind about something she's probably believed for decades now. Certainly not in the span of an hour."

Xandy looked back at Quinn, her look defiant, but after a few moments she blew her breath out, looking defeated. She gave Quinn a mocking annoyed look. "You know, you could at least try to act like an asshole sometimes."

Quinn grinned, then chuckled. "I'll work on that."

"Good," Xandy said, as the first splats of rain hit the windshield.

Clouds had been gathering in the area that day. There were thunderstorms predicted for that evening. As they made the twenty-eight mile drive back to Wichita, the rain began in earnest. They were relieved to be out of it when they pulled into the garage of the hotel.

They had dinner in the room that evening and watched the lightning light up the sky. Later they watched a movie and when Xandy got tired, Quinn took her in to bed.

"You're not coming to bed?" Xandy asked sleepily.

"I got some things I need to do to help Mackie out with security for the show," Quinn said, leaning down to kiss Xandy softly on the lips. "I'll be in soon."

"Okay," Xandy murmured tiredly, reminding Quinn of little Elly.

A couple of hours later, Quinn was working on her laptop, listening absently to the news that played on the TV when a Breaking News story was announced.

"An F four tornado has just touched down in Harvey County. The tornado touched down in Halstead and traveled east, before veering northward into Newton..."

The reporter continued, but Quinn was out of her chair in a flash, striding into the bedroom.

"Xandy, we gotta go," Quinn announced as she turned on the light.

"What?" Xandy, groggy, sitting up and rubbing her eyes.

"We have to go, babe, get up and throw on some clothes, make sure you wear closed-toe shoes," Quinn said, reaching into her duffel to pull out her leather jacket, and her knife before grabbing the first aid kit from the bathroom. Emptying out her duffel she started shoving in things like towels and blankets, as well as the gear, including her gun.

"What's happening?" Xandy asked, even as she did what Quinn had told her.

Quinn stopped packing the bag, and looked over at Xandy. "Newton just got hit by an F four."

Xandy paled instantly. Newton was the town her Aunt lived in.

"Oh my God…" Xandy whispered.

"I know, babe, but stay with me here okay? We need to get there."

Xandy swallowed convulsively, but nodded continuing to dress hurriedly.

Ten minutes later, they were in the SUV speeding down the freeway. Quinn was figuring there was going to be some difficulties getting to the town, but she had every intention of getting to what was left of Xandy's family. As it turned out, the news story must have broken really quick, as there were very few emergency vehicles in the immediate neighborhood when they arrived. Quinn imagined many had gone to Halstead to start with since that had been where tornado had originally touched down.

She was stunned by the devastation before her. The neighborhood they'd been in earlier that day no longer existed. Quinn couldn't see even one building standing from the road. There was so much debris in the street that Quinn parked in what was supposed to be the parking lot for the local church, but was now a pile of debris. It was a couple of blocks from the house, but she didn't want to risk ending up with a cracked axel or flat tires.

There were power lines down and many of them were sparking wildly. There was surprisingly little movement which only served to scare Quinn more. She hadn't listened to the newscaster after Newton had been mentioned, so she had no idea how many people were thought to be dead. All she knew was that she needed to get to Xandy's family. Regardless of their encounter with Xandy's Aunt Sarah earlier in the day, they were still the only family Xandy had left. Quinn refused to even think about how hard it would be on Xandy if she lost them too.

Getting out of the SUV she reached into the back seat to grab her duffel and her jacket. Glancing over at Xandy as she got out, she nodded her head in the direction of her aunt's house.

"Keep your eyes open," Quinn told her. "Watch out for downed wires, and stay close to me."

Xandy nodded, looking very haunted. Quinn reached out her hand, grasping Xandy's, then began striding toward where the house had been. As they got closer, Quinn could see some movement, and she heard a woman screaming. As they approached, Quinn could make out a woman in a white cotton nightgown pacing and crying out. It hit Quinn almost physically when she realized it was Sarah. Letting go of Xandy's hand, Quinn literally sprinted to Sarah's side.

"Sarah!" Quinn had to yell to be heard over Sarah's screaming. Taking the woman by the shoulders, Quinn shook her slightly to get her attention.

"I can't find her, I can't find her!" Sarah was saying over and over.

Quinn looked around quickly and located a very dirty Bobby. Kneeling, she took Bobby by the shoulders gently, looking him in the face.

"Where are your sisters?" she asked Bobby, her voice as calm as she could make it.

Bobby's eyes were huge saucers as she shook his head. "I don't know... Mom said go to the basement... we were going, but then everything was shaking and I couldn't hold onto her, and...." His voice trailed off as he burst into tears, throwing himself into Quinn's arms crying hysterically.

Quinn looked around and saw Xandy walking up. Standing, she took Bobby over to Xandy, grabbing Sarah's hand leading her over as well.

"Xan," Quinn said, touching Xandy's cheek to make sure she was listening, she seemed almost as dazed as Sarah and Bobby. "Babe, you with me?" Quinn asked, her voice stronger now. "I need you with me."

Xandy nodded, doing her best to focus.

"I need you to keep them back, and I need you to watch for help, okay?" Quinn said and began walking toward the house.

"Okay," Xandy said, nodding, looking more alert now. Xandy looked at Sarah. "Aunt Sarah, is Erin in there too?"

Sarah looked back at Xandy, her look blank; she was definitely in shock. Xandy looked at Bobby.

"Bobby, was Erin home?" she asked the boy.

Bobby shook his head, his eyes still looking terrified.

"Quinn!" Xandy called, "it's just Elly, we're just looking for Elly!"

"Got it!" Quinn said, carrying on toward what was left of the house.

She remembered where the basement door had been, back by the kitchen. She walked around the ruins of the house to the back area, where the kitchen had been, which was now just a pile of debris at least two and a half to three feet high. Quinn pulled on her Harley jacket, thinking that it would serve as some protection against nails or shards of glass. She reached into her pockets, thanking her maker that she always shoved an extra pair of leather riding gloves in the pockets. Pulling on the gloves, she leaned down, starting to carefully pull away debris that could be moved. She tossed the pieces away from her.

"Elly!" she called, her voice loud, pausing she listened intently.

Hearing nothing, she continued to pull pieces away from the area she'd estimated would be near the basement stairs. She knew that staircases were particularly fortified; if Elly had any chance of being alive, it would be near the stairwell. Quinn gritted her teeth as nails pierced her hand through the gloves.

"Elly!" she called again, pausing to listen.

Still she heard nothing, the silence was eerie and it was weighing on her mind that the beautiful blue-eyed girl she'd met earlier in that day could be lying under this debris broken and bleeding out the last of her life.

"Damnit Elly, answer me!" she yelled, her voice angry at the thoughts running through her head.

She was about to reach for another piece of debris when she thought she heard the faintest cry. Pausing, she listened, leaning closer to the pile to try to hear. Nothing.

"Elly! Come on baby girl! You gotta tell me you're there!" she yelled.

That's when she heard the best sound she'd ever heard in her life, a tiny little voice that said, "Kin?"

"Yes, baby girl, it's me! Keep talking, I'm going to get you out of there!" Quinn yelled, then looked back over to where Xandy was stood with Sarah and Bobby. "I can hear her, she's here! Find some help!"

Xandy nodded, looking around and running toward the only people she could see. Quinn braced a booted foot on a piece of foundation, and reached down, grabbing a large piece of debris that was actually part of a door. She pulled back with all her might, careful to make sure she wasn't dislodging something else that could fall on the child, wherever she was in that mess. The piece gave and she yanked it away, feeling a sharp pain in her arm as she did, but ignoring it.

"Elly?" Quinn queried, suddenly feeling a hand on her back. Glancing behind her, she saw Bobby, he looked back at her with a determined set to his jaw.

"I want to help," he said.

Quinn started to tell him to go back to his mother, because she didn't want to take the chance that he could get hurt too. But then she realized that if he didn't get a chance to help rescue his sister, he'd blame himself forever.

"Okay," Quinn said, "but I need you to stay right there, I'll hand you stuff, okay? Just throw it over there," she said, pointing to the part of the backyard she'd been using to discard items.

"Elly!" Bobby called this time.

"Beebee?" came Elly's voice.

"Keep talking to her," Quinn told Bobby, "we need to keep her calm."

"Okay," Bobby said, nodding and moving to kneel next to the debris pile.

"I'm right here, Elly!" Bobby called, as Quinn went back to pulling away the pieces she could.

A few more pieces moved, but then she came to a section where the roof had actually caved downwards on the stairs. Looking around, she didn't see Xandy anywhere. Shaking her head, Quinn knew she was going to have to do this herself. Reaching down, she grasped what had been part of the eaves of the house's roof. Testing the weight of the huge piece, she heaved hard, it gave slightly, but she knew she was going to need more power. Setting the piece back carefully, lest she cause more of a cave in, she looked around for something to use as leverage. Everything was so small, she knew they'd snap if she tried, and that could cause more damage and possibly cave in what was left of the stairs to the basement.

Taking a deep breath, she moved to put her back to the slanted section of the eave, sinking down to a squatting position, she put her shoulder against the wood, and then pushed upward with her shoulder, grunting with the effort, digging the toes of her boots in to give her more power. She felt the section shift. Keeping up the pressure, she brought her feet in closer, one foot at a time, careful not to lose any ground. She could hear Bobby talking to Elly, and Elly's faint replies.

Gathering her strength, and taking in a deep breath, Quinn shoved her shoulder further under the eave, and pushed upward. Driving her feet into the ground, she slowly marched in toward the house, levering the piece of roof up. She was on her feet, but still hunched with the weight of the roof piece, when she heard Xandy yelling her name.

Xandy had seen Quinn lifting the section of roof with her own body and was terrified that the piece would shift and collapse on Quinn herself. She was leading two men that she'd finally located toward Quinn.

"Holy shit!" one of the men exclaimed, seeing Quinn's position.

"She's crazy!" the other guy said, as they moved to try to help.

Quinn was panting at this point and feeling slightly light-headed. Her back was screaming as were her legs, they both shook uncontrollably. As the men ran over, she nodded to them.

"Take it, take it," she grunted to them. "I need to get to her!"

The two men heaved the piece of roof, looking at each other wide-eyed as they realized how much weight this woman had just hefted, it was a strain for both of them to hold it.

As soon as the weight was off her shoulders, Quinn dropped to the ground, and crawled over to the opening that raising the section of roof had exposed. She reached in to feel around to determine how much space there was.

"Elly?" she yelled. "Can you see anything?"

"No!" Elly cried.

"Okay, baby girl, okay," Quinn replied, her voice gentle, but loud enough for the child to hear, "I'm comin' for ya, just hold on, okay?"

"Oh... kay..."

It scared Quinn. Fearing that the child was fading, she needed to get in there now. Reaching through the opening, she could feel a decent sized area. Levering herself up to a kneeling position, she yanked off her jacket, knowing it would impede her progress and possibly get hung up on things. She stripped off her loosely-fitting muscle tee as well, afraid it too would get caught, exposing sinewy muscle and a black sports bra. With that, she moved toward the opening, putting her arms through, and shoving aside the debris that was there. She belly crawled through the opening, unable to see anything.

"Elly?" she queried. "Where are you baby girl?"

"Hea," Elly said softly.

She sounded like she wasn't too far away. Quinn shoved herself forward, wincing as she felt something scrape her skin sharply.

"Reach out your hands baby," Quinn said, "try to find my hands."

"Kin?" Elly queried.

"Yes, baby girl, it's like hide and seek, and you need to find me, okay?"

"Okay," Elly answered, sounding enthusiastic.

Quinn pulled her knees up slightly, using her booted feet to shove her farther into the opening. Feeling something sharp rake her left arm, she tried to shift, but the opening was barely big enough for her, there was no extra room. Remotely she heard sirens, but pushed that away as she reached her hands further into the opening, encountering wires and praying none of them were live. That's when she felt Elly's fingers touch hers.

"There you are!" Quinn cried out joyously.

"Kin!" Elly also cried happily.

"Okay, sweetie, hold on, okay? I got you, just give me a second here," she said, stretching her arm back to the front of the opening, straining to reach her jacket.

She wanted to try and keep Elly from getting hurt by whatever had causing her to bleed. The last thing she wanted was for this child to be scarred further from this incident. She laid her jacked over the debris in front of her. Shoving herself a little bit farther forward, she reached for Elly's hand again.

"Give me your hand again, baby girl," Quinn said.

She immediately felt Elly's little hand touch hers. Quinn slid her hand around Elly's wrist, giving it the gentlest of tugs to determine if the child was trapped, she was surprised when Elly slight weight shifted toward her immediately.

"Elly, are you hurt anywhere?" Quinn asked.

"No…" Elly said, sounding like she was worried that she'd be in trouble.

"Okay, baby girl, here's what we're going to do," Quinn said. "I'm going to hold your hand, and you're going to crawl toward me, okay? Take your time, just edge forward a little at a time…"

She felt Elly moving toward her, reaching up she did her best to pull aside the wires that were thankfully not live. Within a minute, Elly was nose to nose with Quinn.

"Well, there you are…" Quinn said, smiling. "Now we're just going to get out of here together."

Making sure that Elly was fully situated on the Harley jacket, Quinn did her best to pull it around the child. She continued to hold Elly's hand with her other hand, and used her booted toes to dig into the ground and pull them backwards.

"We're coming out!" she called. "Fecking hell!" she screeched unintentionally as she felt a piece of rebar dig into her back and rake open her skin.

"Quinn!" came Xandy's immediate reply from out in the open, her tone almost hysterical.

Quinn had no way of knowing that Xandy had paced back and forth, crying the entire time Quinn had been in that opening. She was terrified that the men would drop the roof on Quinn and Elly and kill them both. Sarah was standing to the side, crying silently, her hands clenching and unclenching unconsciously. Bobby was standing stock still, his eyes never leaving the opening.

A moment later, Quinn's boots appeared at the opening, Xandy ran forward, grabbing Quinn's foot, with the intent on helping her.

"Don't Xan! Don't!" Quinn yelled, her voice laced with pain.

Quinn knew that if Xandy pulled her, the rebar would likely either break a rib, or pierce a lung or something. Carefully Quinn shoved her torso down into the debris under her, careful to dislodge the rebar from her skin, before she continued to move backward. She was also very cognizant of the location of the metal, to make sure that Elly didn't run into it.

After what seemed like forever, Quinn emerged, pulling Elly free. The child literally bowling Quinn over with the last tug Quinn gave her to pull her free. Quinn fell back, holding Elly firmly in her arms, cushioning the child's body from the impact. She felt the wind knocked out of her, but she could hear Xandy calling out.

"I'm okay, I'm okay." Quinn assured her, "get Elly."

Xandy moved to pick Elly up, but the child was clinging to Quinn for dear life.

Quinn felt the panicked clutching of Elly's hands and knew that she wasn't going to let anyone take her. Blowing her breath out, she forced herself to sit up. Using every last ounce of her quickly waning strength she pushed herself up to her feet, still cradling Elly against her with one arm.

Xandy moved to put Quinn's free arm around her shoulders, doing her best to support Quinn's weight.

"I'm okay," Quinn said, her voice reflecting the exhaustion that was settling over her.

Sarah rushed over to them as Quinn carried Elly farther away from the house to make sure they were all a safe distance. When Elly saw her mother she held out her arms to her. Sarah took the child, hugging her tight. Her eyes looked back at Quinn, tears in them as she said, "Thank you."

Quinn nodded, then moved to sit on the curb. She stripped off her riding gloves, noting absently that her hands were bloody too. It was only then, in the light of the headlights of a passing police car, that Xandy saw the blood all over Quinn's back, and trickling from various cuts on her arms.

"Quinn, you're bleeding!" Xandy said horrified.

"I'm okay," Quinn said again, glancing behind her and noting thankfully that there was actually a patch of grass behind her.

Lying back she blew her breath out slowly, feeling every muscle in her back screech in reaction. Xandy stood by watching, completely lost as to what to do. No ambulances had arrived yet, so there was no one to help.

After a few minutes, Quinn moved to get up. It was then that one of the men came by and handed Quinn the shirt she'd discarded and her Harley jacket that was now slightly torn.

"Thanks," Quinn said as she nodded gratefully, and carefully pulled the shirt on, smearing the blood, but at least covering it. She then put her jacket around Sarah's shoulders, since it was obvious she was shivering in the nightgown she wore.

"Let's get them back to the hotel," Quinn told Xandy. "We can get the hotel doctor to check them out."

"And you can get checked out too," Sarah said, her eyes on Quinn's bloodied arms.

Quinn looked at Sarah, her lips curling in a grin, as she nodded. She'd heard the 'mom-tone' in Sarah's voice; she was not going to argue. The group made their way over to the lot two blocks down. Quinn leaned down picking Bobby up, since he was barefoot and she didn't want him to cut his feet. At the SUV, Xandy turned to Quinn.

"I'm going to drive us back," she said, holding her hand out for the keys. "You look dead on your feet."

Quinn considered arguing, but then just nodded as a wave of exhaustion moved over her. She opened the door for Xandy, then opened the door behind the driver's door for Sarah. Quinn then turned and took Elly with the intent of holding her while Sarah got up into the SUV.

Elly wound her arms around Quinn's neck and said, "Me ride with Kin!"

Sarah and Quinn exchanged a comical look at the child's edict.

"Oh-K," Quinn said, not sure if that was going to fly with the child's mother or not.

Sarah shook her head tiredly, then gestured to the back seat. Still holding Elly, Quinn climbed inside, setting Elly on the seat next to her and doing her best to seat belt the child in. Bobby ended up getting into the front passenger seat, and Sarah got in on the other side of Quinn and Elly.

"What about Erin?" Xandy asked glancing back at her aunt as she started the SUV and adjusted the seat to her smaller size.

Sarah looked worried suddenly. "I never know where that girl is these days! She's never home, she's always off with these friends of hers. I can't control her in the slightest…" she said, sounding exasperated.

"Does she have a cell phone?" Quinn asked, tiredly.

"Yes," Sarah said nodding.

"Give Xandy the number," Quinn said, "she can call or text Erin to see where she is. Maybe she can have someone bring her to the hotel, or we can go and get her."

"Sounds like a good plan," Xandy said nodding.

Sarah gave Xandy the number; fortunately the cell phone towers seemed to be working, so she was able to send a text. Xandy included the fact that her mother, brother and sister were all okay, as well as the hotel information.

As they were driving back to Wichita, Xandy continually checked on Quinn in the rearview mirror. Quinn actually seemed a bit dazed, and Xandy was worried she might be going into shock from blood loss. She reminded herself that the cuts didn't seem to be bleeding profusely, though it didn't stop her from worrying all the way back to the hotel.

As they pulled up to the hotel, a valet came to take the vehicle, looking shocked as Quinn climbed out of the truck.

"Ma'am are you okay?" The young man asked, seeing the blood.

Quinn nodded tiredly as she lifted Elly down from the SUV. The group walked inside and was met by a young woman that had to be Erin. She looked like a very tough, short haired version of Xandy.

"Mom!" Erin cried, as she ran up to the group.

Sarah hugged her eldest daughter, who was sixteen and a handful. Erin's eyes took in Quinn in all her battered and bloody glory. Quinn saw the younger girl's eyes widen, but then she was hugging by her sister and brother. Quinn walked over to the front desk, grinning at the predictably shocked looks she was receiving from the staff and hotel guests.

"Just got my ass kicked by a house," Quinn told the young lady at the front desk.

The young woman looked back at her open mouthed in shock.

"Can you send the hotel doc up to the Rock Star Suite?" Quinn asked with a cavalier wink and a smile.

She turned and walked away, putting her arm around Xandy and steered her toward the elevators. Sarah, Bobby, Elly and Erin followed.

"Think that made an impression?" Quinn asked, as the group got onto the elevator.

"Probably," Xandy said, grinning as she hit the button for their floor.

Inside the suite, Xandy ordered Quinn to go and take a shower. "Carefully!" she called after her, she then looked at her family members who were staring around them awestruck.

"My boss did this," Xandy said, gesturing around the room.

"Nice boss," Erin said with a low whistle.

Xandy smiled. "There's a guest bathroom over there," she said, pointing down the hall back toward the doors to the bedroom. "I'm going to have them send up some rollaway beds and whatever else we need."

Sarah nodded, surprised at how commanding her niece was suddenly. Apparently she'd grown up a lot in the years she'd been gone. Taking Elly's hand, Sarah headed for the bathroom Xandy had indicated to.

Xandy reached over and picked up the remote, handing it to Erin. "Go for it," she said, smiling.

Erin clicked the TV on as Xandy called the front desk and asked for beds. Then she went to check on Quinn. She heard the shower and walked into the bathroom. She couldn't stop the audible gasp that came out of her mouth. Quinn was standing with her arms braced on the wall in front of her, her back to Xandy. The water was running down her body; blood trails from at least three wounds slid down her skin, but the worst was the wound on her back. It was a half-inch round with a two inch cut that moved up Quinn's back.

Quinn glanced over her shoulder at Xandy. "Wot?" she asked.

"Your back… Jesus babe…" Xandy responded.

She moved to pick up a wash cloth and kicking off her shoes and taking off her jacket, she walked into the shower, mindless of the water splashing her pants and shirt. She wet the wash cloth and gently touched it to the wound; Quinn jumped at the contact, hissing in pain.

"I'm sorry, babe…" Xandy said her voice tremulous.

Quinn heard the upset in Xandy's voice and turned to face her, pulling her into her arms, and hugging her close.

"It's okay," Quinn said, "we're okay…"

"But you're so cut up…" Xandy said, crying softly now. "I was so scared, Quinn, you could have been killed…"

"I couldn't leave that baby in there."

"I know, I know, but God…" Xandy said, lifting her head to look up at Quinn. "Thank you for doing what you did, I still don't know how you did it…" she said, letting her voice trail off as she shook her head.

Quinn shrugged. "I didn't have a choice."

Xandy pressed her lips together sadly, nodding her head. She knew to Quinn's way of thinking she hadn't had a choice. To Quinn's way of thinking family was the only thing in the world that mattered, and there had been no way that Quinn would have left Elly in that wrecked house as long as she'd had breath in her body. It's just who Quinn was. Still it terrified Xandy that she could have easily lost her that night.

After the shower, Quinn carefully pulled on a pair of boy shorts and a clean black sports bra, and then went to lie on the bed, carefully laying a towel over the sheets, since her back was still bleeding a bit. After changing out of her now wet clothes, Xandy had gone out to see if the doctor had arrived yet.

Quinn was just dozing off when she felt a presence in the room. Opening her eyes, she saw Erin standing at the door. What she didn't see was the way the girl's eyes moved over her leanly muscled body, damaged as it was. She did, however, note the guilty look that crossed the girl's features when she realized that Quinn was looking at her.

"Um," Erin stammered, "Xandy said to tell you that the doctor is here and will be in here in a minute."

Quinn nodded, moving to sit up and groaning out loud as she realized that her back muscles had apparently decided they were done for the night. Erin moved to help her sit up, her hands shaking as she reached out to take Quinn's arm to support her as she moved. Quinn felt the shaking hands and wondered if Erin had been drinking or taking drugs earlier in the evening.

"Babe?" Xandy queried from the door.

"Yeah," Quinn said, nodding to Xandy and glancing up at Erin again, once again noticing a strange look cross her features.

She didn't have time to really think about what was going on because the doctor walked in a moment later.

"I understand that I'm to examine Wonder Woman here..." he said smiling and looking down at Quinn sat on the bed.

Quinn looked askance at Xandy. Erin moved to the side, watching the proceedings.

"The two guys who helped you told some reporters about how you lifted that roof yourself, and that they had a hard time holding it, so they couldn't figure out how you did by yourself. That's prompted replays of the white knight footage..." Xandy winked at her. "You're famous again, babe."

"Son of a…" Quinn muttered, shaking her head.

"Let's take a look here," the doctor said, pulling a chair over to the bed, his eyes already scanning the various cuts Quinn had on her arms and her shoulder. "These don't look bad," he said, taking a bottle and some dressing out of his bag.

He cleaned the cuts, and put a bandage on the ones he felt needed one.

"Show him your back," Xandy said.

Quinn nodded and leaned forward, wincing and sucking her breath in sharply as she did, her muscles protesting wildly.

The doctor leaned forward, touching the area around the wound and felt Quinn jump sharply.

"Oh, I don't like the way this looks," the doctor said, reaching into his bag again, this time drawing out a pouch with tools.

The doctor took a pair of tweezers, leaned in close to Quinn's back, and picked at something in the wound. Quinn did her best not to jump as the metal grazed her. Xandy walked over, taking Quinn's hand squeezing it gently. Quinn gritted her teeth as he seemed to dig into her back. She made a grunting sound when she felt him grab at something clearly stuck in her.

The doctor held up a piece of glass that had been lodged in the wound.

"Normally I would insist you go to a hospital for this kind of wound," he told Quinn, as he set aside the piece of glass. "But I know that the hospitals are flooded with people right now and you don't look like you want to sit anywhere for hours on end," he said, seeing that Quinn was exhausted.

"However," he said, his face indicating that she wasn't going to like what he was going to say next. "We're going to need to clean this thoroughly, it's a pretty nasty puncture wound and they can get infected easily…" He shook his head, looking grim. "It's likely to be unpleasant, but I can give you a shot to help with the pain."

"No, you can't," Quinn said, her look as grim as the doctor's had been.

"You don't like needles?" the doctor assumed.

Quinn gave a short laugh. "I wish it was that easy."

When the doctor looked perplexed Xandy said, "She's allergic, deathly allergic."

"Oh," the doctor said, "well, I can give you some Vicodin…" His voice trailed off as Quinn shook her head to that as well. "Is there anything you can take?"

"Not really, no," Quinn said.

"Erin," Xandy said, suddenly noticing the girl still in the room, "can you go and get the bottle of Jack Daniel's from the bar?"

Erin blinked a couple of times, but then nodded. She walked out of the room and reappearing a few minutes later with the full bottle of Jack Daniel's. She handed the bottle to Xandy, who handed it to Quinn. Quinn twisted off the top, breaking the seal, and tipped the bottle up, chugging a third of it while they looked on.

The doctor looked at Xandy. "The only pain killer she can take?"

"Yep," Xandy said nodding.

Quinn moved to lay face down on the bed, as the alcohol flowed through her veins. Tucking a pillow under her chest, she glanced over her left shoulder.

"Let's get it over with, doc," she said, her Northern Irish accent clear in the room.

Xandy moved to Quinn's right side, her hand on Quinn's shoulder, looking worried. Quinn glanced up at her, wincing sharply as the doctor started to clean the wound.

At one point, Elly came running into the room and clamored up on the bed next to Quinn. Quinn grimaced as the girl's eyes widened at what was obviously going on with Quinn's back.

"Kin hurt?" Elly queried.

"Yeah, just a little bit," she said, as she gasped loudly.

"Stop hurting Kin!" Elly yelled at the doctor. In any other situation this would have been considered cute, but at that moment Quinn just needed her out of the way.

"Xan…" Quinn gritted out, shaking her head.

Erin stepped forward. "Elly, come with me," she said, putting her hand out to the younger girl

"No, stay with Kin," Elly said, her voice petulant.

"Elly," Quinn said, forcing herself to sound normal, "can you please go with Erin?"

Elly looked rebellious.

"Please baby girl?" Quinn asked, gritting her teeth. Fortunately the doctor had stopped for the moment due to the interruption… and being yelled at by a six-year-old.

"Okay," Elly finally said, moving to take Erin's hand.

After the two left the doctor resumed his work on Quinn's back. Quinn clenched and unclenched her fists as he moved, picking bits of debris out of the wound track. At one point Quinn loudly cried out as he had to dig particularly deep into the wound. Xandy went to grab her hand, but Quinn yanked it away.

"No, babe," Quinn gritted out, "I'd break your hand right now." She gasped, the pain radiating throughout her body as the doctor continued to do his work.

Xandy watched in tears as the doctor continued to clean the wound. Sarah, brought to the door by Quinn's cry, moved to Xandy's side, putting her arms around the girl and watching the doctor work, her look concerned.

Finally, the doctor was finished. He looked at Xandy.

"You're going to need to watch this closely," he said as he bandaged the wound. "If it gets red, if there are red streaks from it, or if it appears hot or really painful to the touch around the area, you need to get her to a hospital right away. An infection here will be debilitating, and can result in a lot of internal damage."

He stood up, reaching into his bag and pulling out a subscription pad. "I'm going to write a prescription for a heavy duty antibiotic. I can give you one now to start with," he said reaching into his bag and drawing out a bottle. He opened the bottle and hand Quinn a pill. "If you'll get her some water..." he began, but trailed off as Quinn popped the pill into her mouth and swallowed it. "Oh, never mind," he said, grinning, "I forgot I was dealing with Wonder Woman." he winked at Quinn.

The doctor left a list of instructions for treating the wounds. Quinn chugged the rest of the JD bottle and fell into a restless sleep. Out in the living room, Xandy sat with her family for a bit, but then went into check on Quinn. She fell asleep lying next to Quinn, her hand on Quinn's shoulder.

Chapter 10

Most of them slept the next day away. Quinn woke late in the afternoon, her back in a series of knots that had her gasping out loud as she tried to get out of bed. Xandy heard her gasp and turned over immediately.

"Quinn?" Xandy queried, seeing that Quinn was sitting on the edge of the bed, her hands gripping the mattress on either side of her.

Xandy heard Quinn blow her breath out slowly but audibly as she pushed herself up to her feet with a loud groan. She reached out her hand, placing it on the dresser in front of her, bracing herself as she breathed heavily.

Getting up, Xandy stood behind Quinn, touching her shoulder.

"Babe?" she queried softly.

Quinn nodded. "I'm okay, just sore as all hell," she said, her voice reflecting the pain she was in.

"I'll call the doctor, ask him to prescribe some muscle relaxers, those should be okay, right?" Xandy asked.

Quinn nodded. "I'm gonna go take a shower to see if I can soak some of this out."

"Okay," Xandy said nodding.

As it turned out, between the muscle relaxers and the overall exhaustion Quinn was feeling, she ended up eating room service and going back to bed shortly after her shower. Xandy spent time in the living area of the room with her family. At one point while the kids were watching TV with Erin, Xandy and Sarah sat at the dining room table talking.

"I still can't believe what she did," Sarah was saying, speaking about Quinn's feat. "After all that I said... as nasty as I was..." she said, letting her voice trail off as she shook her head.

Xandy grinned. "Well, Quinn isn't one to hold a grudge," she told her aunt, "and she thinks that family is the most important thing in the world, and you're my only family now."

Sarah drew in a breath, looking pained. "And instead of being supportive of you, I was mean."

Xandy gave her a direct look. "Yes, you were," she said, but there was no tone of accusation in her voice.

"I'm sorry for that," Sarah said, looking like she truly was. "I don't know what I would have done if you two hadn't shown up..." she said, shaking her head. "With Elly stuck where she was, I don't know if anyone would have gotten to us in time. There's no way I could have done what Quinn did."

Xandy nodded, understanding exactly how her aunt felt, because she'd been thinking the same thing since the night before. There hadn't been any emergency services on-site, not only when they'd gotten to the scene, but even after Quinn had already gotten Elly out. Who knows how long it would have taken for someone to be there to help?

"No one seems to understand how she did what she did," Erin said, walking over to the table and sitting down with them.

She'd heard them talking and wanted to hear what they were saying. She too was extremely grateful to Quinn for saving her little sister. Every newscast she'd seen on the incident had stated that what Quinn had done was not only heroic, but somehow almost superhuman. Naturally, to a woman lifting a car off her baby had been made, and adrenaline and the power of it had also been discussed by others on the newscasts. Regardless, Quinn Kavanaugh was being held up as a hero, and the phone had been ringing all morning asking Quinn for interviews. Xandy had finally asked the desk to block the calls to the room. Xandy knew Quinn, it wasn't likely she'd do an interview, and if she did, it wouldn't be any time soon.

"I told her I didn't understand how she did it, when those two huge men could barely hold that section of roof together," Xandy said.

"What did she say?" Sarah asked.

"That she 'had to.' " Xandy said simply, shaking her head.

"Why?" Erin asked, looking perplexed. "Elly isn't her family, and no matter how much she loves you, that doesn't change that."

"Erin!" Sarah exclaimed shocked at her daughter's forthright comments.

"Well, hell, Mom," Erin said, "from what I'm hearing, you were a royal bitch to both of them, so why would this woman who barely knows any of us take the chance of being crushed to save one little girl?"

Sarah stared back at her daughter open-mouthed, though she had to admit, it was along the lines she'd been thinking. Leave it to her headstrong, impossible daughter to say it the way she had.

Xandy shook her head, looking full of pride for the woman that slept in the other room. "Because that's who Quinn Kavanaugh is."

The other two women looked back at her, each quite surprised by the statement.

"Well, we're damned lucky she is who she is, then," Erin stated indisputably.

"Indeed," Sarah said, nodding.

The rest of the day was spent with the kids, trying to keep them entertained and away from Quinn. Both Bobby and Elly wanted to check on Quinn often, but Xandy knew that Quinn needed to rest and recharge, so she limited the amount of times the door to the bedroom was opened.

Later that night Xandy told everyone good night and went into the bedroom. She looked over at Quinn who lay on her right side, her arms extended out in front of her, the bandage on her left arm from a nasty cut white against her skin. Moving as quietly as she possibly could, Xandy changed her clothes to more comfortable sleeping attire. By the time she walked toward the bed, Quinn's eyes were open.

"Hi," Xandy said, smiling.

"Hi," Quinn said, smiling tiredly, opening her arms to invite Xandy to lie down.

Xandy lay down in front of Quinn as carefully as she could, putting her back to Quinn's chest. Quinn's arms encircled her pulling her closer. She smiled as Quinn nuzzled her neck with her lips. They fell asleep lying that way.

Quinn started awake to the feel of a touch to her wrist. Opening her eyes, she saw Bobby standing next to the bed, his eyes on her.

"Bobby," Quinn whispered, "what's up?"

"What is this?" Bobby asked, touching the tattoo on her wrist.

Quinn grinned; kids ask the damndest things in the middle of the night.

"It's Irish Gaelic," she told him.

"Oh," Bobby said, nodding, "what does it say?"

"It says 'An làmb a bheir, 's i a gheibh.' " she grinned as she remembered a similar conversation with Xandy about this very tattoo.

Bobby's eyes widened in awe at the way Quinn said the Gaelic words. "So what does that mean?"

"It means 'the hand that gives is the hand that gets,' " Quinn told him and seeing he didn't understand that she said, "Basically do good things and good things will happen to you."

Bobby nodded again, then pinned Quinn with a direct look. "Like saving my sister?"

Quinn drew in a breath, nodding slowly.

"Even when my mom was mean to you," Bobby said, remembering what his mother had said, and that cousin Xandy had told his mom she'd been mean.

Quinn smiled ruefully. "Yes, even then."

"Why was she mean to you?" Bobby asked.

Quinn pressed her lips together, trying to decide what she wanted to say.

"I think she was scared," Quinn said simply and honestly.

"Of you?" Bobby asked, but looking like he could believe that.

"Yes," Quinn said, but reached out to touch his arm, "but I don't mean in the way you think. I mean that she's probably never met anyone like me before," she said, holding up her tattooed arms, gesturing to her short hair. "So that scared her."

Bobby looked like he was considering the idea. "But she likes you now?"

Quinn drew in a breath, then blew it out. "I guess," she said, "I don't know for sure really. I think she's probably really grateful that I got Elly out, but that doesn't mean she likes me."

"Well, I like you," Bobby said, his look firm.

Quinn smiled. "I like you too."

Bobby glanced to the windows in the room as lightning shot across the sky, his look fearful. Quinn glanced over her shoulder seeing the lightning as well.

"Bobby, are you afraid of the storm?" Quinn asked gently, not wanting to insult him, but sensing that it was what had drawn him into the bedroom in the first place.

Bobby looked back at her, at first his look was brave, but then he sagged slightly, lowering his head and nodding.

"It's okay, you know," Quinn told him. "Those storms scare me too."

He looked back at her wide-eyed. "They do?"

"Yeah," Quinn said nodding, she canted her head slightly. "Did you want to stay in here with us?"

"Do you think I could?" Bobby asked.

"You should check with your mom," Quinn said wisely.

"Okay," Bobby said and was off in a flash.

In the living room, Sarah was sleeping on the rollaway bed with Elly next to her, and Erin was sleeping on the couch. Bobby climbed up on the bed, shaking his mother's shoulder roughly in his need to ask his question.

"What is it Bobby?" Sarah asked, trying to blink open her eyes as she did.

"Is it okay if I go sleep in Quinn and Xandy's room? Quinn said I had to ask you."

Sarah thought about it for a moment, then nodded. "As long as it's okay with them, then yes, you can."

"Great!" Bobby exclaimed loudly and jumped off the bed, running back to the bedroom of the hotel room.

Elly turned over rubbing her eyes sleepily as he left.

Back in the bedroom, Bobby walked over to the bed, hoping Quinn wasn't asleep again. Quinn's eyes were open and looking at him.

"Mom says as long as it's okay with you," Bobby said.

"That works for me," Quinn said, winking, "go 'round there," she said, pointing to the end of the bed.

Bobby nodded, and went around the bed, climbing in behind her and Xandy. It was a king sized bed; Quinn and Xandy were only on a very small portion of it, so there was plenty of room. Quinn turned over onto her back wincing as she did, but she looked over at Bobby. His head was on a pillow a foot away. He smiled at her, and she smiled back at him. Then they both closed their eyes. A minute later, Quinn felt movement, and glancing down she saw Elly climbing up on the bed. The child climbed right between Bobby and Quinn, snuggling between Quinn's left arm and her body, putting her head on Quinn's shoulder.

Quinn looked back into the big blue eyes that now stared back at her.

"Hello little one," Quinn said, grinning.

"Seep here," Elly pronounced firmly.

"Okay then," Quinn said, nodding with a grin.

Xandy, awakened by Quinn's movement and the subsequent talking looked over at her two cousins, then down at Quinn.

"Apparently we're having a sleep over," Quinn told her.

"Apparently," Xandy said, smiling.

It warmed Xandy's heart that the kids seemed to naturally gravitate to Quinn. Regardless of her tough exterior, Quinn had a huge heart and the fact that the children recognized that in her, said a lot. It was too bad adults didn't have that innate instinct about people, seeing beyond outward appearances. A few minutes later the four were asleep again.

Erin stuck her head around the door checking on the kids per her mom's request. She'd heard Elly leave the living area. She saw the way the four were laid together. Xandy lay with her head in the hollow of Quinn's right shoulder, and Quinn's arm was around her shoulders. On Quinn's left side, Elly was lying much like Xandy, her tiny hand on Quinn's shoulder. Bobby lay on the other side of Elly, farther up on the bed, so he too could put his hand on Quinn's shoulder right next to his sister's hand.

Erin stood there staring at the picture they made, thinking about what her mom and Xandy had said about Quinn earlier in the day. Quinn Kavanaugh certainly had a quality about her that drew people to her; it was a quality Erin couldn't put her finger on, but she knew that it was powerful.

The next day Sarah carefully opened the door to the bedroom and saw her children sleeping with Quinn and Xandy. She saw the way both Bobby and Elly seemed to need a physical connection with the woman. All her life Sarah had been raised to believe that homosexuality was an abomination and that people who were gay were sick and should never be tolerated. If it hadn't been for this particular homosexual, her baby daughter would likely be lying in a morgue at the Harvey County Coroner's office, instead of here in a fancy hotel room with her savior. Sarah knew that she'd been completely wrong to judge Quinn by her appearance and the fact that she preferred women over men.

She noticed with a start that Quinn's eyes were open and looking at her.

Walking over to the side of the bed, she whispered, "Good morning," with a soft smile.

"Mornin'," Quinn said, grinning as she glanced at the kids to her left; neither had moved an inch.

"I can take them…" Sarah said softly, shaking her head.

"They're fine," Quinn said, smiling warmly.

Moving carefully to sit up, Quinn stretched, wincing as her muscles protested. She climbed carefully out of bed, doing her best not to disturb any of the three still lying there. Xandy stirred, glancing up at her.

"Getting up?" Xandy asked.

"Yeah," Quinn said, "you sleep though, babe, you have a long day ahead of you."

Xandy nodded tiredly, and went back to sleep.

Quinn nodded toward the bedroom door and gestured for Sarah to precede her. Sarah noted the gallant gesture and realized that Quinn did that kind of thing a lot.

Out in the main part of the room, Erin was still asleep on the couch. Quinn walked over to the Keurig coffee maker and stood staring at it like it was a foreign object.

"I've got it for you," Sarah said, grinning at Quinn. "We've kind of been playing with it."

Quinn nodded moving out of the way.

"What would you like?" Sarah asked. "There's pretty much everything: hot chocolate, hot tea, French roast coffee, espresso, Cinnabon coffee, vanilla nut…"

"Good God," Quinn said, rolling her eyes, "is there just regular jet fuel level coffee?"

"Aw,' Sarah said, nodding. "I think that would be this," she said holding up a K-Cup marked "Bitch Slap."

Quinn read the name and laughed out loud, nodding. "Yeah, that'll do it."

A few minutes later Quinn was seated at the dining room table with a cup of "Bitch Slap" in her hands. Sarah sat down in the chair next to her. Quinn's chair was turned to the side, so they faced each other.

Sarah canted her head slightly looking at Quinn. "You should know that my kids don't usually attach themselves to someone as quickly as they have with you."

Quinn looked considering. "I'm sure their lives aren't usually in complete upheaval like this either."

Sarah looked back at Quinn, thinking that this woman sure didn't take credit for things easily.

"They took to you that very first time you visited," Sarah told Quinn, "and even that was unusual for them." She grimaced thinking that it was probably because of her sour disposition over the last few years since their father had left them.

Quinn could see the guilt on Sarah's face and wondered at it.

"It seems like things have been hard for you," Quinn said. Her tone held no judgment.

Sarah drew in a deep breath, blowing it out as she nodded. "Making ends meet is always really hard."

"Do you mind me asking where their father is? Does he contribute at all?" Quinn asked gently.

Sarah smiled at her attempt to be gentle. "No, he's gone with his new family."

Quinn grimaced. "I'm sorry."

Sarah shrugged. "He was a louse for years," she said. "I just kept thinking that if he got that next job, or we had another baby, or if I was a better wife…"

Quinn shook her head. "You can't control anyone but yourself."

Sarah looked back at Quinn, thinking about that, then she nodded her head. "If that's true, then I haven't even been doing that well."

"What do you mean?" Quinn asked.

"I mean, I've let my sour attitude affect my kids," Sarah said, looking mournful. "I just can't help it sometimes. It's like I can't see a way out, and I just get so unhappy that I just want to curl up into a ball and cry…"

"Sarah," Quinn said, sitting forward, "Xandy is being treated for depression. Is it possible that's what's happening with you too?"

Sarah looked surprised by the question and started to shake her head.

"What do you know about depression?" Quinn asked her.

Sarah shook her head again. "Not much."

"It's probably something you should check out."

"Xandy has it?" Sarah asked, looking concerned. "Is it bad?"

Quinn looked back at her for a long moment, then held up her right hand exposing her palm. Sarah could see the still red line from the heel of her hand to just under her thumb.

"I got this when I slapped the razor blade out of Xandy's hand. The one she used to slice open her wrist."

"Oh my lord…" Sarah breathed looking sad.

"It wasn't the first time she'd tried it either," Quinn told her.

Sarah breathed in deeply, looking shaky, but nodded. "I guess bad doesn't begin to cover it," she said.

"She's better now," Quinn said, "but she's seeing a counselor and she's on medication."

"And she has you," Sarah said, her look direct.

Quinn smiled, nodding.

"So you saved her life," Sarah said.

Quinn nodded, not looking too impressed with herself.

"And you saved my child," Sarah said, wanting to make sure Quinn really saw the whole picture.

Quinn looked back at Sarah, sensing what she was trying to do.

Sarah shook her head. "So much humility… and to think I thought you were a Godless heathen," she said, her eyes sparkling.

Quinn chuckled at the term. "I've actually been called worse."

Sarah smiled, but could tell that Quinn was serious about part of what she'd said. She shook her head, not able to imagine being treated badly simply for her appearance and for what people, like Sarah herself, thought that meant in terms of her quality of character.

"She's also a bad ass," Erin said from the couch.

Quinn and Sarah looked over to where the girl sat on the couch, not realizing she'd woken at some point during the conversation. In truth, Erin had heard the entire conversation.

"Erin!" Sarah chided her. "Such language."

"Oh come off it Mom," Erin said rolling her eyes, "that's what they're calling her on the news and on YouTube. Quinn's famous!"

Sarah looked over at Quinn, seeing the way the other woman dropped her head, shaking it ruefully.

"I'm guessing you don't want to be famous?" Sarah asked.

Quinn sighed loudly. "Uh, no, that's your niece's area."

Sarah smiled glancing over at Erin who also smiled, Quinn Kavanaugh certainly wasn't any kind of attention seeker. Like Xandy had said, Quinn was who she was, and she wasn't looking for any kind of award for it.

Later in the morning, Mackie arrived from California to prepare for the concert; the first of which was that night. He'd heard what Quinn had done, having seen the news and he'd also heard from BJ that Quinn was somewhat out of commission. Mackie knew that Quinn would want to make sure Xandy was protected during her sound check and rehearsals at the arena that afternoon, so he'd come early. The other bands would be arriving later that afternoon, but they had their own security details; Quinn was unofficially still Xandy's protection.

When Mackie arrived, Quinn was back in the bedroom, trying to rest her back so she'd be up for the show that night. Mackie walked in, after knocking lightly and being bid to come in by Quinn.

"Hey, it's Ms. Badassery herself," he said, smiling at the woman who was sitting up in bed.

"Feck ya," Quinn said, shaking her head smiling all the while.

"How ya doin'?" Mackie asked assessing her.

"Muscle relaxants are doing the trick," Quinn said. "Thanks for handling this today though."

"You know you ain't getting paid to be her protection at this point, right?" Mackie said, no question in his voice.

"And you know that don't mean shite to me, right?" Quinn countered.

Mackie grinned. "Pretty much."

"Good," Quinn said. "'Cause if she gets hurt, it's your head I'm takin' off," she informed him mildly, but Mackie knew she meant it.

"Got it." Mackie nodded.

Normally he would discount most threats, being over six foot and two hundred pounds of pure muscle. Combined with his Navy Seal training, he was more dangerous than most. Quinn Kavanaugh, however, wasn't someone he would want to mess with; the woman was a definite force to be reckoned with. He wasn't going to test that by letting himself be lax with Xandy's protection.

Xandy and Mackie left the hotel room a few minutes later, with Xandy kissing Quinn and asking her to rest, which Quinn agreed to.

"We're taking the kids and Sarah with us, so you should be able to rest completely," Xandy told her.

"Yes, ma'am."

Five minutes after they'd left the hotel room, Quinn heard a knock on the bedroom door.

"Yeah?" Quinn queried, wondering if maybe the maid was trying to clean the room or something.

The door opened and Erin stuck her head inside. "Can I talk to you?"

"I thought you all left with Xandy?"

"No, I stayed behind."

"Oh… Kay…" Quinn said, and then gestured, "yeah, come on in."

Erin walked into the room. Quinn looked at the girl; she wore tattered faded jeans, and a dirty white tank top with a black bra underneath. Her eyes were smeared with black eyeliner and she wore dark lipstick, she had a rat's nest of short blond hair. The kid was definitely going for the grungy unwashed teenager look.

"So what's up?" Quinn asked.

Erin looked hesitant now that she was there.

Quinn waited patiently. She sat with her knees up, feet planted on the bed, arms draped over her knees. She was dying for cigarette, but since she couldn't smoke in the room, she'd been off them for two full days now. With Erin's continued silence, Quinn decided that maybe it was too tough for her to talk when Quinn was sitting in bed, looking like an invalid.

"Come on," Quinn said, reaching over to pick up her pack of cigarettes and her lighter.

Erin followed her. Quinn wore her black lounge pants and green football sleeveless jersey, her feet were bare. They walked out onto the balcony of the room. Quinn moved to sit in one of the chairs, bringing one knee up to her chest, her foot on the chair as she reached for a cigarette. She lit up and took a deep drag on the cigarette, making a sound of pleasure as she did.

"Christ that's good…" she said, grinning as she motioned for Erin to have a seat.

Erin sat down, her eyes on Quinn, but hesitation still clear on her face.

"Erin," Quinn said, "tell me what's going on."

"Um," Erin began, "well, I wanted to ask you…"

Quinn waited as the girls voice trailed off.

"You know you actually have to ask the question, right?" Quinn said, grinning. "I'm not psychic."

Erin laughed in spite of herself. "I'm sure they're going to say you are soon."

Quinn made a face. "Okay, but for right now, let's assume I'm not."

Erin took a deep breath, sighing. "How did you know you were gay?"

Quinn stared back at the girl, feeling like she'd had this conversation far too recently to be having it again with a different member of the same family.

"How do you know you're straight?" she asked in her usual offhanded manner when it came to this question.

"I don't think I am. That's the thing." Erin said.

Quinn stared back at the girl for a full minute, then sat back and took another drag off her cigarette.

"Well, that's another thing, isn't it?" Quinn asked, her tone more gentle this time.

Erin looked sad suddenly.

Quinn canted her head. "Is that why you've been runnin' off on your mom?"

Erin pulled both her knees up to her chest, her head lowered as she nodded.

Quinn nodded too, starting to understand a little better.

"Obviously she doesn't know..." Quinn said.

Erin snickered. "She wouldn't know if I shoved a rainbow up her nose."

Quinn grimaced. "So you obviously don't need my help in figuring out if you're gay…"

Erin shook her head. "I know I'm gay," she said. "I guess that was just trying to figure out how to ask what I wanted to ask."

"So, what did you want to ask me, then?" Quinn asked

"I guess I just don't know what to do," Erin said.

"What do you want to do?"

Erin shrugged. "Sometimes I just want to run away and be able to be myself where no one knows me. Other times…"

Quinn narrowed her eyes slightly, afraid she already knew the answer. "Other times wot, Erin?"

Erin shrugged, picking at the thread bared knees of her jeans, her eyes cast downward.

Stubbing out her cigarette Quinn stood up, walking over to the girl. When Erin still didn't look at her, Quinn knelt down, looking up into the girls face.

"Other times wot?" Quinn asked again.

Erin stared really hard at her knees, but Quinn could see tears welling up in her eyes. Quinn put her hand on Erin's leg, and that's when the water works really started. Quinn moved to stand, leaning over to hug the girl as she cried.

"Your cousin will tell you that I suck with crying women," Quinn said.

Erin laughed, her face still buried against Quinn's shirt. After a couple of minutes, Erin seemed to calm down a bit. Quinn pulled her chair closer to where Erin sat and sat down.

"You never have to get to that place," Quinn told her, "you have options."

Erin shook her head sadly. "Not really."

"Why do you say that?"

"Because if my mom finds out she'll kick me out."

"Then you'll come live in LA with us," Quinn answered.

Erin's head snapped up, and the amount of hope in her eyes was almost painful to Quinn.

"You'd let me do that?" she asked

Quinn nodded. "Obviously it wouldn't be the best option, it would be better if you told your mom and the two of you could work things out."

"I don't know if that's going to happen," Erin said.

"Well, we'll just have to see."

"We?"

Quinn nodded. "We."

By the time Xandy and the group got back to the hotel room, Quinn and Erin were watching Women's Soccer on the living room TV. As the group walked in, both Quinn and Erin yelled in triumph at a goal that was just made.

"I see you got a lot of rest," Xandy said, grinning at Quinn as she moved to kiss her.

"Well, there was soccer…" Quinn said, grinning.

"Uh-huh…" Xandy said nodding and winking at Erin.

Elly and Bobby ran over to Quinn throwing themselves at her, hugging her.

"Did you two have a good time?" Quinn asked.

"Yeah!" they both said joyously.

Quinn dropped her head to the back of the couch, looking back at Mackie. "Everything go okay?"

"Ten-four," Mackie said, grinning. "I'll be back at five to pick you guys up. You gonna be up for the show?"

"I am," Quinn said, nodding. Moving to stand she walked around the couch and extended her hand to Mackie. "Thanks man."

"You got it," Mackie said, shaking her hand and nodding to Xandy as he left the room.

Quinn walked over to Xandy putting her hand out to her. "Can I talk to you for a sec?"

Xandy looked surprised, but nodded as she took Quinn's hand letting her pull her into the bedroom. Quinn kicked the door closed, seeing Erin looking concerned as she did.

"What's wrong?" Xandy asked.

"Nothing," Quinn said, pulling her close and kissing her, "but, I need to tell you something."

"What?" Xandy asked.

Quinn hesitated for a minute, and then said, "Erin's gay."

Xandy looked back at her for a long moment, her eyes wide. "Okay…"

"She wanted to talk to me about it," Quinn said. "Xan she's thought about suicide over it."

"Oh my God…" Xandy said, shaking her head. "Apparently depression isn't limited to me in this family, huh?"

Quinn gave her an odd look, which had her asking, "What?"

"Sounds like your aunt might have a bit of it herself," she said.

Xandy thought about it, and nodded, it made sense.

"What can we do to help Erin? And my aunt?"

"Well, I can tell you that Erin's concern is that if Sarah finds out, she'll kick her out," she said, leaning back against the door to the room. "I told her if that happened, then she could come live with us in LA."

Xandy looked surprised by that, but then realized she shouldn't be. Quinn would do whatever it took to protect her family, it was apparent that now Quinn considered Xandy's family as her own.

"Speaking of which…" Xandy said, taking Quinn's hand and leading her over to the bed, pulling her down to sit with her. "I wanted to talk to you about something."

"Okay," Quinn said.

"I want to invite my aunt to come stay with us in LA while we figure things out here."

Quinn nodded, expecting more. Xandy looked at her waiting for an answer.

Quinn gave her a quizzical look. "Are you asking me if you can do that?"

"Yes," Xandy said.

"Xan, it's your house," Quinn told her.

"Well, yeah, but you live there with me now and I don't want to put you in a position where you're stuck with my family and wishing to God you'd kept your apartment."

Quinn chuckled at that, but then gave Xandy a serious look. "Babe, they're your family, of course you need to offer them help, and you offer them whatever you want."

Xandy looked back at her and smiled. "Have I told you how much I love you yet today?"

"I don't think you have…" Quinn said, grinning.

"How about I show you instead?" Xandy said, suggestively moving toward the door and locking it.

Walking back over to Quinn, Xandy moved to straddle Quinn's lap and leaned down to kiss her deeply. Quinn's hands slid around Xandy's waist, pulling her closer and sliding up under her shirt. Things got heated pretty quickly since it had been days since they'd made love. Xandy had just pushed Quinn back on the bed, having pulled off her jersey, when there was a knock on the door; a knock that sounded like that of a tiny little fist. Quinn and Xandy looked toward the door, pausing what they were doing. They heard Erin call to Elly to come back and watch cartoons. Quinn and Xandy exchanged a grin, pretty sure that Erin was aware of what was going on.

They made love, but had to make sure they stayed quiet so as not to give away their secret. They laughed about it afterwards.

"So that's what it's like to be a parent," Quinn said, grinning as they both pulled their clothes back on.

"I guess so," Xandy said, giggling.

At five that evening, Mackie arrived to take them to the show. Quinn wore black leather pants with two inch heeled Harley Davidson boots and a rich emerald-green button down shirt. Over that she wore a black leather Harley Davidson jacket that was cut to fit perfectly. The jacket had Harley Davidson stitched across the chest in silver and emerald, and the back featured a black and emerald set of angel wings. Xandy was stunned by her girlfriend's appearance, falling in lust with her all over again.

"Oh my…" Xandy said, running her hand over the stitching on the jacket, her eyes showing very obvious appreciation for Quinn's ensemble.

Quinn grinned, she didn't dress up very often, and she hadn't really done so for Xandy yet. She did, however, thoroughly enjoy Xandy's reaction.

Xandy wore a well cut lace and silk dress that was the same color as her eyes. It emphasized her tiny waist and perfect tiny shape, and with heels she was a little closer to Quinn's height.

"I have to say you look pretty damned good too, babe," Quinn grinned.

Xandy smiled brightly. "Thanks!"

When they walked out of the bedroom together, Sarah and Erin were stunned and made noises to reflect that. Bobby and Elly were awestruck as well.

The group proceeded the mere two blocks to the arena, arriving through the back. Both Mackie and Quinn were acting as Xandy's security as they entered. Back stage they met up with Jordan, the members of Fast Lane, as well as Devlin McGregor and Tabitha.

"Beege is running late, as usual," Devlin said, grinning.

"Such a princess…" said one of the members of Fast Lane.

"Did you learn nothing from that last tour?" Jordan said, grinning.

The man leaned forward extending his hand to Quinn. "I'm Tommy. I've heard about you," he said winking.

Quinn shook her head, closing her eyes for a moment. "It's just never going to stop, is it?"

Tommy laughed, as did the rest of the group.

"Unintentional star," Tommy said, "sucks, huh?"

"And I can't sing worth a damn," Quinn said, grinning.

Later during the concert, BJ Sparks made a speech about why they were there. When he introduced Xandy people cheered wildly. Xandy walked out on stage, smiling and waving to the audience.

"As many of you know, I'm from around here," Xandy said, smiling, "and some of you may know that a couple of nights ago, my family was once again affected by the plague of Kansas. Fortunately, everyone made it out okay. That was with the help of someone very special to me…" she said, turning to look side stage to wink at Quinn who was standing off to her left.

"Quinn!" someone yelled, and others repeated the name. Suddenly everyone was chanting Quinn's name.

Backstage Quinn shook her head, rolling her eyes. For her, this was a nightmare; she never wanted to be in the spotlight.

BJ walked over to her. "You know they're not going to shut up until you go out there, right?"

"Are you fecking kidding me?" Quinn said. Unfortunately she didn't realize that BJ had a mike in his hand which had picked up what she said. The crowd just laughed.

Someone backstage yelled, "Mike's on!"

BJ laughed, looking at Quinn. She knew in an instant he'd done it on purpose.

"I'm gonna kill ya, you maggot bastard!" Quinn said, shaking her head, even as she couldn't help but smile.

BJ laughed out loud. "Yeah, I know. Now go," he said, nodding his head toward the stage.

Finally Quinn strode out on stage, shaking her head. She strode right up to Xandy, and as she reached her, she slid her hand around Xandy's neck, and pulled Xandy to her, leaning down and taking possession of her lips in a hungry kiss; her other hand reaching up to cup Xandy's face gently. The crowd went wild, especially when Xandy melted into Quinn's arms, and slid her arms up Quinn's chest, grabbing two handfuls of the leather jacket. The cameras caught every second and projected the moment on the wide-screens in the arena.

They kissed for what seemed like forever, and the crowd continued to scream and cheer. When Quinn finally broke the kiss, Xandy stared up at her dazed, but her eyes sparkling as she started to smile. Quinn continued to look down into her eyes, ignoring the crowd, her hand was still at Xandy's cheek, her thumb brushed upward over her cheekbone.

She leaned in once again, kissing Xandy on the temple and whispering, "I love you."

With that, she stepped back and without ever even glancing at the crowd turned and strode back off stage. Xandy stood where she was, watching Quinn's retreat like the dazed lover that she was.

Finally she turned back to the crowd. "Yeah, that was Quinn," she said, her proud smile a mile wide.

Backstage, Quinn continued to walk, intent on going out to smoke. Tommy and Devlin both held their hands up for a high five as she walked by them. She laughed, high fiving both men as she walked past.

"Very classy," Jordan said, nodding appreciatively.

"Very hot," Cassie Roads said, smiling widely.

Quinn got outside of the doors to the arena, pulling out a cigarette and lighting it. She was still smoking five minutes later when BJ emerged.

"Nicely done," he said, "it's taken her this long to calm them down. I finally had to send Devlin out there to do a riff to shut them up."

Quinn chuckled, shaking her head.

"You better know that action probably just sold her millions of albums worldwide."

Quinn shook her head again. "Didn't do it for effect."

"That's what I love about you," BJ said. "You are all action all the time."

"What the hell was that?" Mackie asked as he walked through the door.

Quinn laughed out loud, taking a long drag on her cigarette.

"That," Quinn said, pointing back toward the stage with her cigarette, "was me not letting my girl down."

"I don't think there was a dry seat in the house," Mackie said, with a salacious grin.

BJ slapped his leg. "And that's the makings of a star," he said, winking at Quinn.

"Forget it," Quinn said, narrowing her eyes at him. "Can't sing for shit."

BJ snickered. "I can make anyone into a singer, what I can't create is stage presence and you got that in spades."

"Fuck you BJ, no," Quinn said simply.

BJ and Mackie exchanged a look, each grinning. They both liked Quinn Kavanaugh a great deal.

A few minutes later, the three went back into the arena and the show truly began. Quinn watched in awe of Xandy as she sang and danced. Her voice hit notes that Quinn didn't know existed, and she found herself immensely proud to be dating this beautiful girl with so much talent.

The second show, the next night, had sold out just as quickly as the first. The numerous phone videos and the feed from the first concert showing Xandy and Quinn had already gone viral. So by the time BJ called Xandy out on stage, the crowd was already clamoring for Quinn to appear. This time Quinn leaned against a wall backstage, crossing her arms and her legs at the ankle, refusing to budge. At the prompting of everyone in the two bands, and Jordan Tate, she was pushed to the edge of the stage in the wings. Still, she absolutely refused to step onto stage. On this night she was dressed in jeans and a black leather vest that laced up in the front with her motorcycle boots with lower heels. Her tattoos were on full display, not that she'd ever had any intention of being on camera again that night.

Quinn stood her feet braced wide apart, her arms crossed in front of her chest, looking out at the stage where Xandy stood. The cameras in the stadium were trained on both Quinn and Xandy. Quinn was chewing gum, in an effort to curb the urge for a cigarette inside the arena. She narrowed her eyes at BJ as he called her name and then shook her head slowly.

Xandy smiled and shook her head at Quinn, knowing that Quinn had no intention of walking onto that stage. As she stood looking at this woman who she loved so much, she found that she suddenly didn't care about the crowd either. Instead, she became enthralled with this beautiful wild woman, her lips parted and she handed BJ her mike.

Taking a couple of steps toward Quinn, she saw Quinn drop her arms, giving her a curious look. Xandy bit her lip, having no idea how her brilliant blue eyes shone in that moment. Quinn felt her insides turn over and Xandy gave her a very slow, very seductive smile. As everyone in the arena quieted down to watch what was happening, Xandy lifted her hand, and crooked her index finger, beckoning Quinn to her.

Quinn's chin came up, doing her best to resist the sudden seductress she was dating. Then Xandy licked her lips and Quinn knew she was done. She took a couple of steps onto the stage then stopped, not wanting to end up in another scene. Their eyes connected and Xandy walked the extra steps to get to Quinn. Sliding her arms up around Quinn's neck, she pulled her down, her lips seeking Quinn's. They kissed and the crowd predictably went wild. The crowd went wilder still when Quinn reached down, picked Xandy up in her arms and carried her off stage as they continued to kiss.

Onstage BJ shook his head and chuckled, motioning to Jordan to get out on stage with him. Off stage, Quinn finally set Xandy down.

"I'm sorry," Xandy said, smiling up at Quinn, "I just got... caught up..."

Quinn chuckled. "S'okay babe, I knew I couldn't leave you hanging... but where the hell did that other woman come from?" she asked, smiling widely.

"What woman?" Xandy asked, perplexed.

"The one that seduced me in front of god only knows how many fecking people!" Quinn said, shaking her head.

"Oh!" Xandy said, laughing. "You like her, do you?"

"She's pretty damned hot," Quinn said, winking at her.

"Hmmm..." Xandy murmured as Devlin walked up.

"Never seen anyone upstage BJ like that before," Devlin said, grinning widely. "That was just awesome," he said, nodding his head, "and I'm betting completely unplanned..."

"I wasn't goin' out there again..." Quinn said, curling her lips in disgust at her lack of control.

"You should probably try staying on the other side of the country from her then," Tabitha put in, winking at Xandy.

It was another great night. After the show there was an after party that lasted until the wee hours of the morning. BJ did his best to try and talk Quinn into a life on-stage. Quinn absolutely refused, walking away from him a number of times. Xandy was doing her best to hold

BJ off, but he was determined. They were still laughing about it as they returned to the hotel room that morning. Sarah and the kids had long since retired to the room. Xandy and Quinn did their best to be quiet. Erin, naturally, caught them sneaking in.

"Late night, huh?" she asked, grinning at the two.

"BJ wants to make Quinn famous," Xandy said, smiling.

"Wow…" Erin said, looking at Quinn. "You want to be famous?"

"Nope," Quinn said, shaking her head.

With that she led Xandy into the bedroom where they showered, made love and fell asleep.

They slept until the next afternoon. Xandy and Quinn got up and showered, and Xandy finally did the one thing she hadn't done the entire trip: visit her family's graves. It was an emotional experience for Xandy; she cleared away leaves and weeds that had grown around the headstones. Quinn handed her the flowers they'd brought to lay on the graves.

Xandy noticed the huge difference in how she felt this time, versus when they'd laid her family to rest. This time, even though she felt very sad at the loss, she didn't get the overwhelming feeling that she should be resting there as well. Now she had a purpose and she also had Quinn with her, and she could feel Quinn's presence giving her strength.

When Xandy would start to feel overwhelmed, somehow Quinn would know and she would step up behind her, touching her. Sometimes Xandy would turn and rest her head against Quinn's chest, other times Quinn would slide her arms around Xandy's waist, holding her from behind. Xandy would lean back letting the feeling of Quinn's presence hold her steady.

They'd gotten the results from the shows; an amazing $60 million had been raised so far, and money was still coming in. Xandy knew she'd done a lot of good with the concert. She attributed it all to BJ Sparks and his support. Xandy's pre-release album sales were also amassing a great deal of interest. Good things had come out of the concert and the trip to Kansas, not the least of which was Xandy finally reuniting with the rest of her family.

That evening Xandy and Quinn arranged for Erin to stay with the kids up in the room. They took Sarah to dinner in the hotel restaurant. After they ordered, Xandy reached over touching her aunt's hand.

"You know that Quinn and I are scheduled to go back to LA tomorrow."

Sarah nodded, she'd already been thinking about what she was going to do with herself and the kids now that they no longer had a place to live.

"I wanted to talk to you about that. I found a shelter..." she began, hoping she could convince Xandy and Quinn to give them a ride to the shelter that was a couple of counties over from Witchita.

"That may not be necessary," Quinn said, grinning.

"What? Why?" Sarah asked, not understanding.

"Well, we'd like you guys to come back to LA with us," Xandy said, biting her lip. "At least for the time being."

"We can't do that..." Sarah said, shaking her head.

"Why?" Quinn asked.

Sarah hesitated. "Well, I mean, I don't have money for plane tickets, for one thing," she said, feeling embarrassed.

"We're flying on BJ's private jet, no tickets required," Xandy said smiling.

Sarah looked shocked by that answer, but then shook her head. "Xandy, it's really sweet of you to offer, but there's four of us, that's just too much…"

"She has a five bedroom house," Quinn told Sarah with a smile.

"But…" Sarah said, looking lost.

"Please let me do this for you," Xandy asked, taking her aunt's hand. "There was nothing I could do for my family, but bury them," she said with tears in her eyes. "This time I can do something, please let me."

Sarah looked back at her niece, then over at Quinn who nodded to her, affirming that she'd be helping Xandy put her ghosts to rest by accepting her offer. Finally she nodded.

"It would be really nice to see Los Angeles, and where you two live," she said smiling.

The next morning the six of them were on a plane flying back to Los Angeles.

Chapter 11

Bobby stood waiting in anticipation, he was dancing in place he was so excited. As Quinn clicked the automatic garage door opener, he squealed with delight. When he caught sight of the midnight-blue Mach 1 and the black Dodge Charger, he gasped in sheer ecstasy. He clapped his hands and ran into the garage. Quinn stood back glancing at Xandy and Erin who were both smiling widely. Sarah watched from the porch, holding Elly who had no true interests in cars.

"Quinn!" Bobby called from the garage, prompting Quinn to follow him in.

She and Bobby spent the next hour talking about the cars, and going through the differences between the cars. Quinn even popped the hoods and showed him different aspects of the engines. And then it was time for a ride, but not before Bobby spied the Harley also parked in the garage.

"You have a motorcycle too!" Bobby cried overwhelmed, but loving every second.

"Yep," Quinn said, nodding.

"Can we ride that too?" he asked, his eyes wide.

Quinn looked back toward the open garage, where Sarah had joined Erin and Xandy. Elly sat on the ground playing with dolls. She canted her head at Sarah, her way of saying, *it's up to you.*

"Helmets?" Sarah asked.

"Always," Quinn said nodding.

Sarah nodded, trusting Quinn with her son. It amazed her constantly that someone she'd been prepared to completely hate had turned out to be the most incredibly nice person. There were a number of times during the last week in Los Angeles that Sarah had seen where the appeal of Quinn was for Xandy. Quinn was very gallant, unbelievably gentle and an extremely attentive partner to Xandy. Whenever Xandy needed something, Quinn was there; if she needed to reach something in the kitchen, or to pick up a box, or if something needed fixing, Quinn took care of it. When Xandy cut her finger slicing vegetables for dinner, Quinn took care of cleaning it and putting on a band-aid. It wasn't that Xandy couldn't do things for herself, but that Quinn seemed to take pleasure in doing things for Xandy.

When Xandy had been home for her family's funeral, she'd brought Tommy with her. There hadn't been anything redeeming about Tommy that Sarah had seen. When Xandy had needed support the most, Tommy seemed more interested in his phone; he was on it constantly during the week before the funeral and even at the funeral itself. Sarah had sensed that Tommy's support didn't occur in private either.

In Quinn's case, she'd seen someone who was completely dedicated to her partner, and it spoke volumes to Sarah, changing her heart a little more every day. The fact that Quinn actually seemed to be becoming the father figure that Bobby sorely missed warmed her heart even further. The kids' father had never been what she would consider an exemplary male role model, but at least they'd had someone.

Quinn actually seemed much more patient than his father had been, and more willing to explain things to Bobby.

"Well, you'll need to pick which one we take a ride in first," Quinn said to Bobby, causing a quandary in the little boy.

"Um…" Bobby stammered, looking from one car to the next then back at the bike, indecision clear on his face. "But we get to ride in them all today?"

Quinn looked back at him for a long moment, knowing that if she gave him too much rope he'd take more. She knew she needed to set some boundaries for the boy.

"One today," she said, holding up her hand to forestall the protest instantly on Bobby's lips, "but we'll do the other two sometime this week, okay?"

Bobby looked like he really wanted to protest, but he'd already sensed that Quinn was no-nonsense about things. When she said it, she meant it. Nothing he said would change her mind, and protesting could even get the invitation taken away. He really wanted to sit in one of these cars and ride around, so he couldn't take the chance of throwing a fit.

Finally he pointed to the Mach 1 Mustang.

Quinn smiled. "Okay," she said nodding her head, "hop in. Any other takers?" she asked the girls.

"I'll go!" Erin said, holding up her hand excitedly.

Xandy smiled at Quinn, knowing that her young cousin wanted to be wherever Quinn was these days. They'd quickly formed a close bond after their chat, and Erin felt really comfortable around Quinn, safe in fact.

"Sarah?" Quinn queried with a grin.

Sarah laughed, shaking her head. "I'll stay behind and look after Elly."

"Had your chance," Quinn said, winking at her.

Reaching into her jeans, Quinn pulled out the keys to the Mustang, jingling them at Bobby. "You want to start her up?"

"Yeah!" he yelled, excited beyond belief.

Quinn motioned him around to the driver's side. She showed him how to put the key into the ignition and push in the clutch. "Now you have to hold it in," she told him, "then turn that key."

The car chugged, but didn't start. Quinn bent down, checking where Bobby's foot was on the clutch, she made an adjustment to the seat so he was closer.

"Okay, try it again, keep that clutch in," she told Bobby.

The boy pushed down as hard as he could on the clutch and reached to turn the key. When the car turned over he let out a "whoop!" He also took his foot off the clutch and the car bucked as it stalled. Because he was too close to the steering wheel, his face was on a direct path with it. Fortunately, Quinn was faster and put her hand out to stop him from colliding with the wheel. Bobby paled, and stiffened, glancing up at Quinn in near terror.

"It's okay," Quinn said, smiling at him, "it happens to me sometimes. Let's try this," she said, moving to reach around him. "Put your hand here." She put her hand on the stick shift, and Bobby did what she told him to. "Okay, now see how you can't move this right now?" she said, using her hand to help him wiggle the stick shift around.

"Yeah," Bobby said, nodding.

"Okay, that's because it's in gear," Quinn told him, "and when it's in gear and you're stopped, you have to have the clutch in," she told him, pointing to his foot that still touched the clutch pedal. "Otherwise it does what it did just now. So, let's take it out of gear before starting it this time."

"How do I do that?" Bobby asked, his face the picture of rapt curiosity.

"You hold on to the stick," Quinn said, touching her hand to his again, "and you push that clutch in, all the way down... right, just like that. Now you shift it out of gear," she used her hand to guide his smaller one, taking the car out of gear. "You see how it can wiggle back and forth freely now?" Bobby nodded. "That means it's in neutral. Now let's try starting her up again."

Bobby repeated the starting process without being told what to do, which caused Quinn to grin proudly, and the car started with a roar once again. This time it didn't stall, and Bobby threw his arms around Quinn hugging her.

Xandy and Sarah exchanged a look, both women smiling. Erin, who'd been standing on the passenger side, smiled too. It made her happy to see her little brother so happy. She knew it had everything to do with the time Quinn was taking with him. Their father had never bothered. Erin knew that she wanted to be like Quinn, she admired everything about the woman and felt like she was definitely someone to emulate.

Later, on the drive, Erin sat in the backseat so Bobby could right shotgun with Quinn. Erin noticed the easy way Quinn handled the car even at exhilarating speeds, and she noticed how her fingers drummed on the steering wheel to whatever rock song was on. She also saw, at one point that Quinn kept looking in her review mirror and checking the side mirrors. They'd been on the freeway, and Quinn took an exit near some factory building. Again she checked her rearview mirror, and Erin could see that she was suddenly tense.

"Everything okay?" Erin asked.

Quinn didn't answer for a moment. She turned a corner, glancing at Erin as she did. The look on Quinn's face was narrowed, and Erin knew something was wrong but she figured that Quinn didn't want to worry Bobby.

Quinn looked at Bobby, smiling. "Okay, now, I need you to hold on, okay?" she said, glancing back at Erin. "Both of you."

When both kids had secured a hold, Quinn put her foot down on the pedal and the car shot forward with a surprising amount of speed. Bobby let out a yell of excitement, and Erin found herself smiling, but she was also watching Quinn in the rearview mirror and she could see that Quinn was concentrating on her driving. They came to a corner, sliding slightly as Quinn slowed and then gunned the engine into the curve. She did this for a few minutes, always watching the area ahead to ensure safety. When she slowed again, she was checking her mirrors, and finally seemed satisfied.

Back at the house, Bobby hopped out of the car running to tell his mother about the experience. Erin moved to lean her arms on the seat right behind Quinn.

"What was that about?" Erin asked.

Quinn glanced back at the younger woman, her look assessing, then she shrugged. "Just wanted to check something."

Erin nodded, knowing Quinn wasn't telling her the whole story, but she also knew that Quinn wasn't one to over dramatize things, so she left it alone.

That evening, Quinn said she was headed to the gym after dinner, and Erin asked if she could go. Quinn agreed. After dinner the two walked to the car, Quinn chose to take the Charger this time. In the car the song The Vengeful One came on, Erin listened to it for a while and on the chorus recognized it.

"Isn't that the song you got famous for?" she asked, grinning.

"Oh yeah," Quinn said, rolling her eyes, "my fifteen minutes of fame."

"Seems like it's lasted a lot longer than fifteen minutes…" Erin said.

Quinn made a disgusted noise in the back of her throat, but grinned. "Much to my dismay," she replied with a wintery smile.

Erin grinned "You're not really into fame, are you?"

"Definitely not," Quinn said.

Erin nodded. They were both quiet for a few minutes, then Erin looked over at Quinn again.

"Can I ask you a question?" she said.

"Sure."

Erin hesitated for a few moments, but then blurted out her question. "So you're like butch right?"

Quinn grinned, inclining her head. "Yes, I would be considered quite butch."

"And that's because of the no makeup, tattoos, short hair thing?"

Quinn laughed, this was not the first time she'd had questions like this. She shook her head.

"It's not about makeup and tattoos, or hair for that matter," she told Erin. "It's more about what you do, how you act. I've seen the most girlie looking woman be a serious bad ass before."

"So what does being butch mean?" Erin asked.

Quinn thought about it for a long moment. She knew that Erin was searching for her identity in the gay community and she was looking to her to help, she didn't want to give the girl bad information.

"I guess it's about taking on some more masculine roles than most women do," she said. "Girls that are butch tend to be better with stuff like working on machinery, cars, bikes, trucks, stuff like that. Butch girls tend to work in areas where men are usually dominant."

"But it's not like you want to be a guy, right?" Erin asked, her tone confident on that.

"Exactly," Quinn said, "contrary to what a lot of men would like to think, we butch women don't really wish we had a penis, or wish we were really guys. Some women do wish for that, but that isn't what defines them as butch. There are tomboys all over the world that aren't gay; it's just that some of us that are tomboys are gay."

Erin nodded.

"But," Quinn added, holding up her hand, "don't take that to mean that a woman that wears makeup can't be butch, it's about how they act; are they stronger personalities, do they take charge, are they in the middle of the shit when they need to be?"

Erin looked confused. "So a woman can be butch and femme at the same time?"

"Yeah," Quinn said, "I know a couple of women just like that. They ride motorcycles, they'll throw down with the biggest and baddest of them all, and they put their lipstick on using the chrome on their Harley."

"So there's not just one definition of butch or femme."

"Nope, people are all different, and all women are different. You have to figure out what works for you, what feels right and true to who you are and go with that."

"I want to be like you," Erin said.

Quinn glanced over at the girl, thinking she had to be joking, but Erin looked quite serious.

"Why?" Quinn asked perplexed.

"Because you're friggin' awesome!" Erin said.

"Awww," Quinn stammered.

Erin shook her head grinning. "My mom's right you don't even know how people see you, do you?"

Quinn glanced out her side window, having no idea how to address that question.

Erin chuckled. "And you don't like to talk about yourself too much either."

Quinn looked over at the girl, her look indicating Erin was right about that.

"Okay, so can I ask you a question about sex? Or is that too personal?" Erin asked.

Quinn hesitated, grinning as she realized that being a parent had to be the hardest job on the planet.

"Ask," Quinn said then.

"Do you always initiate sex?" Erin asked with no hesitation.

Quinn started coughing as she laughed out loud. "Wow, you don't candy coat your questions do you?"

"Should I have?" Erin asked, looking like she was unsure.

"No, no," Quinn said, waving her hand in a dismissive gesture, "it just caught me off guard. And no, I don't always initiate sex." Quinn said. "Are you asking that as a butch woman I always initiate it? I mean, I assume you don't mean me personally."

Erin's lips twitched at the question, but then she said, "Well, yeah, I mean, do butch lesbians tend to initiate sex?"

Quinn caught the look on Erin's face, but didn't comment on it. "Well, no, not always, because there are femme women who are just as aggressive about sex as any man could be. So no, it's never safe to assume that because someone's butch that they're always going to initiate sex."

"Does my cousin initiate sex with you?" Erin asked.

"Now, that's personal," Quinn said, her look mild, but her tone serious.

"Okay, I'm sorry," Erin said, looking contrite.

"It's alright, but that's another thing a true butch doesn't do; she doesn't kiss and tell," Quinn said with a wink.

Erin grinned, nodding her head.

"So you and Xandy are the real deal, right?" Erin asked a few minutes later.

"How do you mean?" Quinn asked.

"Like you're going to be in her life for a really long time, right?" Erin asked.

"That's the plan, yeah," Quinn said, grinning, "but you never know."

Erin drew in a deep breath, biting her lip.

"Why?" Quinn asked.

"Well, you know that my brother and sister are really attached to you."

Quinn grinned. "Yeah, I'm finding myself pretty attached to them too."

Erin nodded, then gave Quinn a sideway glance. "And I am too."

Quinn caught the odd tone in Erin's voice and glanced over at the young woman.

"Okay…" Quinn said, her tone leading.

Erin looked back at her for a long moment, then shrugged, looking out the window. "I guess you could call it a crush."

"A wot?" Quinn replied, her tone sharper than she'd meant it to be.

Erin winced at the tone, then looked over at Quinn. "A crush," she said timidly.

Quinn looked back at the girl, having come to a red light. "Okay, well, you know that I'm way too old for you, and in love with your cousin, right?"

Erin nodded, biting her lip.

"Okay," Quinn said, her tone more gentle, "you'll find the right one for you, Erin. You just have to make sure you know who you are and what you want."

Erin nodded again. They arrived at the gym a few minutes later.

On the drive home, Erin sat with her head back on the seat, she was exhausted. She'd told Quinn she wanted to get into the kind of shape she was in, she'd had no idea how hard Quinn worked at the body she had. She did now, and she was beyond exhausted!

Quinn grinned at the girl's posture, she had told her to slow down a few times, but she'd insisted and trying to keep up. Quinn pulled out of the parking lot. A few minutes down the road she glanced in her rearview and saw it again, the black SUV that had been following them earlier in the day. At least she thought it might be. As she drove, she kept tabs on the SUV; she noticed it would drop back for a while, and then get closer again.

She took a couple of turns to see if the SUV would remain with her, and it did. Erin lifted her head after a few turns and looked over at Quinn, seeing her looking in the rearview mirror again.

"What's going on?" she asked.

Quinn glanced at her. "Well, I think we're being followed."

At that point the SUV turned off the street. She narrowed her eyes, but didn't stop looking. After a few minutes and at another stop light she caught sight of the nose of the SUV on a side street.

"There you are little fucker," Quinn muttered. "Think you're slick…"

"What do we do?" Erin asked, looking worried.

"Well," Quinn said, watching as the vehicle pulled onto the main road again, "now we're gonna draw him in closer…"

"Closer?" Erin asked, looking alarmed.

"Just to get a plate number, Erin, nothing to worry about."

"Oh, okay."

"Can you take it down for me?" Quinn asked.

"Sure," Erin said, pulling out her phone, "whenever you're ready."

Quinn read off the numbers and letters. Erin put them in her phone.

When they got back to the house, Quinn went out into the backyard and made some calls. When she hung up, she had Mackie working with Joe Sinclair to get the plate run. Sitting down she pulled out a cigarette and lit it, taking a deep drag.

"Everything okay?" Xandy asked, walking out onto the patio.

Quinn glanced back at her, smiling. "Yeah, I'm working on it."

Xandy nodded, knowing that if Quinn was handling the problem, it would get handled and she didn't need to press further.

"The kids are down for the night," Xandy said. "Erin wants to talk to her mom now."

Quinn widened her eyes slightly, but nodded moving to stand.

"No, we're coming out here," Xandy said to forestall her.

"Okay," Quinn said, nodding.

Xandy, Erin and Sarah came outside. Xandy handed Quinn a beer from the fridge as she moved past her. Quinn grinned; she figured this was Xandy's way of trying to help calm her nerves.

"So what's going on?" Sarah asked, looking worried.

Quinn looked at Erin who looked completely nervous, then she looked at Xandy and she looked equally nervous. *Up to me to start then,* Quinn thought to herself.

"Sarah, Erin has something she needs to talk to you about," she said, looking over at Erin again.

With that Quinn sat back, smoking her cigarette, but when Erin didn't start she prompted, "Go ahead Erin, it's okay."

Erin looked over at Quinn, not looking very sure of that at all.

"Oh my God, you're not pregnant are you?" Sarah asked, her biggest fear coming to bare.

Erin laughed. "No, Mom, I'm just gay."

She said it so casually that it took a few seconds for the words to sink in. Quinn was sure she could hear it click in Sarah's head.

"You're what?" Sarah asked, the shock evident on her face.

"You heard me Mom," Erin said, her look direct, ready for a fight.

Sarah nodded. She had heard her, she'd just hoped she'd heard her wrong. She looked over at Quinn and then at Xandy.

"You both knew," she said, her tone holding a note of accusation.

Quinn nodded, her look unchanged.

"Why didn't you tell me?" Sarah asked, feeling betrayed.

Quinn shook her head. "Not our place to tell you that."

"You're other adults!" Sarah responded, her voice raising.

Quinn looked back at Sarah, her emerald-green eyes very bright in the dying afternoon sunlight. "Your daughter needed to tell you when she was ready."

Sarah looked back at Quinn, struggling with the shock, but also remembering that she'd seen so much good in Quinn. She knew it wasn't fair to blame Quinn and Xandy for her relationship with her daughter; they hadn't been close for years. Maybe that's why this had happened. Erin had been attached to Quinn from the beginning, just like Elly and Bobby had been.

Finally she nodded, blowing her breath out. "It's me, I know that."

Quinn's look was very circumspect. "What's you?" she asked Sarah.

"It's my fault," Sarah explained.

Quinn grinned. "No, Sarah, it's not anyone's *fault*," she said, her voice emphasizing the word "fault."

"It's who your daughter is," she said, as she glanced at Erin.

"And there's nothing wrong with that," Xandy added, reaching over to touch Sarah's arm.

Sarah looked at both of them, indecision clear on her face.

"This is all so much to take in," Sarah said, sighing. "I just don't understand," she said, shaking her head remorsefully.

"It's a lot," Quinn agreed, but her look pointed, "but you should know that in the event you can't handle this about Erin." Quinn looked over at the girl, then back at her mother. "We've offered her a place to stay."

"Here?" Sarah said, her tone shocked.

"Yes, here," Quinn said, grinning, wanting to say *where else?* but knowing it wouldn't be in the least bit productive to provoke Sarah. She wanted to help Erin, not make it impossible for her to stay with her mother.

"So you have it all planned out," Sarah said, her tone cold suddenly.

"No," Quinn said, her tone still mild. "We're trying to help you understand, but at the same time we're trying to help Erin."

"And you were pretty clear early on how you felt about gay people," Xandy put in.

"Yeah, Mom, and they haven't even heard all the shit you used to say," Erin said, her voice strident.

Quinn reached over putting her hand on Erin's arm, trying to tell her, *don't antagonize her right now.* Erin seemed to get the message, because she dropped her eyes from her mother's.

Sarah noticed the gesture and seeing Erin's reaction only irritated her more.

"Of course, I'm the bad guy here right?" Sarah snapped, standing up, wanting to get away from this whole conversation.

"No," Quinn said, her voice reasoning, "we're just trying to make you understand how important this is and that what you say right now isn't something you can take back later."

Sarah's eyes went to Quinn, her look angry, but she was met with Quinn's unshakably calm look. She wanted to scream, she wanted this not to be happening, but she knew she had no control over it. She clenched and unclenched her fists in a gesture of futility.

Quinn and Xandy exchanged a look, somehow communicating without speaking. Quinn looked over at Erin.

"Tell her the rest."

Erin looked at her, confused at first, and then with Quinn's look, she suddenly understood. She started to shake her head; she didn't want her mother to know that.

"Erin, tell her," Quinn said again, her tone stronger now.

Erin shook her head again.

"Tell her, or I will," Quinn said, stronger still.

Erin's eyes widened at Quinn's tone as well as what she'd said. Quinn gave her a narrowed look and Erin knew what she was doing.

Turning to her mother Erin said, "I knew that telling you was going to do this," she said, her voice sad, "and I just couldn't face it…I seriously thought about giving up." She shrugging, her face reflected the pain of that admission.

"Oh Erin…" Sarah said, tears in her eyes instantly.

"And *that* is why we are determined to help your daughter," Quinn said.

Sarah looked at Quinn and then at Xandy who nodded in agreement. Sarah herself nodded too, sitting down, her eyes going back to her daughter.

"Okay," she said. "Okay." She reached out to touch her daughter's hand. "I love you, and I will always love you, no matter what. We will figure this out."

Quinn smiled at Sarah. "Great answer Mom," she said winking.

Sarah and Erin went inside to continue talking, Xandy and Quinn stayed outside while Quinn finished her cigarette.

"So how do you think that went?" Xandy asked.

"Good, better than I expected, actually."

"Me too," Xandy said.

"You should know, that your cousin said she has a crush on me," Quinn said, grinning.

"She what!" Xandy exclaimed sharply.

Quinn laughed.

"She can't have you," Xandy told her.

"Really?" Quinn asked, her look wry.

Xandy opened her mouth to respond, then saw the twinkle in Quinn's eyes. "You brat!"

Quinn laughed again, lighting another cigarette. "She also asked me about sex," she told Xandy, giving her a wink.

"Oh my God!" Xandy said, "I'm so sorry!"

Quinn grinned. "It's okay, Xan, she doesn't have any way of knowing, and it ain't like they address this kind of thing on those after school specials or anything."

"Well, that's true," Xandy said. "What did she ask you?"

"About who initiates sex," she said. "She wanted to know if butch women are always the initiators. I told her no, and that I've met femme women who are more aggressive about sex than any butch I've ever met…" She let her voice trail off, and then she added, "she asked if you initiate sex."

"What?" Xandy exclaimed again. "What did you tell her?"

"I told her you've always got yer hands all over me," Quinn said, with a wink.

"You did not!"

Quinn chuckled. "I told her that a true butch never kisses and tells."

"That's more like it," Xandy said, then canted her head. "So you're a true butch?"

"Oh yeah,"

"And that would make me…" Xandy said, her voice trailing off.

"Very, very, femme," Quinn said.

"Very, very huh?" Xandy asked with a grin.

"I'd add another very, but I haven't seen you around spiders yet," Quinn said, winking at her.

"I hate spiders!" Xandy said with a shudder.

"Add another very, got it,"

Xandy gave her a narrowed look, and then laughed.

The next day Quinn talked to Mackie. The vehicle that had been following her had been tracked back to a company, and Mackie was trying to get more information. Quinn didn't see the vehicle that day as she, Xandy, and Erin went to West Hollywood. Erin had wanted to see the area that was considered "gay" in LA. They had lunch, did people watching, much like Xandy and Quinn had done months before.

Xandy found herself very proud to be holding Quinn's hand at the restaurant and she didn't care who saw it. The publicity she'd received from the Kansas concert had been very supportive and well-received. There'd been some negative comments too, but not from anywhere surprising. BJ told her that her presales were through the roof. It made Xandy happy to know that her relationship with Quinn was not only not bad for her career, but actually seemed to be helping it. She'd told Quinn honestly, though, that if it had been bad for her career, she wouldn't have cared.

"I'd rather be with you, than be famous for anything," she'd told Quinn.

They were sitting at an outside café watching people pass by, when they were interrupted.

"Well, well..." said a woman's voice from behind them.

Quinn winced, knowing exactly who it was before she even turned her head. Xandy turned around to see Valerie standing there, her hands on her hips. Valerie wore black leather from head to toe, and spiked heels. Her long hair was pulled back in a braid. When Quinn did turn her head she merely grinned and raised an eyebrow.

"Oh, hi Val," she said, casually.

"Hi, Quinn," Valerie said, making Quinn's name somehow sound like a cuss word. Her cold eyes skipped over to Xandy. "Xandy," she said, her tone flat, and then gestured to Erin, "And I don't know who you are," she said dismissively.

"Pretend you have manners," Quinn said, her tone even.

"Fuck you, Quinn," Valerie shot back, her look openly hostile.

"Watch it..." Quinn cautioned, her eyes narrowing.

"So tough..." Valerie sighed.

Quinn just looked back at Valerie, refusing to rise to her bait. Instead, Quinn leaned back in her chair, her green eyes looking up at Valerie as if she was a waitress who had just interrupted their meal.

Valerie knew Quinn's style well, and she knew that Quinn was waiting her out. Somehow she just couldn't stop herself.

"Why haven't you bothered to call me back?" she asked angrily.

"What was there to say?" Quinn asked, turning in her chair to face her and purposely putting herself slightly in front of Xandy, protectively.

"Quinn..." Xandy said from behind her, wanting to keep anything from escalating. Unfortunately that was exactly what escalated things.

"You stay the fuck out of this!" Valerie screeched, shocking people around them. She also made the mistake of taking a step toward Xandy.

Like a flash Quinn was out of her chair and in front of Valerie, blocking her path, her eyes flashing green fire suddenly.

"Back up," Quinn said, her tone far from mild now. When Valerie didn't do so immediately, Quinn took a menacing step toward her, causing Valerie to back up involuntarily, her chin coming up.

"What're you gonna do?" Valerie asked her tone snide. "You won't hit me."

"Don't gotta hit ya, babe," Quinn said, her tone still low and threatening.

She was satisfied to see true fear flash in Valerie's brown eyes, but she quickly recovered.

"That would hurt your white knight image, Quinn, you don't want that."

"Like I fucking care," Quinn said, her words measured and uttered in practically a growl.

"You'd do that to protect *her*?" Valerie asked, her voice breaking on the last word, tears glazing her eyes suddenly.

Quinn narrowed her eyes slightly. She knew Valerie was a consummate actress who knew her weakness for crying women. Her lips curled into a disgusted grin as she shook her head, turning away. That's when Valerie's hand lashed out raking her neck. Quinn's hand came up just as quickly, grabbing her wrist and stopped her from doing any further damage. They were eye to eye then, and even as Quinn's eyes blazed in controlled fury, she could read excitement in Valerie's eyes.

Dropping Valerie's hand, she turned and stepped back to the table, not looking at her again. It looked like she'd dismissed Valerie, but when Valerie launched herself at her, Quinn quickly spun around grabbing Valerie's hands. In one swift movement shed she put Valerie's back against her chest, holding both of her wrists. Valerie struggled, screaming in frustration, and Quinn simply applied pressure to her wrists until she subsided.

"Now," Quinn said, lowering her head so her lips were right at Valerie's ear, "get out of here before I put you on the floor." This time there was no mistaking the threat, and Valerie knew Quinn meant it.

Quinn let her go, and stepped back, ensuring that Valerie wouldn't be able to wheel on her again. Valerie left the restaurant with no further comment. People around them looked at Quinn as she sat down.

"Oh babe…" Xandy said reaching out to touch her neck where Valerie had managed to draw blood, again.

"Every damned time!" Quinn said, touching at the blood, shaking her head. Then she glanced over at Erin. "See? Women are sometimes like that."

"That's what I'm afraid of," Erin said, still wide-eyed from the confrontation.

Quinn laughed at that, as did Xandy.

John Machiavelli was sat in his office when his phone rang.

Mackie," he answered. "Yeah what'd ya got? Who? Wait, go back who?" Mackie asked then, listening closely. "He about five ten, blond hair? Son of a fucking bitch! Okay thanks!" he said and hung up.

Minutes later he hung up and grabbed his jacket, heading out the door, even as he dialed Quinn's cell phone number.

Quinn, Xandy and Erin were on their way back to the house when Quinn's phone rang. She was still going over the scene at the café in her head. Picking up her phone she glanced around to see if there were any cops, and that's when she caught sight of the black SUV again.

"Quinn, it's Mackie. It's Jason that's been following you, you need to—"

"Too fucking late!" Quinn yelled, dropping the phone. "Hold on!" she had time to yell before the SUV came alongside them and slammed into the side of the car, shoving them off the road onto the wide dirt shoulder. Xandy screamed and Quinn reached out to hold her back since the Charger didn't have shoulder harnesses yet. The Charger spun once, and came to a stop. Quinn's head hit the side of the molding, causing a deep gash. She had no time to worry about that.

Glancing over her shoulder Quinn saw Jason getting out of the SUV. Reaching up under the back of her shirt, she pulled her gun out of its holster, handing it to Xandy.

"If he gets anywhere near this car, you shoot his ass, do you understand?" Quinn told Xandy who still looked dazed. "Xandy!" Quinn yelled to snap her out of it. "I need you to tell me you understand!"

Xandy nodded, taking the gun with shaking hands. With that assurance, Quinn was out of the car in a flash, not wanting Jason to have a chance to get near Xandy. Unfortunately, she wasn't fast enough and Jason's fist sent her flying back. She surprised him though, by getting back onto her feet quickly. She thanked the gods that be that she'd resisted the urge to wear shorts and sandals that day even though it was hot. Something had stopped her. Fate had once again helped her out.

"Come fight me, you fucking coward," Quinn taunted Jason as he moved toward the car and his prize.

Jason glanced at her, surprised; he hadn't really expected her to get up, certainly not that quickly. Even so, he dismissed her with a sneer and turned toward the car door. Quinn hit him at a dead run, knocking him to the ground. He shifted quickly to get out from under her; fortunately for her she was more agile than his bulk allowed, so she was able to bring her arm around to elbow him in the face.

"Fucking dyke bitch!" he screamed as her elbow connected with his nose.

He brought his hand back through, hitting Quinn in the face. She shifted to the right, trying to miss the blow, but still caught most of it in the face. She spun away from him to keep him from getting his hands on her. That's when she caught sight of the smoke from the engine of the Charger.

"Fuck!" she yelled, running over to the car, yanking at the passenger door. "Xandy get out, get Erin out, damned things on fire!"

Jason tackled her, and Quinn knew she was in trouble. Jason was twice her size, and now on top of her, she had no real hope of fighting his massive weight.

"Fucking dyke bitch," he growled, reaching between them to grab her face in his hand. "If you just want a dick, you should go get that operation," he sneered at her.

"That's just it," Quinn said, surprising him, "I don't want one!"

"Yeah, that's what you all say," he said, his tone knowing.

"Well, see," Quinn said, her tone conversational now, as she relaxed a bit, influencing his actions as well. "If I had a dick, you'd be able to do this" she said, jamming her knee up between his now relaxed legs, catching him sharply in the nuts.

Jason howled in pain and rolled off of her involuntarily. Quinn jumped up, and turned to check on Xandy. Jason reached out grabbing one of her feet. Spinning, she kicked his arm and got away, but he was up and moving again. He ran straight at her, grabbing her by the throat and backing her up against the Charger, his eyes were blazing in anger now.

Quinn could feel him squeezing and knew she had to do something quickly before she was unconscious. She lashed out with a booted foot, catching him in the knee, he loosened his grip long enough for her to wrench her neck out of his hands and spin away from him. She turned then, putting her back to where Xandy and Erin now stood. Standing in a fighter's stance she watched him pace, she could see this wasn't going the way he wanted it to. Even as she watched him she felt her vision swim a bit. Gritting her teeth, she forced the feeling away, mentally shoving it down.

Finally he stopped pacing and looked over at her, his look downright evil as he drew out a hunting knife.

"Fuckin' Americans, always cheating in a fair fight," Quinn said snidely.

"You wanna fuck with me, you dyke bitch?" Jason said, his voice gravelly from exertion.

"You keep saying that like it's somehow an insult," Quinn told him, wryly.

That brought Jason up short for a minute; he did think it was an insult.

"You see," Quinn said, "I am technically a dyke, and the bitch part is always a compliment, so, really you're paying me a compliment." She canted her head at him then. "Are you making a pass at me?"

"Fucking bitch!" Jason yelled, charging at Quinn knife in hand.

Quinn waited, calculating his movement. As the tip of the knife came toward her, she shocked him by stepping toward him, using all her might to bring her arm down, chopping the small bones in his wrist as hard as she possibly could. She was fairly sure she felt one break as he yelled in pain. She then brought her other arm through punching him in the face, and then jumped back as he tried to take a backward swing at her. What surprised her was that he still had the knife in his hand. The knife extended his reach by about six inches, and he caught her in the shoulder, but she was able to spin away to keep from any major damage from being done.

Xandy screamed when she saw the knife connect with Quinn's shoulder. Quinn shook her head, she couldn't be distracted right then. Jason came at her, trying to grab her throat again. Quinn lowered her head, as he came close she brought it up, hard and fast, catching him in the chin, and once again bringing her knee up to knee him in the balls.

"Don't learn too fast, do ya?"

This time Jason went down, and Quinn was done fighting fair; she kicked him in the head as hard as she could. He was down for that count then. Just then a Cadillac Escalade came skidding to a stop.

Mackie ran over as Quinn made it back to Xandy.

"Guess you didn't need me," Mackie said, grinning.

Right about then, Jason stirred and started to get up. Mackie put a foot on him. "I wouldn't advise that," he told Jason.

"Oh my god, are you okay?" Xandy said, reaching for Quinn as she walked over.

Everything hit Quinn all at once and she dropped to her knees and passed out, causing Xandy to scream. It was the last thing Quinn heard before her vision went black.

Quinn woke up in the hospital an hour later. An ambulance had been summoned when Quinn couldn't be awoken at the scene. Xandy had been beside herself after seeing all the blood on the side of Quinn's head, not to mention her shoulder. The paramedics had attempted to wake Quinn with no success, so they'd taken her to the hospital.

Opening her eyes, Quinn groaned at the pain in her head.

"Quinn?" Xandy queried from beside her.

Quinn turned her head, slowly locating Xandy. "Are you okay?"

"Yes, as usual, I'm perfectly fine and Erin's fine," Xandy said, shaking her head. "You on the other hand took the brunt of it again."

"That's her job," Mackie said as he walked into Quinn's room, his grin in place.

"Technically," Quinn said, wincing slightly, "I was no longer on the job."

"Well, I'll let BJ know he doesn't need to have your car fixed then," Mackie replied, pulling his cell phone off his belt.

"No, no, no," Quinn said, holding up her hands to forestall his action, "don't do that…"

Mackie laughed, putting his phone away.

"The Charger has already been towed to a shop to have everything fixed, 'better than new' was the instructions they were given by BJ," Mackie said, smiling.

"Is my engine toast?" Quinn asked, grimacing at the thought.

"Nope, it was just a rotor or something causing the smoke," Mackie said.

Quinn visibly relaxed.

Xandy shook her head whistling. "So as long as the car's okay, you're fine?"

"No," Quinn said, narrowing her eyes, "as long as you're okay, I'm fine, but my car being okay is a nice bonus." She winked. She looked at Mackie again. "And Jason?"

"Jason is being booked into county jail as we speak," Mackie said, grinning. "Joe took him there himself. He's being charged with attempted murder, attempted vehicular homicide, and thanks to you getting his information yesterday when he was essentially stalking you, we can considered it pre-meditated. He's going away for a long time."

Quinn looked over at Xandy. "That means it's really over this time."

"As long as you stop getting hurt!" Xandy said, shaking her head in exasperation.

Sarah, Bobby, Elly and Erin walked into the room at that point. Elly ran to Xandy and held her arms out to be picked up.

"I'm gonna go," Mackie said, holding up his hands.

"Thanks man," Quinn said, nodding to Mackie.

"Well, ya didn't need the backup Wonder Woman, but I'm glad you're okay," he said with a wink.

Quinn chuckled, shaking her head, and regretting it a moment later.

"Kin hurt?" Elly asked, from Xandy's arms.

Quinn looked at Elly. "Yeah, just a little bit though."

"They said you have a concussion," Xandy told her, "some nasty bruises and the cut on your shoulder."

"I'm always gettin' bloody around you," Quinn said, winking at her.

"Well, if you'd just stay out of trouble..." Xandy replied, rolling her eyes.

"Ha!" Quinn said, grinning.

"Kin stop getting hurt," Elly said, her look quite serious.

"Yes ma'am," Quinn answered, equally as serious.

A month later, there was a party at Xandy and Quinn's house, celebrating Quinn's birthday. Devin and Skyler were there, as were a few others that Quinn had known while she was with Valerie. Jerry Castle, a model of notoriety and her current girlfriend, Rachel. No one had gotten Rachel's last name, so they figured that meant she wouldn't be around long. There was also Jovina, a local song writer, and a woman she'd called at the last minute to ask about bringing. That had Quinn curious; the Latin beauty went through women fairly quickly, this one must mean something to her.

The doorbell rang, and Quinn answered it. Jovina, with her jet black hair flowing around her shoulders, and her honey colored eyes sparkling brightly, stood there with a beautiful blond. Quinn had to hand it to Jovina, this one was definitely a hottie.

"Quinn," Jovina said, smiling. "Happy birthday!" She leaning up to hug Quinn and kissed her on the lips.

"Thank you," Quinn said, her eyes going to the blond.

"This is Catalina Roché," Jovina said, putting her hand on the other woman's shoulder. "Cat, this is Quinn Kavanaugh."

"The White Knight herself," Cat said, smiling as she did.

"Gah!" Quinn said, rolling her eyes. "Never gettin' past that, am I?"

Cat laughed a very sexy laugh. "Don't worry," she said, winking at Quinn, "I won't hold it against ya, I've made that mistake myself a few times. I just didn't get caught on YouTube with it."

Quinn grinned, she liked this one. "Good," Quinn said, opening the door wider, "then you can come in."

Cat smiled, her sapphire-blue eyes sparkling mischievously. As she walked by, Quinn glanced at Jovina, and gave her a silent 'Wow!' Jovina nodded, grinning.

Inside shots were being poured, and Quinn was quickly pressed to the bar in the kitchen.

"Okay!" Quinn said, taking a shot and handing it to Jovina, and then one to Cat. Then she took one herself. "What to?"

"I have one," Jerry said. "May you live a hundred years," she said, lifting her glass, and then winking at Quinn, "with one year to repent."

Quinn laughed as did everyone else and they drank.

A little while later, Erin arrived, with a diminutive Asian girl in tow. She made a bee-line for Quinn, leading the girl by the hand.

"Quinn," Erin said, smiling up at her, "I want you to meet Kimberly. Kimberly this is Quinn."

Quinn extended her hand to Kimberly, who took it shyly.

"It's nice to meet you Kimberly," Quinn said, softening her voice to keep from scaring the girl.

"You too," Kimberly said, biting her lip.

"Go on outside there," Erin said. "I'll be out in a minute," she said, leaning in to kiss the girl softly on the lips.

Kimberly nodded, looking around her at all the women talking and drinking. She looked overwhelmed, but she made her way to the back door.

"Cute," Quinn told Erin, with a smile.

"Yeah," Erin said, smiling as well.

Quinn nodded to the girl, happy to see that she had at least found someone for the time being. The crush she'd had on Quinn had only increased after the accident, and it had taken Xandy putting her foot down and telling Erin she needed to stop mooning after Quinn to make the girl finally move on.

Sarah and the kids, including Erin, had decided to stay in LA after all. Xandy had sold her parent's land and given the money to Sarah to buy a house, which she had in a nearby community. Sarah had also gotten a job working for the City of Los Angeles as a secretary and was doing well. Erin and Sarah seemed closer than ever, the accident having cemented Sarah's commitment to stand by her daughter through this transition in her life. Elly and Bobby still spent as much time with Quinn as possible. Bobby and Quinn were working on a Harley for him; not that he'd be riding it anytime soon, since it was only a frame and a very shot engine, but it was a project. Elly constantly reminded Quinn that she was no longer allowed to get hurt. Quinn consistently promised that she'd do her best.

In the end, Erin and Kimberly didn't stay long. Kimberly wasn't big on crowds, Erin had explained to Xandy and Quinn. Before they left, Erin hugged Quinn, kissing her on the cheek.

"Happy birthday, CQ," she said, smiling.

"CQ?" Xandy queried.

"Cousin Quinn," Quinn supplied with a grin.

"Ohhh…" Xandy said, nodding and smiling.

"You two have fun," Quinn told Erin. "Just not too much," she added with a wink.

"Uh-huh…" Erin said, grinning, her eyes, so much like Xandy's, twinkling.

Later, Quinn was standing with Jovina, Cat and Skyler, they were all out back smoking. Jerry Castle joined them.

"You smoking again?" Quinn asked Jerry.

"Yeah, work is shit right now," Jerry said, but she was looking at Cat oddly.

"I know you from somewhere," Jerry said to Cat. "Where are you from?"

Cat looked back at Jerry, grinning. She knew exactly who Jerry was.

"I met you at a club in San Diego," Cat said. "I was dating Kana at the time."

"Oh my God yes!" Jerry said, nodding her head. "How is Kana?"

"She's good," Cat said, smiling.

"I never see Palani these days," Jerry said. Glancing at Skyler and Quinn she elaborated, "Kana's wife. Also a model, like me."

Quinn and Skyler nodded.

"Probably because she's pregnant," Cat said, grinning.

"Holy shit, she is?" Jerry asked.

"Yep," Cat said, smiling.

"Wait," Skyler said, putting out her hand. "Is this Kana Sorbinno, Kana? Like the Attorney General's bodyguard?"

"Yes, that one," Cat said, nodding.

"And how do you know her?" Quinn asked, trying to figure out the connection.

"I work for San Diego PD, like Kana did before," Cat said, "and I dated K for a little bit."

"Impressive," Skyler murmured, and then she looked at Jovina. "And how do you two know each other?"

"We grew up together," Jovina said, "in the Castro."

There was a round of, "Ohs…" as everyone recognized the gay district in San Francisco.

"So what are you doing in LA?" Quinn asked.

"I'm going to be doing some bodyguard work here for a bit," Cat said.

Quinn raised an eyebrow, this petite girl was going to do bodyguard work?

Cat looked back at Quinn, her blue eyes direct and unblinking. Quinn pressed her lips together, nodding. "Who you protecting?"

"Some executive," Cat said, "but Mackie claims he wants a bodyguard that doesn't look like a bodyguard."

"Mackie?" Quinn queried.

"Yeah," Cat said, grinning, knowing that Quinn worked for Mackie.

"Well, if you need anything, let me know," Quinn said, nodding.

If Cat was working for Mackie, she must have something, because Mackie didn't employ just anyone.

Later, as everyone sat around drinking and talking, Quinn walked over to where Xandy stood in the kitchen. She was opening another bottle of wine and surveying the group. She smiled as Quinn walked over to her, Quinn leaned in, kissing her temple softly.

"This is fun," Xandy said, smiling softly.

"Mmmmhmmm," Quinn murmured.

"I really like your friends," Xandy said.

"I'm glad," Quinn said, "they're kind of the family I have here."

"Did I hear that the girl your friend Jovina brought is working for Mackie too?"

"You did," Quinn nodded.

'Interesting," Xandy said, looking mystified.

"Yeah, I can't fathom it either," Quinn said, "but Mackie doesn't mess around, so she's got something…"

"Speaking of Mackie," Xandy said, "I heard from Joe Sinclair yesterday that Jason pleaded guilty and was sentenced to thirty to fifty years."

"Good," Quinn said, nodding. She was glad that Xandy wouldn't have to go through a trial. "So we're finally clear there."

Xandy nodded. "Yeah, it's a nice break in the storm."

CPSIA information can be obtained
at www.ICGtesting.com
Printed in the USA
BVHW072106130919
558291BV00001B/35/P

9 781910 780367